86

A T-Shaped World

This is the story of a frustrated, embittered man of thirty who slowly, unperceived by him, falls under the influence of his eleven-year-old niece. When his wife, a self-confessed animal, leaves him, he comes to rely more and more on the small, perhaps precocious, schoolgirl. Deaths in the family also help to make uncle and niece indispensable to each other. A man who had once envisaged a dangerous career in espionage now finds his life centred round a young girl. In the Somerset village where he is the bored manager of her parents' farm also lives a middle-aged man with a strong predilection for raping little girls.

If it is a novel's object to fascinate the reader and keep him on tenterhooks, Mr. de Polnay—with his mastery of his art and deep understanding of human beings, young or mature—succeeds marvellously in this book, which is distinguished by his highly professional touch and literary finesse.

PETER DE POLNAY

A T-Shaped World

W. H. ALLEN
LONDON
1971

© PETER DE POLNAY, 1971

PRINTED IN GREAT BRITAIN BY
THE ANCHOR PRESS LTD., TIPTREE, ESSEX
FOR THE PUBLISHERS W. H. ALLEN & CO. LTD.,
ESSEX STREET, LONDON WC2R 3JG.
BOUND IN TIPTREE BY
WM. BRENDON & SON LTD.

ISBN 0 491 00397 8

A T-Shaped World

I

The village was T-shaped. It consisted of two streets, one running from the church to the Court, the other down the middle to the stream which the villagers proudly referred to as the river. Beyond the bridge the Yeovil road began. From the house half way between the church and the Court Patsy could see old Fred emerging from his cottage, mounting his bicycle and riding off to Yeovil, where he was the gardener at a school. Patsy was holding the receiver to her ear, listening in deep boredom coupled with annoyance to her sister-in-law who was speaking from London. Her dark eyes followed old Fred till he vanished down the slope. Then they became unemployed till a labrador puppy bolted from a cottage.

Allan Ramshorn sat on the round table, his arms and legs crossed, watching Patsy, but, as he often reminded himself, he never ceased watching Patsy as though he still had to make up his mind about her. It was strange, he mused, that in his thoughts she remained slim even when she was present. Nobody could have called her slim, though she wasn't fat by any means. Her figure could have been described as stately if there had been anything stately about her. It was really the figure of an overdeveloped girl who hadn't had time to shed her baby fat or was too lazy to do so. Her long, uncombed black hair half covered her pale face, the dress she wore was the one she used in summer in lieu of a dressing gown. It was now two in the afternoon, which had no significance where the dress was concerned, for it often happened that she kept it on till she went to bed after the television screen had nothing more to offer her. Look at that dress poor Patsy has to wear, Allan said to himself. Beside him on the table lay one of the innumerable magazines Patsy bought just to glance at them. On the open page a girl smiled past him. She wore a dress costing £33.19. Value for your money, the magazine said. Value for whose money? Not his because he never had any. Next to the smiling girl a travel agency announced a cruise for only £150, a cheap way of spending your summer holiday. It also had a round-the-world tour for £500, an unforgettable experience. It must be unforgettable, Allan reflected, though not for those who had five hundred pounds to spend. Only he and the other penniless wretches were not allowed to forget that they hadn't five hundred pounds. Take the dress Patsy was wearing. They couldn't forget it because they couldn't afford a light dressing gown. That there were some light dressing gowns that cost about the price of a bottle of whisky was one of those glaring, sordid facts that both he and Patsy preferred to overlook. It would have disrupted the permanent moan that their existence had become.

Imagine, he said to the magazine page, that I inherited some enormous fortune from a non-existent relative, or held up a bank lousy with ten-pound notes. He would buy Patsy fifty dresses and a mink coat. She would look so slim in a mink coat. Patsy put down the receiver and said in her fast deep voice, 'The cheek of it.'

'What did she want?' Allan asked, uncrossing his arms.

'We'll have the pleasure and the privilege of entertaining her daughter Theresa for the whole of the summer hols.'

'Never.'

'She's paying a fiver a week plus all extras.'

'Why didn't you ask for six?'

'Because like all the other disinherited of this earth I'm not greedy.'

'We are dreamers of dreams,' observed Allan. 'Hence we are incapable of being greedy.' Patsy yawned, showing her large teeth. 'When is that horrible precocious child coming?'

'Tomorrow,' said Patsy, then yawned again. 'She'll arrive at 4 p.m. You'll have to fetch her at Yeovil station.'

'Justin can do that.'

'Justin will be drunk. Tomorrow's Wednesday, and that means The Beech Tree. You'll have to get her.'

'We ought to kidnap Theresa and tell brother Harold and his Elisabeth that either they pay ten thousand pounds or . . .'

'. . . we'll keep that horrible girl for ever. I prefer things to stay as they are.'

'You don't mean that.'

8

'I don't mean what?' asked Patsy, yawning for a third time.

'That things should stay as they are,' said Allan, getting off the table, then stretching himself.

'I do and I don't, and what's the good of it if I don't?'

'One should never admit failure.' His eyes were on his reflection in the looking glass that hung on the wall between the two windows. He was a handsome man with a fine moustache and thick brown hair, but his looks meant nothing to him, in fact were a reminder of the featureless ugliness of his brother Harold, one of the City's most successful chartered accountants. Had Harold his good looks he would have got nowhere either. 'And why are they sending that girl here?'

'Because they're going to America, combining business with pleasure.' Patsy imitated her sister-in-law's voice, not an accurate imitation as she was no good at imitating other people's voices. She just drawled, and it was the same drawl whomever she imitated, including the Somerset accent of the villagers. 'We are invited everywhere,' Patsy drawled. 'Country houses mostly and a ranch in Texas. It would be so tiring for Theresa. Besides, children should remain cabbages as long as possible.'

'You're wonderful,' said Allan.

'We'll also stay with the Shitbuggers in the Rockies and the Hambuggers in their log cabin, then with the Arsebuggers we'll hunt the tuna fish in and out of the tin . . . she sees herself at Camp David as the President's special guest.'

'If they go on like that,' Allan said gloomily, 'they'll work their way there too.'

His eldest brother's financial advancement had been the constant puzzle of his life. Harold was twelve years older than he, thus they had not shared the same childhood. Still, they had been well acquainted, and he was convinced that Harold was just a fool, and a dry one at that. When he had decided to become a chartered accountant their father, an actor who had never got far, told him that he was off his head. 'One must get on in life,' Harold answered, 'and the future lies with scientists and chartered accountants.' The father sneered, but old Raymond Ramshorn was given to sneering, also to exercising no authority over his three sons, convinced that if a father hadn't the financial means to enforce his will it was preferable to keep, as it were, his will to himself. 'You won't inherit a penny from me,' he often said, 'because I'll never have one.

So you have no reason to listen to me.' Then he would add dramatically, 'No money, no father.'

Harold went his way, and now at the age of forty-two he was simply coining it as the senior partner in a firm of chartered accountants. His wife was one of his best assets in so far as she, the daughter of a poor Highland schoolmaster who had strayed to Birmingham, where he had taught in a grammar school, re-polished herself on every rung of the ladder on their swift climb to the top. When Harold was still struggling she was the nice, honest, cheerful housewife; when Harold had ceased to struggle, that is, the road became straight, she was the bridge-playing wife in suburbia who drove her husband to the station in the morning and fetched him in the evening; and when he had reached his present position she presented herself to the world of chairmen, partners and managing directors as the elegant woman who knew how to entertain her own and her husband's equals. For nothing on earth would he, Allan, have changed Patsy for her. If he had had his brother's money Patsy would still forget to comb her hair and would yawn into anybody's face. 'You look tired,' he said.

'I want a nap,' she said.

'I'm coming too,' he said, glancing at the table at the other end of the room on which were dirty plates and an empty beer bottle. 'What about cleaning up?'

'When we get up,' said Patsy.

The house, which was a square red brick Victorian building, did possess a dining room. However, Patsy and Allan preferred to eat either in the kitchen or in the sitting room because they had declared the dining room too narrow. Justin, Allan's other brother, who lived with them as their lodger and cooked his own meals which were invariably sausages and mash, feasted in the dining room in solitary state, for Justin saw himself as a country gentleman of the old school. Patsy was all for it, since Justin's presence tired her in spite of his treating her with respect and devotion. The point with Patsy was that she either disliked or was indifferent to most people.

She climbed up the stairs to the bedroom, which was right above the sitting room. Next to it was the room they would have to give Harold's daughter; Justin's was at the end of the passage beside the bathroom. Patsy's bed wasn't made. Today being Tuesday Mrs. Bramm, the cowman's wife, hadn't come as it was her cleaning day at the vicarage. Anyway, Patsy didn't care for the Mondays, Wednesdays and Fridays when Mrs. Bramm appeared, since that meant getting up before nine. She drew the curtain, took off her dress, pulling it over her head. She wore nothing underneath. No fashion designer would have admired her figure, though a sculptor might have been fascinated by it. Hers was an undisciplined, one might almost say unorganised, body, the breasts small and round, the buttocks too large, and the long slim legs should have belonged to a less expanding body. She lay down on the bed, waiting, and, with her, waiting was akin to a command. There was no nonsense in the dark eyes : they said come, let's get going, and her entire body seemed to swell in anticipation. She looked nearly twice her size by the time Allan got down on her.

When he made love to her it was bliss and a deep ache, the ache often stronger than the bliss. Her open mouth and open eyes were like an unfathomable mystery, one that he would never solve, and frequently while sitting with her or walking at her side that ache would grip him and hopeless it remained even if he rushed her to bed. Nothing could assuage it.

'That's what I needed,' she smiled.

Allan wondered what he needed.

She turned on her side, fell asleep, and soon she was lightly snoring, hers the snores of a contented puppy. Allan didn't bother to close his eyes. It was too hot, a tractor was droning in a nearby field, and one of those damned helicopters from Yeovil was adding to the noise. What he needed was money and the independence money gave you. He didn't want to go round the world, log cabins had no attraction for him : all he wanted was to be independent, and if he felt like buying a new car or having a couple of nights out with Patsy in London not to have to consider either as a fantastic dream. Poverty held them on a short leash. If he could cut that leash they wouldn't have a worry left in the world. His hand was stroking Patsy's back. It would be fun if he could suddenly shake her, wake her and say, 'I've got twenty thousand quid, dress and we'll get out of this damned village without bothering to pack anything.' The letter he would write Harold. 'I am no longer your agent or bailiff or farm manager, and to tell you the truth I am no longer your brother either. In short I resign from my position of a slave.' Or perhaps he wouldn't bother, just call in Simson and tell him that he was going to London and wouldn't come back, so he had better inform Harold. Simson with his red bovine face would say, 'I understand you, Mr. Allan,' without understanding a word of it. Anyhow, what had Simson to do with his daydreams?

There was money about, otherwise there wouldn't be Rollses and round-the-world tours, diamonds at jewellers' and take-over bids. And there would be no Harold either. It wasn't so much a case of money being important as of money existing at all. If nobody were rich he wouldn't feel desperate about being poor. It was really a case of others getting hold of it while he and Patsy had just nothing. Yet they were no bigger fools than the others.

The sun had sneaked in through a hole in the curtain, and Patsy was sweating like a horse. He found the room insuffer-ably hot, so got out of bed as silently as he could, dressed, and carrying his shoes he tiptoed out of the room. Downstairs in the sitting room the sun was lording it. They should have drawn the curtains before they went up. But why should they? Because of the Aubusson? They had one old rug, all that was left of an old pile carpet. Or because of the Sheraton furni-ture? When Harold bought the house with the farm as an investment he declared in that low monotonous voice of his that the rickety furniture should do. The previous owner had gone bust and sold all the decent stuff he had. Frankly, there was no reason whatever to keep the blasted sun out. He looked at the dirty plates and the empty beer bottle. With a sudden, almost superhuman effort he took the lot to the kitchen. The breakfast things lay unwashed in the sink. Let the others join them. He lit a cigarette as he contemplated the sink.

'Your job,' Harold had said when he brought him down to the village as his farm manager, 'will be to see that I'm not robbed. The whole secret of success is not to be robbed. Any great plan can miscarry if one's robbed.' Did Simson rob him? Possibly he did, possibly he didn't. In any case the farm showed no profit, but probably that suited Harold's income tax, tax losses or whatever one called them. He heard Simson coming through the unkempt garden. Now what could he want, he asked himself as the red bovine face appeared in the doorway. Simson wore rubber boots even in high summer, as if to show that he belonged to field and meadow like a cow or a horse.

'I think you ought to ring for the vet, sir,' Simson said.

'That bull calf again?'

'Looks very seedy.'

'I'll ring him, then I'll come to the cowshed.'

It was a mixed farm. Mixed rubbish, Allan often said to himself; but he did like cattle and had suggested to Harold that they breed Hereford bulls for export. Since Harold refused to listen to advice or suggestions they continued with the Friesians, and Allan's revenge was that he kept the bull calves, with the result that there was less milk to sell and most of the bull calves died on him. That made him think of vets who coined it too. In fact, everybody did except him. Still, he would have his own back on Harold when he sold the three young bulls which were already eighteen months old. He would get a stunning price for them when they were two years old. That would learn him.

'We'll have to fence in the three big ones,' Simson said. 'We can't keep them with the rest any more. They bugger all the others. You ought to sell them before long.'

'I'm waiting for the right moment,' said Allan.

Simson was a shrewd devil who had guessed that Harold didn't care for extra expense. Generally speaking, Simson had guessed from the start Allan's exact position in Harold's scheme of things. He spoke again, but Allan was no longer listening because he heard Patsy coming down the stairs. She came into the kitchen, still in the same dress, her hair falling over her face. 'I'll come out in a minute,' Allan said.

'I said to Mr. Allan,' Simson said, 'that them young bulls ought to go into the old paddock and be fenced in. You don't want to get between their horns one day, madam.'

'It might be fun,' said Patsy, frowning at the sink.

'I'd better ring the vet,' said Allan who wanted to be rid of Simson. 'Then I'll come and see you.'

But he went out only after five. When he and Patsy were together they had so much to say to each other, especially when they had other things to do, that time flew on fast wings. In the evenings it was different because of television, though not so very different, for in the middle of a play or a film they would start chatting, forget the play or the film, yet never bother to switch the set off. After Allan had gone Patsy sat down in the armchair beside the telephone with her eyes on the street running down to the bridge. Two young girls came past, both of them dressed in the latest Yeovil fashion, their long skirts churning up the dust. They were the garage keeper's daughters, both of them working in Yeovil. Patsy had never spoken to them. She kept aloof from the village's life because she saw no reason why she should enter it. She found it hard enough to speak to Mrs. Bramm on the days she came to clean. She wished the magazine weren't on the round table. To fetch it meant heaving herself out of the armchair, and it was still so hot.

Suddenly she stiffened: there was Peggy with her two blasted dogs, strutting to the grocers-cum-post-office. Why couldn't a grande dame like her leave it to the Swiss maid or the Austrian cook to do the shopping? However, Peggy was as mean as hell in spite of the Court, her handmade shoes and the whole bag of tricks of the rich. Peggy Latham was as thin as a rake yet had a double chin. Patsy touched her own: well, she hadn't a double chin. She smiled a strange selfsatisfied smile, thinking, if only that poor goose could guess. Of course, she would look in. Peggy looked in every day, and as far as the Lathams were concerned the two poor Ramshorns could have gone to the Court every evening for a drink, though not for a meal, as that was too much trouble. To spite Peggy she decided to go upstairs, and then Peggy would knock in vain. However, that meant an effort, so when Peggy appeared on the doorstep she called to her to come in.

Peggy wore a tweed jacket and skirt, the heat notwithstanding. She had short auburn hair, pale blue eyes and the mouth of a Dresden doll. Her dogs were Great Danes, they filled the room and knocked against the furniture. She carried a straw shopping basket, its only contents a jar of jam and a sliced loaf. She should have taken the Bentley to fetch them, said Patsy to herself.

'Such splendid news,' Peggy said. 'Hector's back from Lagos.'

'Is he?'

'Got back at three. He'll be here in a minute.'

'I'll see if we've any whisky left.'

'Don't bother, dear.'

14

Pushing the Great Danes aside Patsy went to the battered chest of drawers at the other end of the room. 'There's a little left,' she said, lifting the bottle, 'but there's no soda. It'll have to be water.' She walked past Peggy on her way to the kitchen, then stopped, and turned round. 'Our life has been properly messed up. My brother-in-law, the rich one, not Justin, is sending his awful little daughter here for the whole summer hols.'

'How old is she?'

'Eleven, but you ought to see her. You could take her for a grown-up woman, nothing of the child about her. So self-possessed, such self-control and such serene manners, a bloody little conceited ass . . . oh my God!'

'What is it?' Peggy asked anxiously, and Patsy's loud cry stopped the dogs knocking into the furniture, in fact they came up to their mistress as if to find out what the trouble was.

'My sister-in-law, the awful girl's mother, is a bigoted Highland Catholic. You know the sort. Her crofter ancestors were out in the '45, the King across the water, and when they turned from Latin to English she was terribly shocked and said, "We used to die for the Mass". Just like that. Now Allan or I will have to take the brat to the Catholic church in Yeovil.'

'Is your brother-in-law a Catholic too?' asked Peggy, who was given to putting questions without being unduly interested in the answers they would produce.

'He's nothing. God and religion leave him cold, though I'm quite certain that he wouldn't say no to the Church Commissioners if they asked him to help them with their accounts.' Patsy laughed, showing her large teeth.

'Here's Hector,' Peggy joyfully exclaimed.

Hector was tall and breezy and had, so he believed, mocking, twinkling eyes. He thought he possessed the magic wand, and had many reasons to think so. After he left the Navy as a lieutenant-commander for whom no future loomed on the horizon or nearer home he entered a huge firm of engineers without knowing too much of engineering, yet within a couple of years he became their roving ambassador to undeveloped countries. Dams, bridges and new ports were the articles he sold. 'I have an instinct for bribing the right person,' was his modest explanation of his success. He had married Peggy while still serving, and she brought the Court and four thousand a year as her dowry. 'I'm not the sort that lives on a woman,' he said after he had started earning fabulous sums. He always smiled, dressed well, and considered his breezy presence a tonic for all. His hair was silver-grey above the temples.

'Well, Patsy,' he said, coming into the sitting room. 'You stand there as though you wanted to clout me with that bottle.'

Patsy put the bottle on the chimneypiece, then said, 'I was telling Peggy that my rich brother-in-law's awful daughter will spend her whole summer vacation here.'

'Isn't Patsy wonderful?' said Hector. 'I come back after two long months from darkest Africa and she speaks as if she'd seen me in the morning.'

'Why not?' said Patsy, pushing her hair out of her face.

'I don't complain. May I ask how are you both?'

'Bearing up,' said Patsy.

'You always do. Did you get my postcard?'

She nodded, her eyes on the street, her hand reaching out for the bottle, then forgetting it. Two farm labourers were on their way to the Golden Hind, the only pub in the village. She heard Allan coming in through the back entrance. 'I don't think there's anything wrong with that bull calf,' he said. 'I bet Simson is in league with the vet. Isn't it lucky that I forgot to ring him?' He waited for Patsy to nod her approval before turning to Hector. 'Bramm told me you were back.'

'I think we ought to go,' said Peggy. 'I asked the Ackworths for a drink before I knew that Hector would be back today.'

'Why don't you come too?' Hector asked.

'I don't feel like changing,' said Patsy.

'Come tomorrow.'

'That's an idea,' she said. 'I hope your dogs will frighten our dear niece.'

'These two don't frighten a fly,' laughed Peggy.

Patsy remembered that she hadn't been out the whole day, so followed the Lathams into the street. She sniffed the air, which smelt of roses and stocks and dung. She stood arms akimbo, Peggy was a little in front of her, speaking to Allan, the two big dogs between them. A tractor noised past them as Hector moved to Patsy's side. 'I love you,' he said in a low voice, and for once he didn't smile. Patsy threw her head back,

16

then turned it away. Hector joined Peggy, called back, 'Don't forget tomorrow,' and walked off with Peggy and the panting dogs.

'Those dogs are like me,' Patsy said. 'They never run or chase about, yet they're always tired.'

'What we need is to get away from here,' said Allan.

When they went in she lifted the whisky bottle off the chimneypiece. 'Do we put it back or do we polish it off?'

'We'll polish it off.'

2

Justin came in at seven sharp, left his briefcase in his room, then went out, taking himself to the parlour of the Golden Hind, where he sat down at the only table in the middle of that small room, and read the evening paper. Nelson, the publican, had heard him enter, so drew a pint of bitter and brought it to Justin. 'How's Mr. Ramshorn?' he asked. Justin gave him a vague smile and went on reading.

There was much noise, guffawing and general good humour in the public bar, but not for Justin who as a country gentleman of the old school wouldn't put his foot into it. The poorer you are the more you have to keep up appearances, was his motto. The Ramshorn brothers resembled each other neither in looks nor in temperament. Harold was pale with pinched cheeks, Allan was downright handsome, and Justin had a moon-like countenance which was as red as the setting sun. He was the regional representative of a large brewery, a job he had got through Harold, who was the brewers' chartered accountant. Justin was grateful to Harold, for this was so much better than sitting in a City timber merchant's office, though he heartily despised most of the other reps whom he would meet tomorrow at the Beech Tree, which was a free house. He shook the little bell, Nelson fetched his empty mug and went to fill it.

'The visiting dart team's arrived,' Nelson said. Justin nodded, Nelson went, and when he had finished the paper Justin rose and paced the parlour. 'Commander Latham is back,' said Nelson when he brought the third pint.

At nine sharp Justin left the Golden Hind. The day had died and the smell of cow dung had swallowed the scent of the flowers. The village was quiet, only the sounds of television could be heard as he walked past houses and cottages, mostly cottages. He went in through the back entrance straight to the kitchen, where he prepared his evening meal. While the potatoes boiled he laid the table in the dining room. Patsy appeared, saying, 'Can you fetch your niece Theresa tomorrow at four at Yeovil station? She's going to spend her hols here. The mighty Harold's order.'

'I'd do anything for you, Patsy,' said Justin without looking at her.

'Don't be too tight when you fetch her. She's very sharp, the little bitch.'

'It's not my habit to get tight.'

'You just get sloshed professionally,' she said, and went back to the television set.

Justin took his dinner to the dining room, and ate slowly, thinking of Patsy who, without making any effort, was for him the essence of the house. He didn't want to admit that she was of his life too. He had never sat with her in the dining room, from which she kept aloof, none the less it was as though she sat there on his right. He clearly saw her thick mane, the two hills that her breasts made, and her two hands which were seldom quiet. He was certain that she was incredibly shallow and hadn't a thought in her head. Yet his mind remained full of her. He woke with her, carried her about with him, and at night she walked in and out of his dreams. When Allan told him that he had a met a strange girl whom he wanted to marry Justin asked what she was like. 'Like nobody you and I know.' Justin inquired what they discussed when they were together. Allan thought hard, then said, 'She asked why I spelt Allan with two ls.' Justin could almost hear Allan answering, 'Not a clue.' They were indubitably made for each other.

Justin didn't despise Allan for the weakling he was; he had no admiration for Harold because he was doing so well : his own existence and routine took up all his spare time, that is, the time he didn't spend thinking of Patsy. Only a door separated the dining room from the sitting room, and at odd moments he could hear their voices rising above the television sounds.

'I'll give her supper in the kitchen, then pack her off to bed,' Patsy was saying.

'You'd better come quietly,' said the television set.

'Isn't she too old for that?' Allan asked.

'Go through his pockets,' said the set.

'She'll probably get herself raped and Harold will chuck us out,' Patsy said.

'That would be the making of us,' said Allan.

'Theresa being raped?' laughed Patsy.

A shot was fired followed by a groan.

'What a fool,' said Patsy. 'He should have known that he was armed.'

Justin cleared the table, took the tray to the kitchen, washed up without touching or even looking at their dirty plates, then went up to his bedroom. He smoked a short cigar in bed, expanding with every puff, a sense of wellbeing overtaking him, and he decided to get a bottle of port and keep it in the wardrobe. If he left it downstairs those two might drink it, believing that it was Spanish burgundy. He tried to imagine what it would be like to be married to Patsy. His big chief at the brewery would dislike her, and what would she do while he went his daily rounds? 'I don't think,' she said one day, 'that there's much difference between a rep and a milkman.' She could say such things without it occurring to her that she was offensive. What would she do while he was out? Do nothing, of course. She wasn't made to be a wife, and that must have been the reason why Allan chose her.

He heard them come upstairs, Patsy going straight to the bathroom. He heard her running her bath, then exclaiming, 'Bugger it,' because she had knocked against something. He stabbed out his cigar and listened. She got into the bath, then he heard her splashing. Now she was standing up better to wash herself. She sat down, and came a noise as you hear in the Zoo as she heaved herself out of the water. She ran bare-footed along the passage, and Justin wiped his forehead. There had been a night when he crept up to their bedroom door and listened to their love-making. Next day Patsy looked at him so strangely that he didn't do it again.

Tonight for the first time since last autumn he lay with her in his dream, but it was not as satisfying as it had been on that October night. He woke up to the shrill ring of the alarm clock, jumped out of bed and rushed to the bathroom as if this were a boarding house and the other lodgers would soon be knocking on the door. The bathroom window overlooked the cowsheds, and before them stood Simson talking to Bramm, both of them innocent of hurry and industry. Half a dozen cows or so seemed to be listening to them. 'I'm getting too fat,' said Justin in a loud voice as he got into the bath. But what else could he expect with all the professional drinking he had to do?

Before going down to prepare his breakfast he wrote into his business diary next to three cases of ginger ale for the Red Dragon, '4 p.m. Theresa, Yeovil station.' Not a sound came from Patsy's and Allan's room. Allan would be the first to rise, and go unshaved and still half asleep to join Simson and Bramm for a few minutes' chat before returning to the bedroom to have his and Patsy's first long conversation of the day. As Justin came out of the house Simson called to him, 'The bull calf's dead.'

'Not my pigeon,' answered Justin.

He drove to several pubs as today was the day for taking orders in the Yeovil district. He visited one where the tenant had died four weeks ago, and the widow feared that because she was a woman the brewers wouldn't let her have the licence. He knew that they wouldn't, but it wasn't his job to tell her. He encouraged her, thinking he would have made an excellent family doctor, if such a thing still existed. After he had reassured her without committing his masters she wiped her eyes as a preliminary to talking of her husband. 'When you come in here, Mr. Ramshorn, don't you expect to see my Bill behind the counter?'

'As a matter of fact I do.'

'Isn't it a shame?'

'The Great Reaper is a shameful person.'

'I could wring his neck,' said the widow.

The heat lay heavy on Somerset, already the cattle clustered round the trees, and the hedgerows were lifeless under the cumulus clouds. The next stop was on the outskirts of Yeovil, the publican nearly eighty years old, rather deaf and ill-tempered. However, the brewers kept him on, saying you can't put out a tenant after fifty years, and their eyes were moist with their philanthropy.

At one sharp Justin reached the Beech Tree. Mrs. Neeves, the owner, received the reps on Wednesdays. On other days they could come only as clients, which was a pleasure all of them abstained from. For Mrs. Neeves was a domineering woman with hair dyed lilac and teeth like tombstones in a

Turkish cemetery. Nobody quite knew who Mr. Neeves had been, and among them the reps referred to her as the unmarried widow. Still, they made up to her, hoping for her orders. At one o'clock the bar clients had ceased to exist for Mrs. Neeves who had become the gay empress, holding court and ruling her subjects, those eager men who wanted to sell her their particular brands of rum, whisky, gin, bitter, light ale, stout and soft drinks. Justin timed his entrance to be the last to arrive.

'Hullo, Justin,' said Mrs. Neeves.

'Hullo, Jenny,' he said, hating her. She insisted on being called Jenny by the reps because they were men, and men were born to admire her white bosom, of which she showed as much as convention tolerated. She was also enamoured of her naked arms, wearing sleeveless dresses even in winter.

'Hi,' said McDougall's Gold Heather Whisky. 'I was just telling Jenny a very riskay story I heard, one about a little girl and an old gentleman. Know it, Justin?'

'It's ever so funny,' said Mrs. Neeves.

Little girl, thought Justin. Plenty of time till four.

'Not as funny as the one Jenny told us,' said Three Sheaves Ale.

They oozed bonhomie, were gay cavaliers and drank like fish. Towards two o'clock there was a political argument between Bright Star London Gin and Anita Rum. 'I'm telling you both parties have the same programme,' Bright Star maintained.

'I don't say you're unintelligent, Bertie,' said Anita Rum, 'but all I say is that intelligent men don't generalise.'

'Now I don't want any politics here, boys,' Mrs. Neeves said. 'No politics and no religion. We're friends here, all of us, so we don't want any politics or religion.'

'I did tell you, didn't I?' said Ye Olde Crofters Whisky, 'that we provide baby fridges with our new raspberry ale? Very handy, you can keep the ale cool under the counter.'

'I do nothing under the counter,' laughed Mrs. Neeves, showing the tombstone teeth. 'Anyway, you sent me a ton of printed stuff on it.'

'It's a good thing to remind the client,' said Ye Olde Crofters.

'I'm not a client, I'm a friend,' said Mrs. Neeves, who was

drinking as hard as the rest. The only two bona fide customers stood subdued at the other end of the bar. 'Justin is very quiet today. Anything ails you, dear?'

'He's probably contemplating marriage,' laughed Anita Rum.

'The heat doesn't agree with me,' said Justin, then wanting to be as gay and hilarious as the others he added, 'The cold doesn't either, and the rain and the wind . . . I need a seasonless world.' One without Patsy, he said to himself.

'There are no seasons up there,' said Bright Star London Gin, pointing at the ceiling.

'I told you, dearie, I don't want religion discussed here,' said Mrs. Neeves severely. 'You can do that at home the lot of you.'

'I think I'm going to sit down for a moment,' said Justin.

Beside the door was a table with an armchair on each side. Justin sat down in the one nearest to the door, took off his tie and unbuttoned his collar. 'Out of the hangman's noose,' he called to the bar, but there the repartees were flying so fast that nobody heeded his words.

'He's asleep,' said Mrs. Neeves after a while.

'Must have had a drop too many last night,' said Gold Heather, for whom everything began and ended with drink.

'I don't like it,' Mrs. Neeves said suddenly, and lifting the hatch she hurried to Justin whose cheeks were no longer their customary red. 'What is it, Justin? Don't you feel well?' She touched his shoulder, he fell forward, and Mrs. Neeves yelled.

3

Theresa stood in the corridor of the train rocking towards Yeovil. She stood near the lavatory because she liked space round her. She was small for a girl of eleven, and, therefore, her serious grown-up face looked out of place on the short body, but she carried herself very straight. Her hair was black, her eyes, her mother had told her, were as grey as a loch, and there was little colour in her cheeks. She had an expensive small bag, and needless to say her parents sent her down first class. A corpulent gentleman approached the lavatory, Theresa politely opened the door for him, and the corpulent gentleman was so taken aback that he nearly jumped. With an encouraging smile Theresa signalled to him to enter which he swiftly did, bolting the door behind him. Theresa was pleased with herself, thinking of Mother Mary Philomena, the mother superior of the convent where she was a weekly boarder, certain that Mother Mary Philomena would have approved of her polite conduct. 'Politeness,' the mother superior was wont to say, 'is the cheapest yet the most agreeable commodity there is.'

Theresa loved three people with all her heart, Mother Mary Philomena, her mother and her father, though she had some reservations about him. His habit of reading business papers during meals she didn't find endearing, and he seemed to make an effort whenever he addressed her. The gentleman emerged from the lavatory, shooting past her, forgetting to close the door in his hurry. With a smile Mother Mary Philomena would have appreciated she shut the banging door. The train stopped at Sherborne as if to regain breath, then hurried on to Yeovil. Theresa returned to her empty compartment, got on the seat, lifted down her suitcase, and let down the window. 'Porter,' she cried.

'My uncle,' she told the porter as they walked side by side

24

to the station entrance, 'is coming to fetch me. So my aunt told my mother.'

'He'll be waiting outside,' said the porter, rather impressed by the self-possessed little person.

'That's what I expect,' said Theresa.

They came out, the sun was there, but she saw neither Allan nor Justin. She had thought that it would be Allan and not Justin because she knew Allan slightly better. 'They're not here,' she said. 'I've two uncles here in Somerset.'

'One of them could have turned up,' said the porter.

'We mustn't be impatient,' Theresa said.

All those who had alighted in Yeovil had left, and only a couple of taxis remained outside the station. 'Strange,' said Theresa after a quarter of an hour. 'My uncle must have been delayed, or perhaps my aunt got it wrong and is expecting me by a later train.' The porter wanted to go off, yet to his surprise he remained glued to the spot. 'That's it,' said Theresa after another ten minutes. 'They got it wrong. When's the next train from London?'

'At six-thirty.'

'I can't keep you that long, and I'm sure you have other things to do. I'll take a taxi. Could you call that one? The first. One must always take the first.'

The porter waved to the first taxi, then carried the suitcase over, the driver took it, and Theresa opened her bag. Her mother had said that a porter's tip was half a crown; however this porter had spent quite a while with her, so she would give him two half-crowns. What was her father's favourite expression? Equitable. Two half-crowns would be equitable. 'Take these please,' she said. The porter thanked her, she got into the cab, gave the driver the address, then sat back in the seat.

'Bugger thee art,' muttered the porter as the taxi left.

Theresa sat with folded arms, now and then leaning forward to look at a horse or sheep or cattle. 'It's a very hot day,' she said after a while.

'It's summer, miss,' said the driver.

'Last summer it rained most of the time,' said Theresa, 'but then my parents took me to Spain, and there it didn't rain.'

'All these fields were flooded,' said the driver.

'In Spain the land was very dry.' She unfolded her arms. 'We went to a town called Avila because of St Teresa. I am

25

called after her and she's my patron saint. There is a huge, huge wall all round the old town. As I came out through the gate I was pushed aside, but very gently. Do you know who pushed me? You'd never guess. A donkey.' She laughed out loud. 'You'd never have guessed.'

'There's a Mrs. Wall in Yetminster who breeds donkeys,' said the driver.

'Would they push me? I don't think so. You see, St Teresa often rode on a donkey, so perhaps that donkey pushed me because I too am called Theresa.' Her brow puckered as she sought the right word. 'A salutation from the saint.' How pleased Mother Mary Philomena would be with her. A salutation from the saint. 'What a pretty stream this is.'

'We're nearly there,' said the driver in a relieved voice.

Theresa got out and rang the bell; the driver brought the suitcase to the door. 'Nobody,' said Theresa. 'They must have got it all wrong.' She looked up and down : both streets were empty. 'The sleeping village,' she observed. 'I don't want you to stay for my sake. How much do I pay you?'

'Nine bob.'

She gave him ten shillings, then on second thoughts added sixpence. 'You'll be all right?' the driver asked.

'I'll wait on the doorstep.'

He drove off, and Theresa sat down on the doorstep. The afternoon sun was in her eyes, so she took a pair of dark glasses from her bag, and put them on. In a couple of hours' time her parents would be flying to New York. Her mother had promised to cable her when they arrived. Suddenly she looked up, but there were only five cows coming along the street without a human being anywhere. How long would she have to sit there, Theresa wondered.

Shortly after the cows had gone through a gate Bramm came past the house, looked at Theresa, said politely ' 'Ow do thee do,' and entered the vegetable patch beyond the low wall. Only what he knew and what he was accustomed to could raise his curiosity. If Patsy had been sitting on the doorstep he would have asked her why she sat there, but a stranger left him uninterested. Theresa observed the lack of life round her with equanimity. This was the first village she had ever come across, therefore she could form no opinion of it. Her life had been anchored in London, her travels had taken in a few foreign seaside resorts and Italian lakes, also Spain last year, with long journeys in hired cars, her mother complaining of the food and her father hardly touching it. A small boy aged about five ran past, stopped, turned back, gaped at her, and when he saw that she was determined to ignore him he went off with his hands thrust into his pockets.

Suddenly a shadow came between her and the westering sun. She looked up, and saw a tall man with a bald crown surrounded by reddish locks. He was incredibly thin and carried a stick which was like a bishop's crook. 'Good afternoon,' he said in a slightly hoarse voice. 'Are you waiting for someone?'

'For my aunt and uncles,' said Theresa, rising.

'They're not in, but that you must have guessed or ascertained by now. I am afraid they won't be back in a hurry.'

'Why not, please?'

'Family matters,' said the man after brief hesitation. He had a sort of feverish smile which his eyes reflected. 'You're the niece from London, aren't you?'

'I'm the daughter of Mr. and Mrs. Harold Ramshorn. My name is Theresa.'

'Mine is James Lindsey. Would you like to come to my cottage and have tea with me? Less boring than waiting here, don't you think so?'

'Thank you so much, but if they come back?'

'I'll tell Simson that you're coming to have tea with me.'

He went round the house, and returned with Simson a few minutes later. 'We was expecting you, miss,' said Simson. Then he didn't know what else to say, stared at her, then picked up the suitcase. 'I'll tell Mr. Allan when he comes back.' Disapprovingly he watched Lindsey marching off with Theresa at his side. Lindsey's cottage was between the house and the church, and Simson remained motionless till the cottage door closed on the two of them. He shrugged his shoulders before he carried the suitcase to the empty garage. Though the kitchen door was never locked he didn't enter the house when Allan and Patsy were absent. He went in search of Bramm who with a boy aged about fifteen was tinkering with the tractor. He had a lot to say to Bramm about Mr. Lindsey collaring the little girl, but decided to keep it to himself because Bramm was slow in the uptake.

'What do you think?' Bramm asked.

'What about?'

'Mr. Justin.'

'There's nothing to think.'

Bramm nodded, and told the boy to get cracking with the tyre.

'Here they comes,' said Simson, ran round the house and met Allan and Patsy as they climbed out of the Land Rover. 'He's dead all right,' said Patsy. 'His heart. He never told us about it.'

She wished she could feel sorry for Justin, in fact she had wished it ever since they had seen Justin in the hospital to which Anita Rum had driven him after he and the other reps had carried him to the car. 'The quicker you get him there the better,' Mrs. Neeves had said. They all knew by then that Justin was dead, however bustle and speed seemed to belong to the occasion. In the hospital they laid Justin on a stretcher, and Patsy saw him lying on it. Why couldn't he get up? He looked so silly lying there helpless, fully dressed but without his shoes. One of his socks had a hole in it which was so unlike Justin who spent half his time darning his socks.

'It's very sad,' said Simson. 'And in the prime of his life too.' He liked prime of his life, so he repeated it.

'Not even,' said Allan. They had been three brothers, and now there were only two. Would he ever get accustomed to saying, we are two? He doubted it. 'We ought to do something about Theresa. The child must be getting impatient at the station.'

'She's here,' said Simson.

'In the house?' Patsy asked, making for the door.

'Mr. Lindsey took her to have tea with him,' said Simson.

'Lindsey?' Patsy exclaimed. 'That horror? We can't leave her there. Fetch her, Allan, at once.'

'You come with me,' said Allan.

'No, I won't go there, and you must tell Theresa never to speak to him again.'

Allan went off. He must ring up their father and send Harold a cable. Theresa probably knew the address in New York. What a fool Justin had been to die in such a sordid fashion, that is, without having got anything out of life. It would have been better not to have lived at all. Not better, just simpler and fundamentally nothing lost. If Harold had died instead he could have died with the knowledge that he possessed a farm, a house in London, lots of money in the bank, in short he would have been entitled to tell himself that he had not lived in vain. Well, he, Allan, wouldn't live in vain either. Justin's death was the best warning he had ever received.

He didn't feel deep sorrow, for they hadn't been a united family. Their mother had gone off with a Canadian captain when the war ended, and their father was too busy with his unsuccessful stage career to bother about his sons. Besides, there was too big a difference in age between the brothers for any true friendship and understanding. Justin had boarded with him and Patsy because it was convenient for both parties. He could as well have been a total stranger.

Lindsey's cottage had a thatched roof and whitewashed walls, and the window frames were purple. He was a keen gardener, his garden was well kept, and in the middle of the lawn stood a marble Artemis, her left breast slightly chipped. Allan pushed the door open without bothering to ring or knock. He wouldn't have been surprised if he had found Theresa raped and strangled. Such was Lindsey's reputation in the T-shaped village. Since raping and strangling little girls were beyond his ken as he could imagine neither, he said that to himself without ire or being shocked. The door opened on the sitting room which was long and narrow and smelt of incense. On the wall facing the entrance hung a red brocade cloth, somehow the last thing one would have expected in a thatched cottage. Theresa sat on a chair covered in a white material, eating a fruit cake. Lindsey was walking up and down, reaching the door as Allan entered. Thus the two men nearly collided. 'Here's your uncle,' Lindsey called, then lowering his voice, 'I'm terribly sorry. I didn't say a word to her.'

'How did you know?'

'It's all over the place.'

Theresa had risen, put the half-eaten slice of cake on a plate, then came up to Allan, expecting to be kissed. 'Mr. Lindsey very kindly asked me in, Uncle, because you were out when I arrived.' She craned her neck, waiting for the kiss.

'I'm sorry we couldn't fetch you,' said Allan. 'I'll tell you all about it when we get back.'

'Will you have tea?' Lindsey asked.

'We must go back,' said Allan.

'I very much enjoyed chatting with you,' Lindsey said to Theresa. 'You must come and see me again.'

'I should like that very much,' said Theresa, and Allan gave her a long, puzzled look. 'Come on,' he said.

'If I can be of any help . . .' said Lindsey.

'Thanks, we'll manage,' said Allan, took Theresa by the hand, and practically yanked her out of the cottage. 'I don't want you to come here again. Lindsey isn't a man we want you to frequent.'

'I am accustomed to grown-up people's company. I prefer them to children.'

Allan gave her another puzzled look. Some old ventriloquist ought to get hold of this child, put a grey wig on her head and use her as his dummy. 'You'll find plenty of grown-up people here without having to fall back on Lindsey.'

Two old spinsters lived next door to the post office, one of them a retired music teacher, the other, according to Patsy, her girl friend of yore. They were in their tiny garden, and when they caught sight of Allan they trotted up to the gate, saying in unison, 'We're so very sorry, Mr. Ramshorn.' He muttered a few words, they said it was sad to die so young, he nodded, then pushed on. 'Why were they so very sorry?' Theresa asked. Allan looked at her, wanted to say they were sorry for the bull calf that had died in the morning, but instead blurted out the truth. 'Your Uncle Justin, whom you probably don't even remember, died today.'

'I remember him. Was he very ill?'

'It was sudden. That's why we didn't pick you up at the station.'

'You'll have to cable my father, though he won't get it before he and Mother reach New York.'

'Have you the address?'

'I have it here in my bag. It's in my pocket diary. Tonight I'll pray for my uncle. Will you take me to the funeral?'

'I don't think it's for little girls,' he said, adding to himself, little girl, my foot.

'As you like, but I'm no longer a little girl. I'm top of my form, and Mother Mary Philomena, the mother superior, says that many of the much older girls could learn wisdom from me, but I shouldn't repeat it because that is conceit.'

'I agree with the mother superior,' Allan said drily.

'About conceit?'

'About your wisdom.'

Theresa laughed modestly, then said in a grave voice, 'This isn't the moment to laugh.'

'Where are you?' Allan shouted as they entered the house.

'In Justin's room,' shouted Patsy.

'Come down, Theresa is here.'

Patsy came down slowly, almost reluctantly. Disappointed by Allan not having kissed her Theresa didn't approach her, but pushing her hair back Patsy leaned over Theresa and kissed her on the forehead. How thick her hair is, Patsy thought. 'I told her about Justin,' Allan said.

'May I say how very sorry I am?' said Theresa.

'I just can't believe it,' said Patsy, speaking to Allan. 'That room doesn't look like the room of a dead person.'

'Is he the first dead in our family?' Theresa asked.

'I suppose so,' said Patsy. 'Come, I'll show you your room.'

Theresa took Patsy's hand, and Allan watched them mounting the narrow stairs side by side. Then he went to the telephone. Before lifting the receiver he remembered that he hadn't Harold's New York address, so went upstairs to get it from Theresa. The door of Justin's room was open, the wardrobe too, and the sun was sweeping the floor, the luminous shaft on the mean little carpet beside the bed. Theresa and Patsy were both leaning out through the window in Theresa's room. 'Theresa,' Allan called, 'give me that address.' Theresa turned round, lifted her bag off the bed, took her pocket diary, and read out the address. 'I'd better write it down for you,' she said. 'One can so easily forget an address.' Allan felt Patsy's eyes on him, looked at her, she wagged her head, and in answer he shrugged his shoulders.

'I was telling Theresa,' said Patsy, 'that if Lindsey ever asks her to tea again she must say she hasn't time.'

'A pity that,' said Theresa. 'He was so nice and amusing.'

'He can be amusing,' said Patsy, 'but he's not the right company for a little girl.'

By then Allan was telephoning the cable. 'Justin died suddenly of heart attack. Burial on Friday. Allan.' After that he sent a telegram to his father. The old man would find some excuse not to come; still he had done his duty. He went to the field beyond the garden, where Doyle, the farm labourer, was mending a fence. The evening sun was fierce. 'It's a big loss, sir,' said Doyle, making Allan wonder why Doyle, to whom Justin had never spoken, considered it a loss. It was a loss only to Justin, and if he came to think of it not even to him since life had given him so little. 'Very sad,' he said.

'It'll happen to all of us,' said Doyle.

Allan nodded, and went off to the cowsheds, suppressing a yawn. What a bore his own life was, he thought, and yet he clung to life as though it showered gold on him. He had Patsy, the only present he had ever received, and as he said that to himself he became frightened. Imagine if Patsy had died instead of Justin.

'Aunt Patsy said I can come and look at the animals,' said Theresa's voice.

'Don't go too near them. The cows in calf can get very ugly, and we don't want to cable your father and say you were kicked or gored.'

'One cable is enough at a time,' Theresa said.

'Simson,' he called. 'Look after my niece.'

'Come here, miss,' called back Simson, coming out of the shed.

Allan turned round, and hurried upstairs. Patsy was still in Theresa's room in front of the bed on which lay the open suitcase. 'You've never seen anything like it,' she said. 'Four dresses, each of them madly expensive, and shoes to match. The handkerchiefs are Irish linen.'

And I can give you nothing, Allan said to himself. He ran his hand down her back, pinching her strong, large behind. She giggled. 'That girl,' he said, 'terrifies me. She's like a witch, has the brain of an experienced old woman.'

'And we'll have her all the summer.' She made for the door, Allan followed her to Justin's room. The sun was slowly withdrawing. 'What will we do with his things?' he asked.

'Get rid of them. Sell them, but we'll have to wait a little. It wouldn't be decorous to sell them at once.' Patsy laughed. 'Who'll pay for the funeral?'

'He's insured. He was very methodical, poor Justin. In that

drawer are all his papers. Aren't we supposed to go to Peggy?'

'We have a good excuse not to.'

'It might cheer us up.'

'All right, let's go. What are we going to give the witch to eat?'

'There are plenty of sausages in the fridge. Justin's, of course.'

'If we were decent people we wouldn't touch them,' said Allan.

'You can be funny,' she said. 'I'm going to put on my white dress, though I'm getting too fat for it.'

He went with her into their bedroom, and sat on the bed while she changed. He wanted her badly, and there was that ache again. When she was dressed she searched for a handkerchief which she eventually found in a drawer. 'Cheap cotton,' he said. 'That's all I can give you.'

'What does it matter? Tell me, do you really believe that Lindsey runs after little girls?'

'I'd believe anything about him.'

'He gives me the creeps. Fetch Theresa.'

Theresa was chatting with Simson and Bramm, the two men speaking to her without the condescension or fatuity of grown-ups when addressing children. She stood with her head bowed, eyes on the ground, a trick of hers if listening intently. 'We're going to some friends,' said Allan, coming up.

'I'll be glad to meet them,' said Theresa, and Simson winked at Bramm.

They didn't take the Land Rover since the Court was only five hundred yards away. Patsy walked slightly ahead, carrying a flower basket because Peggy always cut flowers for her. In their own garden they had practically none as neither she nor Allan was keen on gardening, too much work and why bother when the Lathams had two gardeners? Theresa trotted at Allan's side, after a while taking his hand. A lorry laden with empty, clattering milk cans churned up the dust, and Theresa asked, 'Where will my uncle be buried?'

'In Yeovil, I suppose,' said Allan, who hadn't thought of that before. He called to Patsy, 'Where will Justin be buried?' The question sounded rather bizarre to him. He could just as well have asked where he and Patsy would be buried. One shouldn't die suddenly. 'The undertaker's chap was there,' she said, stopping. 'The man in spectacles I spoke to. It'll be in Yeovil.'

'You think of everything,' said Allan. 'What did you say to him?'

'It was he who asked me what his religion was. I said C. of E.'

'That's what we are, aren't we?' said Allan.

'Father says he has no religion,' said Theresa, 'but he says if he had religion he'd be a Catholic like mother and me.'

Harold had but one god, thought Allan, the one that was made of gold and was stuffed with bank notes, and they helped each other to get along.

In front of the Court was a cedar tree on a round island of grass. The Court was Palladian with an ugly Victorian orangerie built onto it, the apple of Peggy's eye. The Great Danes rushed out to wag their tails and whimper their friendly greetings. 'They're a bit big,' said Theresa, stepping back.

'They're slophounds,' said Patsy.

'I only heard about it a few minutes ago,' said breezy Hector, coming out. 'I'm so sorry, Patsy. Can I be of any help, Allan?'

'It's all under control,' said Patsy.

Hector took Allan aside, saying in a low voice, 'If by any chance you're short of cash, a funeral is so expensive, I'll be only too glad to help.'

'Justin was insured,' said Allan, 'but thanks all the same.'

'So this is your little niece,' said Hector. 'Poor child, arriving at such a moment.'

Allan fell behind as the others went into the Court. He was deeply humiliated by Hector's offer to lend money to pay for the funeral. Did he, Patsy and the late Justin smell so strongly of poverty? Or was it just the case of Hector having enough money to appreciate that others could be poor? There were two sorts : those who thought that everybody was as rich as they, and the others, who were convinced that everybody else was a beggar compared to them. Hector belonged to the second category, which made him pretty odious; and now Hector was surely thinking that he had behaved handsomely by offering to lend money he didn't need. He wished he had the strength to stop seeing Hector and Peggy, who had nothing to offer except paying for a funeral when it wasn't necessary. He went into the library, where the Lathams entertained people who came in only for a drink. The drawing room was used but on special occasions, such as giving a dinner party for a visiting tropical minister or some big bug from the City.

Peggy couldn't have children, Patsy used the pill. With moist eyes Peggy gazed at Theresa, smiling timidly. She had been married to Hector for twelve years, therefore she could have had a child of her age. 'So you're eleven,' she repeated several times. Theresa accepted a lemon squash, then walked round the library, looking at the sporting prints, of which there were a fair number. When she had examined the lot she went to the book shelves.

'I hardly knew your brother,' Hector was saying. 'I think he came here only once.'

'He wasn't sociable,' said Patsy, 'but I can understand him. All those pubkeepers and their like must have killed all desire to mix with people.'

'Patsy always hits the nail on the head,' said Hector admiringly.

'Would you like to see the orangerie?' Peggy asked Theresa, speaking in a diffident voice. She loved children because she would never be a mother, but had no idea how to approach them. 'I don't know what that is,' answered Theresa, and Patsy chimed in, 'A place where there are orange trees, plenty of plants and flowers.' Peggy looked at her enviously.

'I love flowers,' said Theresa, putting down her empty glass.

Peggy took her along, Patsy followed them, and Allan remained alone with Hector who immediately poured him more whisky, a male conspiracy in the absence of women. 'She's a curious child,' Hector observed.

'She's too grown up for her years, too sure of herself, but I don't think she's a nuisance, just spoilt. Do you know where we found her when we came back from the hospital?' Hector shook his head. 'She took a taxi from Yeovil station, and was apparently sitting on the doorstep waiting for us when Lindsey came past, and took her to his cottage to give her tea.'

'He shouldn't be encouraged,' said Hector. 'Mind you, I don't know whether the gossip about him is true—in a village there is always too much gossiping—but one should never take a risk when a small child might be involved. It's better to think the worst and give him a wide berth.'

Allan thought him unbearable, and yet the earth belonged to men like Hector. 'One of the reasons Lindsey is disliked,' he said, 'is the annoying fact that he keeps to himself, and nobody knows anything about him.'

'Because he surely has something to hide,' said Hector. 'Ah, here they come.' The two women and the child reappeared. 'You look tired, Patsy, but in the circumstances that's understandable.'

That reminded Allan of Justin, not the Justin who had been his brother, but the freshly dead person in the Yeovil hospital. 'Let's go back,' he said.

The Lathams walked with them to the gate, both saying they would come to the funeral. 'Please don't,' said Allan. 'We want it to be as private as possible.'

'I appreciate that,' said Hector. 'Come and see us very soon.'

'Why don't you want them to come?' asked Patsy as they approached the house.

'I just don't want them to come,' said Allan, looking at Theresa who was walking with her head bent. Like a pilgrim or something, he said to himself.

He found a letter on the round table in the sitting room, delivered by hand. It was from a seed merchant whom he hadn't paid and who wanted his money. This meant juggling with the accounts again because Harold must never know that now and then dire need forced him to hold back for his own purpose sums allotted to the farm, and how modest, he thought bitterly, his own purpose was. And there beside him stood Harold's daughter. With a couple of hundred pounds the daughter's father could lift him out of his debts. But was that an answer?

'We'd better have those sausages tonight,' Patsy said.

'I am very fond of sausages,' Theresa said.

'You eat first,' said Patsy. 'You must be tired, so you ought to go early to bed.'

'As you wish, Aunt Patsy.'

Patsy fed her in the kitchen, took her upstairs, came down, switched on the television set, remembered that she had forgotten her packet of cigarettes in Theresa's room, and hurried back. Allan was sitting on the round table when she returned. 'What's wrong?' he asked.

'I opened the door quietly in case she was already asleep,

and there she was, kneeling beside the bed, praying.'

'What did you say?'

'I said nothing, closed the door quietly and came down. It was like catching somebody out. Now I've no cigarettes.'

'I'll go to the pub and get you some.'

There they were, he thought on his way to the pub, living from one packet of cigarettes to the next, never daring to buy more than one at a time because like that it seemed less expensive. Harold and Hector probably bought them by the ton.

'I am ever so sorry, sir,' said Nelson, the publican. 'He used to come 'ere every night. I'll miss 'im something bad.'

There were a few heavy drops of rain as Allan retraced his steps, but they ceased falling before he reached the house. Patsy was seated before the television set. 'This is quite good,' she said, and they started discussing the seed merchant's bill. At eleven they decided to have only a little bread and cheese. 'It can't go on like this for ever,' he said as they went upstairs. He made vehement love because of all the despair he felt in himself. Patsy was thinking of Justin, whom she had once heard tiptoeing up to their door while they were at it.

4

Though she hadn't been to a funeral before, Patsy found it exactly as she had expected. It was a sort of anticlimax without there having been a climax. She overheard one of the gravediggers saying to the other, 'Frank can't come today.' Who was Frank? He appeared more important than the coffin, which could have been anybody's coffin. But Frank was a person, moreover he couldn't come today. Justin couldn't come either, but he was no longer a person, hence he didn't count.

Last night they had received a cable from Harold, saying he was deeply distressed and the funeral should be at his expense. Allan decided to ask the undertaker for a duplicate bill which he would keep against the seed merchant's bill, one worry less. Then he asked her, 'Why don't you despise me?' So they went upstairs and had a jolly good bash. Old Ramshorn had telegraphed to say he was heartbroken, but his lumbago kept him from coming to the funeral. Anyway, Allan had expected that. Theresa had asked her to let her come to the funeral because she felt it was her duty to be present. 'Mother Mary Philomena wouldn't approve if I stayed behind.' She was a frightening girl. The funeral was at ten, Theresa stood beside Patsy, head bowed, never saying a word, and remained silent while they drove back to the village.

Patsy said she had to return to Yeovil to do some shopping because they had run out of food. In Yeovil she entered the car park in the Land Rover, got out, looked round, then hurried to a small yellow car which was usually driven by Peggy who left the Bentley to Hector. Patsy got into it beside Hector, who had borrowed his wife's car as it would make him less conspicuous. She thought that quite funny.

Hector grabbed both her hands, saying, 'Patsy, my love.' His lips sought hers.

'No, Hector,' she said.

'You know I love you.'

'You often say that.' She laughed. 'You say that far too often.'

'Why far too often?'

'Because in the end I'll believe you.'

'And then?' She shrugged her shoulders. His hand touched her breast, which she pretended to ignore. 'I told you,' he went on, frowning at an old woman who parked her car next to Peggy's, 'that for you I'd leave Peggy tonight. You're everything in the world to me . . . you're not listening.'

'I am, Hector.'

'Kiss me.'

'If that's all you want,' she said, leaning forward, her mouth open, her eyes on him. It was she who pulled back first. 'It's terribly hot in here. No shade.'

'It's more than a kiss I want,' he said. 'I want you wholly, completely, because I want to make you happy, give you everything a woman needs to be happy. How can you go on leading that sordid life? It breaks my heart to see you leading such a miserable, wretched existence with a man who is incapable of getting anywhere.'

'I don't mind that.'

'You're lying to yourself. Don't forget it'll get worse every day. He has no guts, he's not entitled to an adorable woman like you.'

'That's our vicar over there,' said Patsy.

'Hang the vicar.'

'We don't want him to see us.'

'Why not? He'll know like everybody else when you leave Allan for me.'

'I'd rather go to bed with you than leave Allan,' Patsy said, watching the vicar drive off. 'He's gone.'

'What did you mean by that?' asked Hector, his hand slowly moving up her thigh. There were a few silky hairs on it, a sort of advance guard. He disliked his heavy voice, for Hector believed in being in complete possession of himself, which, naturally, included his voice as much as his desires. However, so near to Patsy self-control escaped him. 'What did you mean by that?' he repeated.

'Nothing really,' she said, her body beginning to tremble.

'That's Mrs. Holden arriving over there.' She pulled away. 'We can't stay here. Can't we drive somewhere for a few minutes?'

He didn't answer, let in the clutch and drove Peggy's little car out of the town, passing the cemetery where a couple of hours ago Justin had taken up residence. Patsy forgot to glance at it.

'I'd once a lover long before I met Allan,' she said, 'who said I was just an animal.'

'What did he mean by that?'

'That I was just an animal. Perhaps he was right.' She pressed her leg against his as she laughed. 'Take that little road there. One afternoon when Allan and I came back from Weymouth we did it right there in the Land Rover.' She smiled reminiscently. 'I'll show you where. Nobody ever passes here.'

They reached the spot a few minutes later, a row of elms with a high fence running parallel with the lane. There was a wide opening in the fence and enough room between the elms for the car to pass through. The sun beat down on the fallow land, in the distance a cuckoo was repeating itself, and nearby two robins and a blackbird made off only to return to the bush. 'We'd better get into the back,' said Patsy.

Hector hadn't planned it like that. He hadn't imagined that it could be so easy and so quick. He was a slow worker by instinct, one who took his steps one after the other, never running or jumping, refusing to force an issue. He was too modest when he said he knew when and where to tip. In fact, he was a first-class salesman who carefully prepared his terrain, knew how to make the first moves and not to attack too soon. Now Patsy was upsetting his well-conceived plans. Already she had got into the back of the car, and as he turned his head he saw that she had trussed up her skirt, waiting for him. Her mouth was half open, her eyes shone tantalisingly. Hector began to feel the ache to which Allan had accustomed himself. You could make love to her for hours without truly possessing her. He moved to the back seat where the Great Danes usually panted. They made love in the heat, her body burning, he almost wanting to wring her neck in order to obliterate that impersonal light in her eyes. Yet she gave him more pleasure than he could have conceived, pleasure without happiness, though pleasure all the same. 'You're good at it,' she cried. 'More, more, more.' When it was over she wiped the perspiration off her face with her hand. 'Give me a cigarette,' she said without bothering to pull down her skirt. Hector was staring at her. 'Don't worry,' she said, 'I use the pill.'

'It's not that,' he said, shifting his right leg because he feared a cramp. 'I never met such a wonderful girl before. This was the greatest revelation of my life.' All that was left of his plans was to work his way back to where he had wanted to start, even though events had overtaken him. 'I want you to leave Allan, and if you do I'll leave Peggy. She and I have nothing left in common.'

'And what have we?'

'Didn't you feel it?' he asked reproachfully.

'It was very good,' she said, pulling down her skirt. 'We ought to go back.'

'Before we go, my darling Patsy, there are one or two things I want to tell you. The first is that I love you, but you know that. The second that I love you too much to tolerate the life you lead with Allan. You haven't a decent dress, your life is humdrum and monotonous, and it will go on like this as long as you stay with him.' The words came easily : the high-powered salesman at work.

'I never think so far ahead.'

'One never gets anywhere with a short-term policy.'

'I've no policy,' she said in a self-satisfied voice, then yawned. 'We must go back. Allan will be waiting and it's suffocating here.'

He looked at her, saying to himself, I'm already missing her. 'How could we arrange a night together?' he asked. She shook her head, smiling with understanding. 'Can't you say you have to see some relation?'

'I've no relations. Come, Hector, drive me back to the car park.'

On the way back he continued to pound her with vistas of a future that was gilded lilies, or rather roses, all the way. 'I've never known luxury,' she said, 'so it leaves me cold. When I see a fashion show on telly I switch off. I read only magazines, but never look at the dresses. I never had any jewels, and I never ...'

'You say never too often, Patsy darling. There is no such

thing as never. I'd still be tied to Peggy's apron strings if I believed in never. You must divorce him.'

'I can't,' she laughed.

'Why can't you?'

'Because we're not married, but keep that to yourself. His brother would send us packing if they knew. Not so much he as she.'

'That makes it easier.'

'I won't leave him.'

'Just think of it, Patsy. You're not even married to him. I know my English Catholics. They're more puritanical than the Puritans themselves were. If your sister-in-law finds out you'll be left without a home, and what sort of life do you have?' He knew how to press his point and take advantage of any fresh information he gleaned. 'You'll accompany me on all my trips, we'll travel all over the place, won't stagnate in the country but have a flat in London, go to Paris, to Rome, to Greece, to . . .'

'Don't drive into the car park. I'm getting out here.'

'When shall I see you again?'

'I'll try to come in tomorrow around five, but can promise nothing.'

'I'll force Peggy to ask you all to a meal.'

'Not necessary.'

'To be near you, to gaze at you.' She opened the door and got out. 'Did you like it?'

'Very much, otherwise I wouldn't dream of coming in tomorrow.' She hurried to the Land Rover without glancing back. She had been clever, she thought, to have done her shopping before meeting Hector. She shouldn't have promised about tomorrow because she mightn't feel like it. What should she give Theresa for lunch? There were plenty of sausages left, but one couldn't feed the girl on sausages all the time. She would buy three steak and kidney pies in the village shop, and boil some potatoes and runner beans. There was some processed cheese too; the girl would have no cause to complain. Was it wise to tell Hector that they weren't married? She smiled, remembering Justin who though living with them had died under the impression that they were married. She vaguely wished that she could miss him.

To his own astonishment Allan was missing Justin with

whom he had never had a single thought in common. Sitting in the room he called his office, bored stiff with a form he had to fill in, his thoughts were with his dead brother. Luckily Theresa had come for the summer to fill the financial gap Justin's demise had caused. When she went back they would have to look for a new lodger.

He remembered saying one day to Justin that there surely was a way out of poverty if one thought of it hard enough. 'Robbing a bank,' Justin had said in the voice he used when jesting with publicans and their ample-bosomed wives. 'Why not?' Allan observed, and Justin gave him a disapproving look. 'If we're not caught on the premises,' Allan went on, 'nobody will suspect us. Crooks and gangsters are professionals who know the police, and the police know them. The underworld knows them too, but neither police nor the criminal classes know us, consequently we could get away with it if we're not caught. With a little training, careful planning and using our loaves we could do it.' Justin said he considered it an excellent joke, then went up to his room. Frankly, they had had nothing in common, yet here he was missing him. Where was Patsy? She ought to be back by now.

The door was pushed open by Theresa who wore a red linen dress. She held out a book, then asked whether it was the kind of book she should read. Allan looked at it. When he and Patsy had moved into the house they had found about a dozen books the previous owner had forgotten to take with him. This one was a thick volume, a history of the Duchy of Cornwall. 'I think it would bore you stiff,' he said.

'May I try?'

'If you want to. Why did you ask whether it was the kind of book you should read?'

'Mother Mary Philomena says one is always punished when one reads a book one is still too young to read.'

'How is one punished?'

'By not understanding what one reads.'

'I see,' he said, jumping up because he heard the Land Rover. 'Here she is.'

He nearly collided with Patsy in the doorway. 'Gosh, it's hot,' she said.

'Hullo, Aunt Patsy,' said Theresa.

'Hullo,' said Patsy, giving the child a long glance, then turned her head away, for to shake the child with that satisfied smile of hers was too much of a temptation.

'Mrs. Latham telephoned,' said Theresa, 'and asked for you. I said you went shopping to Yeovil.'

'Where was I when she rang?' Allan asked.

'You went out with Mr. Simson to see about fencing in the young bulls.'

Is this weird girl, Patsy asked herself, going to run the house and the farm too? She hurried to the kitchen with Allan in her wake. 'She's driving me crazy,' she said, putting the shopping basket on the table.

'I admit she's quaint,' Allan said, 'but she's no bother. When you drove off to Yeovil she asked me whether she could go for a walk. I said yes as long as she didn't get run over. She said she'd learnt road drill when she was five. She went down to the bridge, so she told me when she came back, looked at the stream, talked to some village lout who wanted to scare her with Snake Country . . .'

'For God's sake don't let her go there. If she gets bitten by a viper your brother Harold will kill us.'

There was no more need, thought Allan, to refer to him as brother Harold, just your brother, since he had no other left. 'They're only grass snakes,' he said. 'Then she inspected the cricket pitch, looked at the church, came back, and informed me that the village is T-shaped. She said she ought really to be T-shaped too because her name began with a T.'

'And you think that's funny?'

'She's quite cute, and no trouble at all.'

'We shall see,' said Patsy, and sat down to peel potatoes.

The door gently opened, and Theresa smiled in on them. 'What will we have for lunch, Aunt Patsy? I hope you don't mind my asking.'

'Steak and kidney pie.'

'That takes a very long time to make.'

'These are ready made,' Patsy said.

'I'm sure they'll be very good. May I help?' She sat down at the kitchen table. 'At the convent we have an old French nun who does most of the cooking. She says it is a fallacy to scratch new potatoes. They ought to be peeled like old ones. I'll peel these the way Mother Sainte-Agnès does.' She chuckled. 'I'll

44

tell you something very funny about steak and kidney pie. During last hols I went to have tea with a girl who's in the same form, Charlotte Coleman, and her grandfather came in, a very kind old gentleman who told us that he once engaged a new cook who said she was very good with pastry. On the first day they'd steak and kidney pie, on the second day the same steak and kidney pie reheated, on the third it was served cold. Well, this is over, thought the old gentleman, but on the fourth day they had a fresh steak and kidney pie.' Theresa laughed, waiting for Patsy to laugh with her. As there was no accompanying laughter she asked, 'Didn't you think that funny, Aunt Patsy?'

'I'm not going to give you steak and kidney pie every day,' snapped Patsy.

'I'm sure you won't,' said Theresa in a soothing voice. 'I only told you about it because the kind old gentleman made us laugh, Charlotte and me.'

'Is the water boiling?' Patsy asked.

'It is,' said Allan.

From the corner of her eye Patsy watched Theresa peeling the potatoes. 'We don't want that many,' she suddenly said. 'I'm too fat to stuff myself with potatoes.'

Theresa laughed again. She has a peculiarly irritating laugh, said Patsy to herself. 'Help me to lay the table here,' she said, 'but first we must clear away the mess.'

'I laid it in the dining room,' said Theresa.

'Who told you to? We always eat either here or in the sitting room.' She felt insulted.

'The sun was shining into the dining room,' said Theresa, 'and it looked so nice in there, but if you want me to . . .'

'For once we can lunch there,' said Allan, and Patsy gave him a baleful look which she had really meant for Theresa. As she was fundamentally far too easygoing and too lazy to stoke the coals of her ire she observed on entering the dining room, 'You were right, Theresa. It is nice in here.' Allan sighed his relief. 'But it's too much work to eat here every time,' she added.

'I'll lay the table and clear it off, so don't worry on that score,' said Theresa, and Patsy disliked her again.

She should, she thought, ring up Peggy to ask her why she had telephoned. The last thing she wanted was to make Peggy suspicious. Suspicious of what? Anyway, it was too hot to bother.

'Your aunt,' said Allan at the end of the meal, 'always has a little rest after lunch. These last two days she was too busy, but today she'll start again. What will you do this afternoon?'

'I'd like to read that book, please,' said Theresa.

'You like reading?' Patsy asked, rising from the table.

'Very much so, but first I'll clear the things away.'

'We'll do that when I come down,' said Patsy.

She mounted the stairs slowly, thinking of Peggy, and thought it was rather cute to have made love with Hector in her runabout. Hector was asking too much of her who hadn't bothered to marry Allan, who in the beginning had tried to insist, though in vain since it would have made no difference. She took off her dress, threw herself on the bed, turned on her side, jumped because a wasp had buzzed its way into the room, chased it with a towel till it flew out, then, feeling completely exhausted, she lay down again, thinking that tomorrow she would tell Hector that it was too complicated to live with Allan and carry on with him. Allan stood beside the bed.

'I won't do it,' she whispered. 'I wouldn't enjoy it with that girl in the house. She gives me the creeps. She might hear us, or come upstairs. Tonight when she's gone to bed.'

'But Patsy.'

'I can't. I'd think of her, and neither of us would like it. I'll make up for it tonight.'

Allan went downstairs, looked into the sitting room, where Theresa sat reading the book on the Duchy of Cornwall, apparently deeply absorbed. He felt like murder. It wasn't Patsy or Theresa he wished to do away with, but only himself. To kill a useless and powerless person like him would be the best piece of work of his life. Would Harold have planted the child on him if he weren't in his clutches? Would Patsy have refused to make love with him if they lived in a house that was large enough for three people? Of course not, and that was why he should take a hammer and bash in his own head. As he came out of the house he saw old Lady Blurthrop sailing past in her chauffeur-driven Rolls-Royce. She lived on the other side of the stream, and had known wealth and power from the day she was born. If they sent her a niece she would put her in the guest wing, or simply refuse to have her. The

Rolls-Royce pulled up, the old woman beckoned to him.

'You havent forgotten about the Conservative fête, I hope, she said. He said he hadn't. 'Oh good. I want you to bring all your yokels, Mr. Ramshorn. The idea, as you know, is to get to the grassroots, ha ha. Tell them there will be all kinds of games and stalls, in short everything to amuse them. And then, ha ha, having done my duty by my son-in-law I'll go to my little house in Grasse.' The son-in-law was the local M.P.

'My three yokels are Tories anyway,' said Allan.

'That's the spirit,' said the old woman, waved, the chauffeur closed the door, and the car moved on. My little house in Grasse, Allan muttered to himself. The car stopped, and the chauffeur blew the horn. Allan turned away. The chauffeur klaxoned, Allan began to walk towards the cowsheds, and as he approached the back gate he heard the chauffeur's voice, 'Her ladyship wants to say something to you, sir.' Allan wished he had the guts to pretend he hadn't heard him; instead he went up to the Rolls-Royce. 'I heard,' she said, 'of your brother's sudden death. I am so sorry, Mr. Ramshorn.' The door closed again, and she was off to the two old spinsters to remind them of the fête. My little house in Grasse, Allan thought bitterly; and why did he say that his yokels were Tories? Why not say they were Anarchists to make that old parchment face grin a little less?

Half an hour later he found himself walking on the edge of the beet. Suddenly he disturbed a covey of partridges that flew off like a cannonball. Lindsey's wall came as far as the field and as he passed, Lindsey, who was working in his garden, hailed him in a loud, cheery voice. Didn't the swine understand that he couldn't stomach him? 'Step in,' said Lindsey. 'I want to show you some of the vegetables I'm giving to the fête.' Allan was still in the little house in Grasse, so stared at him without comprehension. If he had a little house in Grasse he would be in bed with Patsy in a fine bedroom and no creaking springs. 'You were out,' continued Lindsey, 'when I called to condole with you properly, such a sad blow.'

'Very unfortunate,' said Allan without listening to his words. He took a step forward because all he wanted was to get away from Lindsey and back to the little house in Grasse which probably had a dozen bedrooms.

47

'I've got Danish lager in the fridge,' said Lindsey. 'Come in, and we'll have a cool drink.'

'I haven't much time,' Allan said ungraciously.

Again he was shocked by the red brocade cloth on the wall. It looks evil, he said to himself as he stood in the middle of the room, waiting for Lindsey to fetch the beer. A bookcase was bursting with books, a couple of Japanese prints were on the wall facing the red brocade, and the large yellow sofa, covered with cushions of all hues, cut the room nearly in half. If you were on the other side of it you could easily be stopped from reaching the door. A cunning bastard, nodded Allan, and he imagined Theresa on the other side of the sofa with Lindsey blocking the way. 'I sleep on the sofa,' said Lindsey, appearing with a bottle of beer and two glasses. 'The rooms under the roof are too small and poky. Sit yourself down.' Allan sat down in an uncomfortable armchair near the empty grate. 'I honestly don't know why I bought this cottage,' Lindsey continued. 'It has so little to recommend it, though the garden is lovely. I mean I made it lovely.'

'How did you hit on this village?' Allan asked, watching him pour out the beer.

'Through an agent. I was rather browned off at the time. Doesn't that ever happen to you?'

'All the time.'

'You're joking.'

'I'm dead serious. Ever heard of clipped wings? I was born with clipped wings.'

He was annoyed with himself for speaking so openly to a man he despised. If Patsy had let him stay with her he wouldn't be in this blasted cottage.

'You surprise me,' said Lindsey.

'You really imagined that somebody of my age can be contented to lead the life of a sort of honorary farm manager? And employed by his brother?'

'If one isn't in business it's very difficult to get on. Yet look at me. I was in business, but when I inherited a little money I got out, came here to potter about in a small garden. How's that charming little niece of yours? Such an intelligent child.'

'She's very well, thank you,' said Allan, regretting his frank speech. 'And thanks for the beer. I must be moving on.'

'I've another bottle in the fridge.'

48

'Some other time.'

'I'll show you the vegetables. I've marrows as big as an old-fashioned liner, he he, for the fête.'

'Honestly, I haven't time.'

Lindsey walked with him to the gate. 'I'll think about your problem,' he said, and Allan had a good mind to shout at him that his problems were no concern of his, but remembered that it was he who spoke of them first. He was in an even worse mood when he returned to the house. Theresa stood up as he came in. He put on a smile for her benefit. 'Is your aunt still upstairs?'

'And asleep. When I went upstairs to fetch a clean hanky I heard her snoring so very sweetly. I passed the room on tip-toes.'

'You're very considerate,' said Allan, and she thanked him with a sincerely happy smile. He felt that he had been far too long without Patsy. Gently he opened the bedroom door, stopped in the doorway to contemplate her lying naked on her back, eyes closed, legs wide apart and an arm across her eyes. The mouth was half open, the wasp was back but Allan ignored it as he gazed at her. If I never saw her again, he said to himself, this is how I would remember her. The thought of never seeing her again filled him with such an ache that he stepped into the room, and said 'Patsy' in a loud voice which, of course, woke her up. 'A wasp,' she exclaimed. 'They petrify me.' He took a towel and chased the wasp out through the window. She had sat up, and was yawning and stretching her arms.

'What are we going to do with her this afternoon?' she asked.

'She seems quite happy reading,' he said, sat down on the bed, drew her hot body to him, and kissed her desperately. 'Hang the girl,' she said, 'and lock the door. Heat and sleep always make me randy.'

While they were at it the telephone bell rang. Theresa lifted the receiver. Again it was Peggy, asking for Patsy. 'My aunt is sleeping,' Theresa said. 'She's very exhausted. We had to get up so early for Uncle Justin's funeral.'

'Poor you,' said Peggy. 'I mean poor Allan, poor Patsy, and you poor child.'

'And poor Uncle Justin,' said Theresa primly.

She promised to tell Patsy to ring her back, and when Patsy came down, followed by Allan, who didn't look any happier, she informed them of the telephone call. 'First we'll clear the dining room table and wash up,' said Patsy who in her present mood didn't want to be reminded of Hector, hence Peggy could wait.

'I've done the lot,' said Theresa.

'You're very useful round the house,' said Patsy, sitting down in the armchair from which she could survey the street. It must be getting on, for there was old Fred's wife coming out of their cottage and turning towards the bridge. Daily she went to her married daughter who lived beyond the stream. 'What would you like to do, Theresa?'

'What will you do?'

'There's plenty to keep me busy here,' Patsy yawned. 'I'll take you tomorrow to the Crans. They've two children. Today I'm done to the world.'

'May I go for a walk and explore the countryside?'

'Don't go too far.'

Patsy watched Theresa as she walked towards the stream till her attention was caught by a man riding past on a scooter. When she looked down the street again Theresa was out of sight. Patsy yawned and picked up the magazine she had bought before meeting Hector in the car park.

Theresa stopped before the garage, smiled at the garage keeper and a client who were arguing. A small terrier ran out of the garage to bark at her. He received a smile from her too, also a wave of the hand asking him to approach. Wagging his stump the terrier came up, she patted him, then leaned over to kiss the pointed nose. With a loud yap the terrier jumped away, and when he turned round to continue the game he was disappointed to see that she had moved off. This side of the stream three Devon cows were grazing in a meadow. She stopped on the bridge, and leaned over to see whether the water contained fish. She saw no fish, though she caught sight of the same tall boy of about fifteen who in the morning had spoken to her of Snake Country. The boy grinned at her, she bowed to him as she had been taught in the convent, crossed to the other bank and took a lane leading up to a hill. There was an imposing sycamore on top of the hill.

After passing the sycamore she took a narrower lane flanked

by hedges that hadn't been cut level for a long time. Beyond each row of them were bushes, a sort of small jungle, and she was walking in complete shadow till she reached a derelict barn. She stopped, a jay flew over, there must have been a fire here, she said to herself, and moved on. Soon a dilapidated, deserted farm house followed, the windows like empty sockets and the door unhinged. An old rusty kettle lay on the doorstep. 'This is Snake Country,' said a voice behind her. It belonged to the boy, who had followed her from the bridge.

'Now is it?' Theresa said, turning round. 'I've seen no snakes.'

'If you walk on you'll see plenty. If they bite you you die.'

'You're saying this to frighten me.'

'A viper killed a cow here last year.'

'Last year I wasn't here.'

'I dare you to walk on.'

'I will, but I can't go too far because I promised my aunt not to go too far.'

'That's an excuse because you're afraid,' said the boy. He had a flat nose and his flaxen hair hung down his forehead. His cheeks were extremely red.

'To be afraid is never an excuse,' said Theresa. 'I mean it the other way round. If one is afraid one should admit it and not look for excuses.'

'Who told you that?'

'I was told that by a saint. You see, I'm brought up by Mother Mary Philomena who is a saint.'

'There are no saints,' the boy guffawed.

'How can you say that?' Theresa asked indignantly.

'I ought to know. My pa's the vicar, and he knows everything there is to be known on the subject . . . there's a snake. It's coming towards you.'

He waited for her to shriek, to jump and bolt. He waited in vain because she simply said, 'I can't see it.'

'You must be shortsighted.'

'I've very good eyesight, thank you. I am more and more convinced that it's all a fabrication, and if there are snakes here they're grass snakes.'

'Who told you that?'

'My uncle.'

'Who's your uncle?'

'My Uncle Allan Ramshorn.'

'Those people,' said the vicar's son in a despising tone.

'I don't think I want to speak to you any more,' said Theresa, and walked on.

The boy followed her without saying a word. Suddenly his eyes lit up, and he sang out, 'Look, there's one, right under that bush.' He leaped forward, then stopping at her side he pointed at a snake moving fast from a small patch of sunlight into the shadow. 'That's a grass snake,' said Theresa.

'How do you know that?' he asked.

'Because it is one. Anyway, it's gone. Now I'm going to turn back.'

He grabbed her by the shoulder, saying, 'You see, you are a coward.'

'Please take your hand off my shoulder,' she said. He guffawed, but dropped his hand. 'I want to walk back alone.' He followed her, keeping his distance.

She walked with her head high, not once looking back to see if he were in her wake. He kept about ten paces behind her, once or twice letting out a loud guffaw which she ignored. They passed the farm house, then the barn, an old man stood beside the sycamore, smoking a pipe, and when he saw the boy he called to him, 'What are you doing round here, Horace, eh?'

'You mind your business, and I'll mind mine,' the boy answered.

'No better than your dad,' called the old man louder.

The boy sprinted up to Theresa. 'That's a Baptist,' he said, and guffawed. 'You know what a Baptist is?'

'I told you I want to walk back alone.'

'They're chapel people. My pa has no time for them. Now you got me?' He remained at her side till they reached the bridge. 'If you come tomorrow I'll show you a real poisonous snake, and it will bite you.' She didn't answer. 'I was just pulling your leg. If you come tomorrow I'll show you something which you'll like very much. It's a real kennel full of dogs, but it's a little bit farther on.' There was still no answer. 'Will you?'

'You were rude about saints and my uncle, so I don't want to speak to you again.'

'You said that before, but then you spoke to me.'

'Because of the snake,' she said, stepping on the bridge.

He let out a loud guffaw as she hurried away. She found Patsy seated in the same armchair with the magazine on her lap. Evidently she hadn't budged while Theresa visited Snake Country. 'Did you ring the lady?' Theresa asked. 'I mean the one who rang twice?' Patsy's first reaction was to tell her to mind her own business, however the girl looked so intent that she said, 'Mrs. Latham wants us all to supper on Sunday.'

'Thank you so much. It was such a nice house.' Patsy nodded, her eyes on old Fred, bicycling home, his face red because it was uphill work and he had a weak heart. 'The same boy spoke to me again this evening,' Theresa continued. 'He says he's the vicar's son.'

'That's Horace. He's not quite right here.' She tapped her forehead. 'The father's like the son. You keep away from them . . . why are you laughing?'

'Forgive me, Aunt Patsy, but you said the same of Mr. Lindsey.'

'For different reasons. Take my advice and don't talk to anybody in this village when you're not with us. Will you do something for me?' Theresa assured her that she would. 'You go to the pub, that's up the road to the right, but for God's sake don't go into the bar, but ring the bell where it says Parlour. Mr. Nelson, the landlord, will come to the door, tell him I sent you and would he give you a tin of cheese biscuits, and I'll settle with him when I see him next? I'm too tired to move.'

Theresa took her bag and darted out of the house. With her eyes on the street Patsy fell into a reverie. Hector, Allan and Peggy were beckoning to her, each a shadowy figure, all of them moving their lips without her hearing a word they said. How tiring the whole business was. A tractor stopped outside the garage, then the back door opened and closed, and there was Theresa with the tin of biscuits.

'You told him that I'll pay him the next time I see him?' Patsy asked.

'You don't have to, Aunt Patsy. I bought it as a present because you and Uncle Allan are so kind to me.'

Patsy jumped out of the armchair, her cheeks flaming red, fury in her dark eyes. 'How dare you?' she vociferated. 'So your parents told you that we're poor, what? So you want to be charitable to poor people, eh? You dirty little horror, don't you do that to me again.'

Theresa burst into tears. 'I only wanted to give you a present,' she sobbed. 'I never thought of it that way. We're all the same before Our Lord whether we're rich or poor. Oh . . . Oh . . . Forgive me, Aunt Patsy, I only wanted to make you a present. Oh, please, don't be angry with me.'

Though she was easily moved Patsy wasn't yet satisfied. 'But they did tell you that we were poor wretches with no money, didn't they?'

'I mustn't tell lies,' cried Theresa. 'I think mother did say you weren't as lucky as them, but that doesn't matter, and I didn't buy it because of that. I just wanted to give you a present, dear, dear Aunt Patsy.'

The girl's misery was irresistible, and while muttering to herself, so they did tell her, Patsy bent down to kiss her on both cheeks. Then she said, 'Thank you, it was really a kind thought. I was wrong. Don't say a word to your uncle about this. Go and wash your face.' However, Allan appeared before Theresa reached the stairs. 'Look at this,' Patsy said quickly. 'I sent Theresa to fetch it from the pub, naturally I was going to pay for it, and do you know what the sweet girl did? She paid for it because she wanted to make us a present.'

'That was damned decent of you, Theresa,' said Allan. 'You're a very sweet girl. Thanks awfully.'

Theresa was all smiles, but when she reached the bathroom she had a brief sobbing fit, remembering Mother Mary Philomena saying that misunderstanding other people's intentions was the cause of most ill feeling. She washed her face, dried her eyes, combed her hair, and her smile was luminous again as she went downstairs. They had Justin's sausages for supper. 'The last of the lot,' Patsy announced. In order to be nice to Theresa she asked her to watch television with them; the girl preferred to read the book on the Duchy of Cornwall; and so as not to disturb them she would read it in her room. Patsy kissed her good night, vowing that for nothing on earth would she go up to her room since she might find her kneeling beside the bed.

Before turning in Allan entered Justin's room, switched on the light and looked round. On the table lay the local paper, only four days old. It was open on page three, and with a blue pencil Justin had marked a short paragraph. Somehow Allan hadn't the courage to read it, for it would be eavesdropping on the dead. He turned out the light, went to the bedroom, and as he lay down beside Patsy, who already was half asleep, he murmured fiercely, 'You're all I've got in the world.'

5

Rain fell in the night, and old Fred, who took up most of the double bed, leaving little room for his emaciated wife, muttered to himself as he listened to the rain, This is the end of the summer, it'll rain till Michaelmas, the flowers will rot in the herbaceous border, bugger thee art. He wasn't much of a weather prophet, for by the time Lindsey awoke on the yellow sofa the sun was out in all his splendour, and the heat continued.

Lindsey was a slow riser. He lit a cigarette, took a few puffs before smiling at the red brocade, then lay back, sending the smoke up to the low ceiling. The brocade was reassurance for him, that is to say it reminded him of the great days before he buried himself first in a London office, afterwards in the country. It stood for luxury, for a gay and giddy life, and for danger too which he had often skirted. The gay and giddy life he had led after the war when for nearly three years he had been part of the military government of Trieste. And it had been in Trieste where he discovered what he really liked and wanted. The red brocade had hung on the wall of the bedroom in which for the first time he had given vent to his true feelings. Little Marietta must be a fully developed woman by now, over thirty years old, and probably with huge, hanging breasts. The thought made him shudder. When the military government came to its end and he left Trieste he took the red brocade with him, his mascot. He stubbed out the cigarette.

He looked revoltingly ugly with his bald pate and long nose which the sun turned red every day. The hair round the pate was like wire netting. He smoothed it down before getting off the sofa, examined his face in the glass, grinned at himself, then went upstairs with lowered head so as not to knock into the rafters. The bathroom faced the stairs. While he shaved he thought of Allan and their chat of the day before. Since everybody has his moral frontiers he contemplated Allan with moral disgust. The fellow was weak, useless, and reminded him of an Italian with whom he had some dealings in Trieste and who had spied for Tito. Fundamentally that was no business of his, none the less he couldn't resist asking the man how he could work against his own country. The man smiled, shrugged his shoulders, and said, 'One lives as one can.' Allan, he was convinced, would have said the same under similar circumstances. And the woman whom he paraded as his wife. Patsy stood for everything he abhorred, for there was nothing under the sun as loathsome and revolting as a woman in full bloom. Girls should die at the latest at thirteen as after thirteen they became shapeless by growing breasts, getting hairy, in short losing the pristine beauty they had possessed while they were small. Women were eyesores, and Patsy the worst among them. Many times he had seen her walking past his gate with her breasts shaking, her backside sticking out, yet she too had once been a sweet little girl, flat and without appendages. Last night he had seen Theresa running to the pub, what grace, what perfect beauty, and with what ease she moved. Poor girl, to live with the useless fellow and the full-blown slut.

He remembered saying to Allan that he might find a solution to his problems. His subconscious had been quicker than he; and he grinned at himself in the glass, his yellow teeth showing. He hadn't forgotten the tricks he had learnt in Trieste, that then so feverish town with Italians and Yugoslavs working against one another in the dark. Those tricks stood him in good stead long after he had left military government, a perfect example of which was his choosing as his operational headquarters a benighted village like this one. It was no longer benighted since little Theresa had appeared. For a second he was frightened because it was so perfect that it might be a trap fate had set for him. That was going too far, since fate had been pretty lenient with him.

He took a cold shower, put on corduroy slacks and a white and red checked shirt, hurried down, and went out through the front door. A steeple-jack on the church spire loomed like a heavy shadow. He knew the chap, who could at noon drink four pints of rough cider, then climb unflinching on top of the spire without fear or vertigo. 'Good morning, Mr. Lindsey,' said a deep voice. Lindsey turned to the vicar, whom he thoroughly despised. The vicar was the spit of his son, only sturdier and never guffawing. His was a losing battle, which in his intrinsic modesty that amounted to meekness, he no longer bothered to fight. The villagers were Low Church, the gentry Anglican, but the gentry was small in number and hardly bothered to go to church. It often seemed to him that Peggy Latham was his only parishioner. If he felt less gloomy he added Lady Blurthrop who came rarely and was abroad half the year. On top of it he was a widower, plagued by the two old maids in the cottage too near to the vicarage, and had no control over or any sort of relationship with his son, who misinterpreted whatever he said to him.

'It's a lovely day again,' said Lindsey.

'We're lucky with the weather.'

'A gift of the Almighty,' said Lindsey in an ironical voice.

'By every means,' said the vicar, stepping back because he had sensed the nearness of his son Horace hovering only a few paces away, grinning sheepishly. 'He can't even make his own breakfast,' said the vicar more to himself than to Lindsey. 'I must leave you, Mr. Lindsey. I wish you a very happy day.' Why hadn't he the courage to speak to Lindsey as man to man, that is as vicar to parishioner, and find out why he never came to church? He shook his head, then went into the vicarage to prepare Horace's breakfast.

Lindsey, with the plan his subconscious had evolved for him, sauntered towards Allan's house. As he approached it he caught sight of Allan speaking to Simson on the other side of the low wall. 'Ramshorn,' Lindsey called, 'could I have a word with you?' Allan came to the wall. 'Look in on me this evening if you can. I thought of our little chat, and I might have something for you.'

'I just felt gloomy,' said Allan. 'You mustn't take it seriously. Anyway, I can't manage tonight.'

They're all the same, Lindsey thought. They take the first step, then regret it, then sheer necessity or despair forces them to take the second. 'Come in whenever you want. I don't think my idea is a bad one.' His was a cool, aloof voice, and he walked off slowly, stopped to light a cigarette, then still slowly he went towards the Court; half way to it he turned back, and his slowness was rewarded in so far as he had a glimpse of Theresa coming out of the house, wearing a sky-blue dress that set off her jet black hair most becomingly. Should he follow her? He wouldn't because that was going too far. With no ulterior motive he had one day offered the Cran girls a bar of chocolate as one of the old village women passed, and he shook with fury as he saw a nasty glint in her eyes. These village people read only the lowest tabloids, consequently all they knew of life was strangled little girls lying in dark fields, preferably thrown into a bush.

Theresa had entered the post office, so he lingered, hoping to meet her as if by accident. She emerged a few minutes later, coming straight towards him since he was between the house and the post office. 'Good morning, Theresa,' he said in a cheery voice. 'I bet you posted a letter.'

'To Mother Mary Philomena,' said Theresa.

'The mother superior of your convent.'

'So you remember me telling you,' said Theresa with a smile.

'I remember everything. Grown-up people don't listen enough to children, but I'm not like other grown ups. I like children because they often have more sense than grown ups. Do you know why?'

'Please tell me.'

'Because they're unspoilt.'

'Grown-up people can be unspoilt too.'

'Very rarely,' said Lindsey, then saw Patsy, his natural enemy, on the doorstep, so he waved to Theresa, saying, 'Come and see me when you have time. I'm either in the house or in the garden.'

'I told you not to speak to him,' said Patsy.

'But it was Mr. Lindsey who spoke first, and he speaks so kindly.'

'You keep away from him,' said Patsy, and they went into the house together. 'At eleven I'm taking you to the Crans.' Theresa thanked her, then went to the kitchen to get the breakfast going. 'Is there any real ground for the gossip about Lindsey?' Patsy asked Allan when he appeared.

'Frankly, I don't know. He was already here when I arrived, and Simson and Bramm and Mrs. Bramm all said he chased little girls. They could give me no proof, it mightn't even be true though he looks like a satyr, but so many people do, and village people trust their instincts more than you or I would.

That's why they're village people. He never has anybody staying with him, no woman anywhere, smiles at the little girls . . .' He shrugged his shoulders. 'Are you taking Theresa to the Crans?'

Cran was an electronic engineer who was employed in a factory just outside Yeovil, and had brought his family to the village because they couldn't find suitable accommodation in the town. Country life as such had no attraction for them, and their trim garden was proof of their suburban mentality. Cran was in the factory, Mrs. Cran, a short, mousey woman, offered Patsy and Theresa tea in the chintzy sitting room, and the two daughters, one ten, the other nine, stood with their backs to the window, staring at Theresa and nudging each other. Conversation was lame, and never got off the ground.

'You're at school in London?' Mrs. Cran asked.

'I'm a weekly boarder at the convent of Our Lady of the Seven Sorrows.'

'So you're a Catholic?' Theresa assured her that she was. 'Do you like it there?' Theresa loved it there. Mrs. Cran asked Patsy how Mr. Ramshorn was keeping. He was keeping well. That reminded Mrs. Cran that the other Mr. Ramshorn had died, so she condoled with Patsy. 'It must have been a terrible blow,' she added. Then she looked at her daughters. 'Why don't you take your friend to the garden?' She turned to Theresa. 'You'd like to go to the garden, wouldn't you?'

'I'd like to very much,' said Theresa unenthusiastically.

'Take her to the garden,' Mrs. Cran ordered her daughters. They took Theresa with them, and Patsy watched the three of them through the open window.

The Cran girls moved silently at Theresa's side; Theresa pointed at the dove cot; one of the girls spoke; then all three lapsed back into silence. They circled the garden twice, after which, as if by accord, they came back into the room. Mrs. Cran looked disappointed. 'It was too hot, mummy,' said the elder daughter.

'You must bring them to us,' said Patsy, rising. 'Theresa needs the company of girls of her own age.'

Mrs. Cran promised she would, her daughters said nothing, and when they were out in the sun-pounded street Patsy turned on Theresa. 'You weren't sociable at all. That isn't good manners.'

'I'm sorry, Aunt Patsy,' said Theresa, 'but I did my best. I asked them why they had no doves in the cot, and the bigger girl said because they made too much noise in the morning. I said they made a soothing noise, they laughed and didn't speak again. Mother Mary Philomena once said to me that I am too solemn for little girls, and don't know how to play with them. I'd have played with these little girls if they had wanted to play, but I don't think they know how to.'

'You'll be an old woman of sixty by the time you are fifteen.'

'Does that mean to be wise in one's generation?'

'You're a strange child,' said Patsy, and they both turned round as they heard a loud fiendish cackle. 'That's that daft boy.'

'The vicar's son, the one who tries to frighten me with snakes.'

Horace followed them at a distance till they reached the house. 'There's a letter here from your mother,' Allan said. Theresa took it, and hurried up to her room to read it. 'Hector was here.'

'What did he want?'

'Frankly nothing. He walked three times round the room, then asked me to go to the pub and have a drink with him, but I said I had too much work here.' He laughed. 'The best lie ever. Then he went off.'

Patsy nodded. 'I imagine he's bored when he's down here. This afternoon I'm going into Yeovil. We really must give the girl a proper meal.'

'You were in Yeovil yesterday.'

'I don't want her to write to her mother and say all we give her is sausages. I'll get chops.'

Allan looked at her with his sad, hurt eyes, then went into the office. Hector, Patsy thought, must have been disappointed not to find her in. Why did she say she was going to Yeovil? She had decided to drop Hector as it was becoming too complicated, chiefly because Hector wanted the lot. If he had only wanted an occasional bash that would have harmed nobody, but he was asking too much from her. The trouble was that the butcher wouldn't come before tomorrow in his van. If he had come today she could have forgotten about Yeovil. She shook her head because it was a pity that the butcher's day was tomorrow and not today.

Theresa laid the table again in the dining room, with Patsy no longer objecting. 'Mother sends you both her love,' Theresa said at lunch. 'They're flying to Texas today. Mother went to St. Andrew's Cathedral, but says she prefers the Oratory. She thinks that I wouldn't like the extreme heat and bustle and not knowing my way about. She envies me for being here in the village. When they come back in September they'll take me to Morocco before I go back to the convent. That's very kind of them, isn't it?'

'Very,' said Allan.

'Father wants me to describe in my next letter all that is going on on the farm.' Allan frowned. 'Will you help me to write that letter, Uncle Allan? You know all that's going on on the farm. I don't, and father always says, never speak of a subject if you don't know it well.' Allan's brow cleared, and he said, 'I'll help you with the letter.'

'That's very kind of you,' said Theresa.

'One can't put in a word edgeways,' said Patsy after Theresa went to the kitchen with a tray on which the dirty plates were piled.

'She's all right. Are you going upstairs?'

'Not this afternoon,' said Patsy. 'I'm getting really too fat, and I read in a magazine that nothing fattens more than sleeping in the afternoon.' She saw the disappointment in his eyes. 'I'll make up for it tonight.'

She helped Theresa half-heartedly with the washing up. Then she went into the sitting room, sat down in the armchair facing the window, and fell immediately asleep. Allan looked in, gazed at her, shook his head as he smiled at his sleeping love, took a magazine, and seated himself on the round table, hardly reading, lifting his head every five minutes or so to gaze at her. She slept for an hour and a half. 'What's the time?' she cried, waking with a start. 'Why did you let me sleep? I told you I didn't want to sleep.' She ran upstairs, and changed into her white dress. 'You do make yourself pretty for the butcher,' laughed Allan when she returned. 'Why don't you take Theresa with you?'

That, thought Patsy, was a good excuse not to dally with Hector. However, she remembered Hector's excitement and ecstasy as he made love to her in the back of Peggy's car, so said, 'I want a little holiday from her.'

'You shouldn't say that. She's doing all she can to fit in and be helpful. Don't forget that in London they have two servants.'

'She isn't bad,' said Patsy, ready to take her along to Yeovil, but at that very moment Simson knocked loudly on the door. 'Come in.'

'I hope I'm not disturbing,' Simson said. 'The missus would be ever so pleased if the little miss could come and have a cupper with her. Can I take her?'

'Of course, take her,' said Allan. 'Theresa,' he called, 'come down.'

The hand of fate, said Patsy to herself. 'Well, I'm off.' She beckoned to Allan. 'Can I give the butcher a cheque?'

'You can, it's still on Justin.'

Simson took Theresa to his cottage which was beyond the meadow where the cows were grazing, and near an apple orchard. Lindsey, who was in his garden, saw them climbing a gate. He let out a long, low whistle.

Theresa came back at six, looking delighted with herself. The sun had already been busy with her pale little face. Steak or no steak, thought Allan, life in the village was doing her good. 'Is Aunt Patsy back?'

'She isn't, but she ought to be here any minute now. How did you get on?'

'Mrs. Simson has two budgies which are in a cage on a chair beside the window, and all the time birds fly in and out, even fly round the cage. I saw robins, and blackbirds and thrushes, and I said to Mrs. Simson that they're wicked birds really because they just want to show those budgies that they are free. Free like a bird, isn't that so, Uncle Allan?'

'I bet Mrs. Simson was astonished.'

'Why?'

'I don't think she's accustomed to such remarks.'

'Was it the wrong thing to say?'

She craned her neck as her eyes met his. They were slightly worried eyes, but slowly a light which was akin to a smile spread across them. 'You're a funny little girl,' Allan said, patting her cheek. 'Why funny?' she asked without receiving a reply, for Allan had recognised the rattle of the old Land Rover. He hurried to the garage, reaching it before the car. Patsy gave him her ear to ear grin with practically all her teeth in evidence. 'Don't say I'm late, because I am,' she laughed, 'but I got three juicy chops.' Before he could ask her what had delayed her she climbed out of the Land Rover, saying, 'I promised Simson to get him this.' She held up a can.

'I'll take it to him,' said Allan, and Patsy ran into the house.

She was in an ebullient mood for the rest of the evening, chatted vivaciously with Theresa, made the girl laugh, in short was the life and soul of the little party. Allan beamed on both of them. After the chops she took Theresa for a short walk, and when Theresa went upstairs she accompanied her to her room. Allan could hear both of them laughing in spite of the noise the television film produced. It was a Western full of bang-bangs. He heard Patsy coming down the stairs which creaked as though they were in a ghost-ridden house. She switched off the sound, leaving only the fast-moving shapes, now uncannily dumb, then sat down in her armchair, and said to Allan in a slow matter-of-fact voice, 'I was late because I was thinking. I stopped the Land Rover on the roadside to think even harder.'

'What were you thinking about?'

'I was thinking that we're a bad influence on each other.'

'Don't be funny, Patsy.'

'I'm not being funny, I'm dead serious. We're both too easy going, too damned lazy, I lazier than you. We complain of being perpetually broke, but neither of us has the strength and energy to do something about it. Now if you had an energetic woman who would drive you . . .'

'Nobody could ever drive me, my love. The reason we're a good influence on each other is our never nagging or forcing each other. But where did you get that idea?'

'You're not taking me seriously.'

'I take you very seriously,' Allan said, rising from his armchair, going over to stroke her thick mane. 'Can't you feel it?' he asked bending down, and their lips met. But when he had straightened himself she said with a sigh, 'One can't talk seriously to you.' He sat on the arm of her chair, and his right hand began to caress her left leg. As the hand mounted so her trembling increased, turning into a tremor, her hand pulling his head down. They made love in the sitting room, and anybody who passed could have seen them at it since the curtains weren't drawn. Nobody passed.

'We are a good influence on each other,' Allan said when he rose.

'One can't talk to you,' she said, sighing.

'This was better than talk.'

6

The day of Lady Burthrop's fête was cloudy and hot. 'This is the end of it,' said old Fred to his emaciated wife as he mounted his bicycle. 'A thunderstorm will come and the weather will never be the same, bugger thee art.' There was no thunderstorm.

After breakfast Theresa took herself for a walk. She was wearing the yellow dress. She went down to the bridge, the clouds were low, and before reaching the bridge she was hailed by Mrs. Bramm who asked, 'Is Mrs. Ramshorn taking you to the fête?'

'We're all going,' Theresa said.

Mrs. Bramm hurried on, this being her day at the Crans, and Theresa stopped on the bridge, determined to discover fish in the stream. When last year they were on their way to Avila they had stopped in a village near Pamplona, and in the stream she had seen many trout. She saw no reason why there should be none here. Horace wasn't about. She lingered for a while, disappointed she climbed up to the sycamore, looked back on the bridge which a tractor was crossing, waited till the tractor had vanished round the bend, then set out for Snake Country. What would happen if she met a real poisonous snake? She recalled that St. Francis of Assisi had spoken to a wolf, so why shouldn't she speak to a snake? What would she say to it? 'Brother snake, I mean thee well.' That sounded very good indeed, and the glory that would come her way if the snake bowed, or whatever else a snake did to show its friendliness, followed her back to the house, took up residence in her bedroom and never left her sight. In a large box with holes in it, so that the snake shouldn't suffocate, she would take it back to London, and present it to Mother Mary Philomena. 'This is my brother snake,' she would say.

She saw no snake as she moved between the high untidy

hedges. The barn still looked evil, the farm house more derelict under the clouds, and as she passed it she became aware
of footsteps on the other side of the hedge. On she went, and
so did the footsteps. She stopped, not a sound, a pigeon flew
overhead, she moved on, and there were those creaking sounds
again. She stopped, the footsteps continued. She waited, then
she went on. Suddenly a voice shouted from a large bush
slightly in front of her, 'I'm a big venomous snake,' and a
loud guffaw followed. Stupid boy, Theresa said to herself.

Horace crawled out of the bush. 'I frightened you,' he
declared.

'You didn't frighten me a bit.'

'You're lying.'

'I wouldn't lie to you. Why should I?'

'But you'd lie to someone else?'

'Only if it meant saving a person's life.'

'Do you know anyone whose life you'd want to save?'
Horace asked.

'Plenty. You ought to brush your jeans. They're very dirty.'

'Thanks. Now that was decent of you. You see, if I went
back with my jeans covered in grass my pa would start shouting, "Oh, what have I done, Lord, to have a son like this
one?", and then there would be a sermon lasting two hours
all about my wickedness. If only he could preach to his congregation as he does to me he could be a bishop by now. But
he has no congregation, so I get the lot.'

'What does your mother say?'

'My mother? She doesn't say much because she died when
I was a kid, but he speaks to her. He says, "How could you
have brought into this world a son so unworthy of you?" Then
he looks like crying.'

'So you're an orphan?'

'Only half.'

'I've a mother and a father, but lost an uncle.'

'I knew him,' said Horace. 'Do you want to see that kennel?'

'Yes, please. Are there many puppies?'

'Not one. It's a very special kennel. Now come through this
bush.' He looked back as he reached it. 'If you're not afraid of
the boa constrictor that lurks under it.'

'We're not in the Matto Grosso,' Theresa said coldly.

'I say, you do know a lot.'

67

'I'm the best pupil at the convent.'

'The others must be pretty daft.'

'You say that to annoy me, but I've learnt never to be annoyed.'

'You've learnt a lot.'

'Mother Mary Philomena says it's silly to be annoyed because when one is annoyed one suffers more than the person who annoys one.'

They crawled through the bush, a wooden fence was before them, he bade her climb over it, and when they were across he pointed at the expanse of stubble, whispering, 'Don't make too much noise. This belongs to Farmer Rush who's Chapel, so doesn't like me.' They were a conspicuous pair as they moved along the stubble, neither of them uttering a word. In the distance hummed a tractor, and a cuckoo repeated itself. They reached a gate, beyond it they took a narrow path which skirted a small wood. 'They're elms,' Horace said. She said she knew they were. 'You know everything. They make coffins with elms, cheap ones. Expensive ones are made of oak. Was your uncle buried in an elm or an oak coffin?'

'I could ask.'

'So you don't know.'

'If I don't I ask.'

'You wouldn't be popular at my school.'

'I'm not a boy.'

Horace sighed.

The wood ended, and beyond a large patch of grass were the kennels. Each dog was on his own behind nine-foot wire netting. Each large cell, for that is what they amounted to, was separated from the next with double netting. The dogs began to yap, bark and bay as they caught sight of them. Facing them was a fine bull-mastiff, next to him a dachshund, a chocolate poodle followed, and a poor little papillon shivered and yapped in the fourth, which was far too large for him. Farther on were an Irish setter, a golden retriever, a Doberman pinscher, a German pointer and a majestic Pyrenean sheepdog that lost all his majesty as he ran round his cage, whimpering. 'This is a very funny kennel,' Theres observed.

'I told you it's a very special kennel,' said Horace, approach ing the bull-mastiff, who wagged his tail, stopped barking and looked at them imploringly. 'It's a quarantine kennel. You know what a quarantine kennel is?' He waited with a triumphant smile while the frenzy of the prisoners rose.

'It's a dogs' prison,' Theresa said. 'They're kept for six months because of rabies. When we were last year in Avila there was a very sweet stray dog who followed me everywhere. I said to mother we should take it back to England. She said it wouldn't be fair on that free dog to put him into quarantine for six months.' She gazed at the dogs. 'Poor prisoners, and they think we came to fetch them.'

'Free them,' Horace gleefully corrected.

'They should have made an exception with that little one.' She pointed at the papillon. 'It's too small to be locked up. We mustn't stay, we're only making them unhappy.'

'You're a cry-baby.'

'I'm not,' said Theresa, going nearer to the papillon. The little, long-eared thing nearly collapsed with hope and joy. 'I'm sure you'll soon go home, little one.' Her voice broke, and she wiped her eyes surreptitiously, as she didn't want Horace to notice it.

An enormous kennel maid, looking like a peevish gaoler, appeared on their right, coming to investigate what caused all that barking. 'It's you again,' she said to Horace. 'Push off. Told you not to come here to annoy the dogs. Off you go.'

Theresa expected Horace to give her some fitting answer. However, he slunk off, and still wiping her eyes she followed him. Reaching the path she looked back, to wave to the dogs. The bull-mastiff was staring after her with despair in his eyes. She wiped her eyes again. 'That awful woman is Irish,' said Horace when they were beside the wood. 'Do you know what I'm going to do when I finish school and get away from my pa?' She said she had no idea. 'I'm going to start a quarantine kennel.'

'You're wicked.'

'Let me finish. Has that mother something-or-other never told you to let people finish what they have to say?'

'I'm sorry.'

'At last. I'm going to start a quarantine kennel, fill it with dogs, then when it's chock-a-block with dogs I'll let the lot out. That'll learn all the Irish kennel maids.'

'You're nice and kind,' said Theresa. Then she thought it

over. 'But what will happen to those dogs? They'll either be caught and brought back ...'

'They wouldn't be brought back to me.'

'Has nobody ever told you to let people finish what they have to say? If they aren't caught they'll starve. Dogs have been domesticated for too long to be able to forage for themselves.'

'I know who you are.'

'What do you mean?'

'You're Miss Show-off,' guffawed Horace. 'I don't show off. I don't tell you all I know. I never told you that I knew all about the Gauls. You don't know who the Gauls were.'

'They lived in the centre of France and were defeated by Julius Caesar.'

'Well, I be buggered,' Horace exclaimed.

'I don't know what that word means,' said Theresa, immediately regretting her lie, for she had heard the word used by Simson, Bramm and Doyle. It must be, she was convinced, a swear word.

'At last something you don't know,' said Horace.

'The Gauls had a chief, but I haven't yet learnt his name. It's a very long name.'

'Vercingetorix,' said Horace coldly.

'I said it was a long name, didn't I?'

As they reached the road on their side of the stream a car abruptly stopped, the driver leaned out and called, 'Hullo, miss. How is you keeping?' Theresa went up to the car, Horace stepped back, and stared open-mouthed while Theresa chatted with the driver. When he drove off he waved to her. 'Who was that man?' Horace asked.

'The taxi driver who brought me from Yeovil on the day of my arrival. It was nice of him to remember me.'

'You're so funny that naturally one remembers you.'

'If you think I'm funny you don't have to come for a walk with me.'

'All right, you're not funny.' They crossed the bridge, Horace stopped, for he didn't want to be seen in the village with so small a kid, especially as it was a she-kid. Theresa asked him at what time he would go to the fête. 'I'm not going.'

'Why not?'

'Because I don't like people,' said Horace.

She gave him a smile full of curiosity, then walked up to the house in the midday silence, the village asleep, and nowhere a soul moving. She found Patsy upstairs, lying on the bed, her hair practically covering her face. 'Are you not well?' she asked.

'I've a splitting headache, and I think I've a temperature,' said Patsy. 'Your Uncle Allan will have to take you to the fête. I don't feel well enough to face it. I've sent him to get some ham, and there's plenty of lettuce, and I boiled you each an egg, then there is a little cheese, so you won't die of hunger.'

'Can I do anything for you, Aunt Patsy?'

'You can, Theresa. Pull the curtain and let me rest.'

'I'm so sorry that you're not well.'

'I'll be well by the evening.' Theresa reached the door. 'Theresa.' The girl turned back to face the darkened room. 'Tell your uncle to let me sleep. Don't let him come up. Only sleep can save me.'

But Allan did go upstairs after Theresa had delivered the message, which reminded her of an oft-repeated observation of her mother's, namely that men had no tact, and wanted everything their way. Allan was back two minutes later, saying, 'Your aunt isn't well at all. She promised to call the doctor if she doesn't feel any better by five.'

'She'll be better by then. Cheer up, Uncle Allan.' He smiled at her. 'I got the lunch ready, but I can't find the vinegar and oil for the salad. Mother says I mix a salad quite well.'

'We just pour salad mixture on it.'

'Oil and vinegar are better.'

'Some other time.'

She tried to carry on a conversation at lunch, but got few answers out of him, which was understandable with his thoughts upstairs in the bedroom. He saw Patsy with the clarity only nostalgia can give. When he made love to her he felt that in spite of her passion she wasn't truly near him; when only a door separated them he was convinced that he wouldn't see her again; now it was a ceiling. 'You won't mind, Theresa, if we come back a bit early.'

'If you prefer to stay I'll stay with you. We don't have to go.'

'We're going. The house will be more quiet if she's alone. Anyway, she very much insisted on my taking you.'

The telephone bell rang. 'Shall I answer it?' Theresa asked. He nodded. 'It's Mr. Latham,' she said. 'He wants to speak to you.'

'I just rang to find out if you're going to old Lady Blurthrop's,' said Hector's breezy voice. Allan said he was taking Theresa, though not Patsy, who didn't feel well. 'I'm sorry to hear that. What time will you be there?'

'Half past three.'

'The earlier one goes the less smelly the crowd is, ha ha. I'll try to be there before.'

The crowd wasn't too large at the fête, and consisted mostly of old women, for Lady Blurthrop had had the capital idea of putting on a cat show. 'The cats will be judged by their friendliness and charm,' said the gushing programme. 'The days of pedigrees are over.' That showed that Lady Blurthrop moved with the people if not with the times. It was her son-in-law the M.P. who was to judge the cats. Vegetables and flowers abounded, for they too would be judged. There were different sporting events, mostly for children, but they were few and far between. When Allan and Theresa arrived Lady Blurthrop and a small, fat woman shaped like a tobacco pouch were judging home-made cakes. The general impression one had was that the fête was a sort of tea feast, the marquee the temple of the brew. The manor stood serene and stolid in the background. It had been a Queen Anne manor that was burnt down in 1900 and rebuilt in the Elizabethan style.

Trevor Whitehurst, the M.P., was visibly bored. He looked at a person, his face lit up as though he had spotted an old lost friend, rushed up to him or her, and had little to say. Allan received the full blast of his momentary enthusiasm, and while he spoke to him of the weather and the Labour government's appalling record Theresa detached herself from Allan and went to look at the cakes, then at the vegetables. 'Good afternoon, Theresa,' said Lindsey. 'Come and look at my enormous marrows, or would you like to have tea first?'

'I'd rather look at the vegetables first, Mr. Lindsey.'

'So you remember my name,' said Lindsey, delighted.

'I do,' she said, looking away. Allan and Patsy had so often warned her against visiting Lindsey that it would have been well nigh impossible to forget his name.

What an adorable little face, said Lindsey to himself. Then aloud, 'We'll settle the matter. I'll get you a cake, and you'll eat it while you look at my enormous, gigantic marrows.'

'It's too early for me, thank you so much.'

'You know your own mind,' said Lindsey. 'Come along, my dear.'

They were joined by a flat-faced man with a flat nose and a thick ginger moustache. 'This is my old friend Jonathan Hickman,' Lindsey said, 'and this is Miss Theresa Ramshorn.' Hickman let out a cackle. 'Now would you believe it, Theresa? Jonathan and I were together for years in faraway Trieste which, as you know, is the frontier town between Italy and Yugoslavia. We were both fierce soldiers of the King, sitting in offices with our feet on the desk.' Theresa laughed. More and more adorable, thought Lindsey, his eyes aglow with his kind of tenderness. 'Then our task was over,' he continued, 'and old Jonathan and I lost sight of each other.' Hickman let out another cackle. 'And then suddenly we met here. It wasn't prearranged, it wasn't planned, it was just fate. One day when Jonathan deigns to pay me a visit you must come in too, and you'll have tea or coca-cola, whichever you prefer.'

'Coca-cola,' said Theresa, thinking what a nice and kind man Mr. Lindsey was in spite of Aunt Patsy and Uncle Allan warning her against him. They were surely mistaken.

'I'll see if I can get you a bottle of coca-cola,' said Lindsey, and hurried away, leaving her with Hickman, who smiled vaguely at her, the smile never reaching his cold, light blue eyes.

There was a shout, and in the distance four small children began to run for their lives, encouraged and cheered on by their parents. Theresa turned her back on them. 'Do you live far from here?' she asked.

'A couple of miles only,' said Hickman, then frowned, trying to think of something to say to the little girl with the grown-up face. 'And you, do you live far from here?' was all he managed to bring out.

'I live in London, but now I'm staying with my uncle and aunt in the village.'

'It's a strange little place.'

'It's T-shaped.'

Hickman couldn't think of anything else to say. Lindsey

came back empty-handed. 'All they have is tea and stale buns,' he said. 'I'm sorry to have let you down, Theresa.'

Allan appeared. It had taken him some time to get away from the M.P. Then Lady Blurthrop had collared him to ask him whether he thought that it would be a good idea for her to see his brother the famous accountant, her income tax affairs being in a frightful mess. I'm basking in Harold's blazing sun, he said to himself as he explained that his brother was in America, but would be back in the autumn. He could have added that his famous brother's daughter was here at the fête, yet he didn't feel like it. By the time he reached Theresa he regretted it since the old woman might have invited the child to the manor which probably would have amused her. It was too much bother to go back. He frowned at Lindsey, the frown making no impact as his frowns were unconvincing. 'Haven't you seen the Lathams?' he asked Theresa. She said she hadn't. He looked at Lindsey, who thought they weren't present.

'I must introduce you to my old friend Major Hickman,' said Lindsey. 'We were together in military government in Trieste.' Hickman gave him a curt nod. Looks like a policeman, Allan said to himself. 'One day,' Lindsey went on, 'you must both come in for a drink. Remember our little chat, Allan? You call me James, less ceremonious. Jonathan is one of the cleverest men I know. He may be useful. I mean he always has brilliant ideas.'

As Allan couldn't be rude in front of Theresa he gave Lindsey a distant smile. He wasn't any good with distant smiles either. Lindsey said, 'What about the day after tomorrow? Can you look in around seven in the evening, Jonathan?' Hickman said he could. 'I'll expect you at seven, Allan.' He can expect me till Doomsday, thought Allan. Theresa turned to him, 'Don't you think we ought to go back, Uncle Allan? Aunt Patsy might need us.'

'But you haven't had tea yet,' bleated Lindsey.

'We'll have it when we get back, don't you agree, Uncle Allan?'

'Completely,' said Allan. 'Anyway, we don't want to see the cat show . . .'

'Not really,' said Theresa.

Lindsey reminded Allan about the day after tomorrow,

Allan said he wasn't certain whether he could get away, his eyes scanned the small crowd : the Lathams hadn't come. The cat show was in full swing. Lady Blurthrop and her son-in-law beamed at the cats, most of which had ribbons round their necks, and their owners, elderly women the lot, smiled with their National Health teeth in order to add more friendliness and charm to the proceedings. Three hefty young men were jumping about on one leg. And this amuses them, thought Allan, glancing first at the grinning women, then at the hefty young men. It was understandable that in such a world there was no room for him.

. He drove back in silence. Some of the farmers' wives were better dressed than Patsy who, if she could have come, would have worn the white dress which she already possessed when she came to live with him. Last winter he had bought her a tweed coat and skirt in Yeovil, his sole contribution to her wardrobe. What a wonderful creature she was to stay with him and never utter a word of complaint. When he had met her she was doing nothing. Officially she was a secretary, but at the time wasn't working. 'It's so difficult to get up early,' she had said, and he answered, 'You're the woman for me.' He accelerated because his longing for her had become insupportable. He dropped Theresa before the front door, then took the Land Rover to the garage. He came into the house through the back door, and entering the sitting room he saw Theresa standing on the stairs. 'I don't think Aunt Patsy is in,' she said.

He pushed past her, rushed upstairs, and as he came into their bedroom the first thing that caught his eye was an envelope stuck into the frame of the looking glass above the never-used fireplace. The sun was on it as if to pinpoint it. The wardrobe door was open, and her few dresses, including her tweed skirt and coat, were gone. She is gone, he said to himself. It had happened because he had feared it even while they made ecstatic love. It came to one only if one was certain that it was the last straw. He took the letter, and sat down on the bed to read it. He tried to cross his legs, they didn't seem to respond, and it was an effort to tear open the envelope. The letter wasn't long.

My dear Allan, I tried to speak to you the other night, but it was impossible, and I know that if I had told you today that I was leaving you for good we'd be still arguing or lying in bed. So I chose this simple but certain way out. We were no good for each other. As a friend I hope that you'll find the kind of woman you really need. Goodbye, my dear Allan.

Patsy.

As he was going to re-read the letter Theresa appeared in the doorway, saying that Mrs. Latham wanted to speak to him. 'Tell her I haven't time.' She came back as he reached the second sentence of the letter again. 'She says it's very urgent.'

'Tell her I've gone to the cowshed.'

Theresa went downstairs.

Patsy was right, for if she had told him that she was leaving him they would this moment still be making love or arguing. Hers was a clean sweep, which was the right action in the circumstances. But what were the circumstances? He looked round the room. This, he said to himself. He ran, as it were, over their joint existence. That too. Only the other day she had been compelled to ask whether she could give the butcher a cheque; and rare were the occasions when he could say yes. No woman would waste her life under such circumstances. She was easy-going, hadn't tried to grab; in any case there had been nothing to grab. The worm had turned, lazy though it was. 'What is it, Theresa?'

'At what time is Aunt Patsy coming back?'

'A relation of hers is ill. She lives in London, so she had to rush off to her. Left me a note telling me about it.'

'How long will she be away?'

'I don't know.'

'Can I do anything, Uncle Allan?'

'We'll see later.'

'Poor Aunt Patsy must be very upset.' As she reached the door the telephone tinkled again. She ran down to answer it.

Well, she was gone, and he felt grateful to Justin for having chosen the right moment to die. Imagine him explaining to Justin that Patsy had left him. Justin would ask, did that mean a divorce? And who would divorce whom? The hours Justin would have ruminated on it, never leaving him alone, with his advice and suggestions. What would happen if she suddenly reappeared? They would get into bed, make vehement love, she would moan and cry, 'More, more,' and then she would leave him. 'Mrs. Latham,' said Theresa, 'but I told her that you were still with the cows.'

'Good girl.'

It served no purpose sitting on the bed in which she wouldn't lie again. He stood up, his back as stiff as if he had sat for hours. Beside the open, empty wardrobe lay a handkerchief thick with lipstick. He picked it up, and threw it into the wardrobe, a relic he ought to cherish. It was a cheap cotton handkerchief, bought at Woolworths, and he felt so bitter that he wished Patsy were there to congratulate her on having left him. 'I'm going to the office,' he said.

'What are we going to do about dinner?' Theresa asked. 'At the convent Mother Sainte-Agnès gives us cooking lessons. What would you like me to cook for you?'

He wanted to say that he had given up eating for life; the very idea of food filled him with nausea; but she looked so eager to show that she could cook that he hadn't the heart to disappoint her. 'We'll discuss it later.'

'Won't the shop be closed?'

'You can go in through the back door. Old Mrs. Boyle, the post-mistress, is always at home.' What an unnecessary conversation, he thought, and how unimportant. The years would go by and he would continue to speak of matters that left him cold in this icy world bereft of Patsy.

'May I go for a moment to Mrs. Simson?'

'You do that, Theresa.'

Her grown-up face and manners notwithstanding, Theresa was still a runner. She ran out of the sitting room, and through the window he saw her running past the cowsheds. What would he do about her? He couldn't cable Harold to inform him that Patsy, of whom he hadn't thought much, had gone off like a one-night lay. He would have to invent something that sounded plausible to be able to get rid of the child. He was on his way to the office when Peggy's runabout stopped before the house. She had seen him, and waved to him. He would tell her too that Patsy had gone to a sick relation.

She burst in through the door, wearing a light blue skirt and a white blouse. Thin though she was, she seemed to have lost weight since he saw her last Sunday. Her face looked washed out as if a sponge had been used to obliterate her features, leaving only the long nose which was red and shiny, and her pale eyes which were set in red. 'Allan,' she said in a choking voice, 'I don't know what to say.'

'What about?'

'What about?' she gasped, staring at him. 'Hector and Patsy.'

It was his turn to gasp. 'Hector? What has Hector to do with it?'

'They've gone off together. He left me.' She cried like a child that had been told that it was bad manners and ridiculous to howl. She looked more ludicrous than pathetic. She dabbed her eyes with a handkerchief. Irish linen, he said to himself. On the round table lay a packet of cigarettes, Patsy's. In her hurry she must have forgotten it. Anyway, Hector was rich enough to buy her all the cigarettes in the realm. He helped himself to one before asking, 'How do you know?'

'He told me,' sobbed Peggy, and he nodded because Hector could afford to. Only the weak and the poor had to resort to lies. 'He told me about twenty minutes before he left. He's not coming back.' Well, Patsy wasn't coming back either, so what? 'He said that he and Patsy loved each other, she was the only woman in the world for him.' For him too she had been the only one in the world, so he and Hector had something in common, an interesting thought. 'He said that I owed it to him to set him free. Why do I, Allan?'

'Because thanks to your solid financial background he could climb the ladder.' Her little eyes said that she didn't understand what he meant. 'I was a good, loving wife to him,' she cried. They were still standing near the door which she had forgotten to close properly. He gave it a push with his foot, then asked her to sit down. Of course she chose Patsy's armchair. She blinked before she said, 'But why did Patsy leave you? I always thought that you were such a united couple.'

'We thought the same of you and Hector.'

'There you are,' she sighed. 'He told me that he and Patsy were going abroad. He told me too that if I still cared for him I should tell my solicitor to get in touch with his immediately.'

'Will you?'

'Not on your life.'

'You're wrong. He won't come back.'

'How can you say that?'

'Because Patsy won't come back to me.'

78

'But it's easier for you,' she wept. 'You weren't married.'

'Who told you that?'

'Patsy told Hector.'

Allan laughed. It had been for Patsy's sake that he had pretended that they were married. He was thinking of her position when he told both Harold and Justin that they were husband and wife. True, she didn't care one way or the other, so perhaps he shouldn't have laughed. 'Did he tell you when it started?'

'In Yeovil, where they ran into each other before he went out to Nigeria, but it became serious only after he came back. Why speak of it? What does it matter? All that matters is that he left me cruelly, and left me for a slut . . . I'm sorry, Allan, but now you probably feel the same about her.'

'I feel nothing,' he said. Oh, it was too simple for words. The successful, high-geared salesman offered the poor slut a life of ease and luxury, dresses, jewels, travel, and if they wanted to go on a cruise round the world all Hector needed to do was to write out a cheque. Never did Hector have to dream of a bank robbery. For once she had chosen wisely, therefore nobody was entitled to blame her. He alone deserved blame because he was miserably poor. 'He even wanted to kiss me on the cheek,' said Peggy. 'Let's part as friends, and that sort of thing.' He nodded, thinking that it was easy for Hector to be brutally frank, for there was no fear of her enticing him into bed. One who had tasted of Patsy was bound to become indifferent to Peggy. Moreover, brutal frankness was the prerogative of the rich.

They heard Theresa entering the house, and going straight to the kitchen. 'I told her,' said Allan quickly, 'that Patsy's gone to a sick relative in London, so not a word in front of her.' Theresa came in, smiling blissfully. She made a little convent-taught curtsy to Peggy, then said to Allan, 'Mrs. Simson has given me lots of fresh vegetables out of her garden. Now all we need is something to go with them. She gave me two gorgeous lettuces.'

Peggy had surreptitiously wiped her eyes, and looked at Allan, then at Theresa. 'Would you like to come to the Court tomorrow towards ten o'clock and spend the day with me?'

'That's very kind of you, but won't you need me here, Uncle

Allan? You see, Aunt Patsy's gone away for a few days to a sick relation in London.'

'Your uncle told me,' said Peggy quickly. 'So will you come?'

'If Uncle Allan doesn't need me. If I go he'll be all alone.'

'You go, and I'll fetch you in the evening.'

'Thank you so much. I'll be at the Court at ten,' said Theresa. 'May I go for a moment to the village shop?'

Allan nodded, she ran off, and Peggy explained that the reason she had asked Theresa was to make things easier for him since a small girl was only a nuisance for a lone man. She admitted that she didn't want to be completely alone, and the girl might cheer her up. 'But there is the night,' he said, because he was thinking of the night that faced him. She said she would take a sleeping pill. It was the morning she feared, hence the invitation. He accompanied her to the car, and before driving off she asked, 'What will you do about it?'

'There's nothing I can do.'

She sighed, he watched the car till it turned the corner, then went to the farm. What would Simson and the other two say? Two pigeons came from the spinney, flying side by side. Lucky pigeons. Simson stood arms akimbo, watching the three bull calves; Bramm left the separator and approached them; and Doyle, who was wheeling a wheelbarrow full of muck, stopped and waited.

'It's Martin who drove her to Yeovil station,' Simson said in a low confidential voice. Martin was the local taxi driver, brother-in-law of Mrs. Boyle, the postmistress.

'She had to go to London,' Allan said. So she had become just 'she' as much for him as for Simson. 'A sick relation.' He saw that Simson and the others knew the truth, for their silence said so. Afraid of Simson wanting to enlighten him, he added, 'What's done is done, Simson.'

'Yes, Mr. Allan,' said Simson, and Bramm went back to the separator while Doyle pushed on. 'Any news from Mr. Ramshorn?'

'Damn,' Allan exclaimed. 'There's a letter from my sister-in-law, came by the second post, forgot all about it.'

'You had a heavy day,' said Simson. 'The bull calf there, the one we call Dafty, limps a bit.'

They approached to have a look at it. As pedigree animals the calves all had pompous names which Simson could never remember. 'If,' said Simson after they had examined the bull calf, 'you need any 'elp Mrs. Simson is always willing to give a hand.'

'That's very decent of her,' said Allan, smiled at Simson whose face was the colour of the westering sun, then went back to the house, where Theresa was waiting for him. 'I couldn't get any meat from Mrs. Boyle,' she said in a disappointed voice. He said Mrs. Boyle was no butcher, hers being just a small village store. 'I saw that,' she said ruefully, 'but I did get boiling gammon. She said it's very special gammon. I'm going to boil it. She said to boil it for three-quarters of an hour in its own paper and finish it in the oven, a quarter of an hour. We'll have boiled potatoes and runner beans with it. Will that be enough, Uncle Allan?'

He felt like saying that one bean would suffice for him. However, the keen face was irresistible. 'More than enough,' he said, and she ran to the kitchen.

It was easy for Hector, in fact too easy. Curiously, Allan's anger had evaporated when Peggy told him that Patsy had left him for Hector. Had she left him simply to leave him he would have found it insupportable; her leaving him for successful Hector was akin to losing someone through sickness. It was inevitable, his sole consolation that if he had money she might have remained with him. Nothing succeeds like success. When Harold had married Elisabeth Justin had said, 'He can afford to, as he's on the up and up.' Well, he, Allan, had never been on the up and up : he was bound and gagged by poverty that refused to ease up. He remembered his sister-in-law's letter which was addressed to Mr. and Mrs. Allan Ramshorn. Was he entitled to open it alone, or ought he in the circumstances to seek Hector's permission?

The letter was on top of the bookcase that contained so few books. Elisabeth had an energetic handwriting. He was convinced that it had been less firm before Harold began to coin money. Elisabeth thanked them both for looking after Theresa, who was an exceptional child and deserved all God's blessings. She didn't say that as a mother : she was as impressed by her daughter as all the strangers who met her. Theresa had an excellent brain, was deeply religious and loyal, straightforward and without a fault, and she, her mother, often had the sensation that the child would grow into a saint. She wouldn't be astonished if Theresa performed miracles. 'Wouldn't it be grand,' the letter added, 'to have a saint in the family?'

'Dinner is served, Uncle Allan,' said Theresa from the door.

Allan glanced at the rest of the letter. Theresa didn't like puddings and sweets, none the less they should force her to eat some; Theresa preferred the company of grown ups; it would be better for her to meet girls of her own age if, of course, they were suitable.

'The food will get cold,' called Theresa.

He ought to wire Hector to send back Patsy to force Theresa to eat puddings and sweets. 'Coming,' he called.

The table was laid in the dining room, he sat down and Theresa served him, piling large quantities of food on his plate. 'Far too much,' he said. 'I won't be able to eat all this.'

'Try, Uncle Allan. We'd very little for lunch, and never had tea. When she comes back I don't want Aunt Patsy to say I didn't look after you properly.'

'You're a funny child,' he couldn't help observing.

'I'm serious. Can I sit in Aunt Patsy's place while she's away?'

'If you want to.'

She sat facing him, trying to look solemn, but that didn't last. 'Do you like it?' He said he found it excellent. 'I'm so pleased. This is the first meal I cooked all on my own. It's one thing to be taught to cook, but quite another to cook oneself, isn't that so?' He said it was. 'I was a bit frightened when I put the gammon into the oven. I forgot to ask Mrs. Boyle whether the oven ought to be very hot. So I thought of the golden middle way, Mother Mary Philomena often brings it up, so I did it on a moderate oven.'

'You're a born cook,' he said, thinking they were a strange pair, he the deserted cuckold, and she the tiny saint-to-be, facing each other across the long table. 'I had a letter from your mother.'

'What does Mother say?' asked Theresa, leaning forward. She had put a cushion on the chair, yet even so she hardly rose above the table.

'She says we ought to force you to eat puddings.'

'Don't force me, dear Uncle Allan. I like nothing that's sweet, but I love cheese, good cheese like farmhouse Cheddar, Stilton, and Camembert and Coulommiers, much healthier than stodge. When we went to Spain and stopped everywhere in France I tasted about twenty different cheeses.'

'Next time we go to Yeovil you'll choose any cheese you want.' She thanked him effusively. 'When Aunt Patsy drove you to Mass on Sunday did she stay with you?'

'No, she didn't. She said she would come back to fetch me because she had something to do. Anyway, she's not a Catholic, and it was kind of her to drive me in. She was held up in the traffic, so after Mass I had to wait a little for her.'

That's a good one, he said to himself. While the future saint prayed with all her heart Hector was probably having a bash with Patsy behind a bush. To chase the vivid picture of Patsy, Hector and the bush away, he said, 'At your convent do you ever think of becoming a nun?'

Theresa weighed the question before answering. 'There was a time,' said the eleven-year-old girl, 'when I wanted to be a nun, but that was long ago. Mother Mary Philomena said I hadn't the vocation.'

'Why haven't you? I know so little about it.' Any subject would do as long as it kept his mind off the bush.

'If you have the vocation you mustn't think of anything else. I think of so many, many things. Mother Mary Philomena says I have too curious a mind to be able to,' she frowned as she searched for the word, 'to . . . to concentrate on a vocation.'

'I see,' he said, staring into Patsy's eyes as seen by Hector, listening to her animal cries as heard by Hector.

Theresa went to fetch the salad. 'You must try it,' she said. She stood beside him as he tasted it. 'Like it?' He said it was good. 'I bought oil and vinegar from Mrs. Boyle. Isn't it better than salad mixture out of a bottle?'

'Much better,' he said, his eyes on the open window. The night had nearly arrived, and it was the night that he feared. Yet let it come, for in the stillness and darkness he could fight it out with himself. Theresa fetched the fruit, and while she was out of the room he decided to ask Peggy to keep her at the Court for the rest of her stay. He would have to invent some cock-and-bull story for Harold and Elisabeth, or better still, not say a word. Theresa brought a plate of apricots, and as she put them before him she said, 'I'm doing my best, Uncle Allan, aren't I?'

'You are.'

'We get on quite well alone. Now you'll want coffee.'

'Coffee keeps me awake,' he said, and could have laughed at himself. Coffee or no coffee he would spend a pretty sleepless night.

'But we do get on quite well alone. Of course, I know it's not the same without Aunt Patsy. Mother always says nothing is the same when father is away. Nowadays he often goes to Geneva because he has an office there too.'

Expanding, thought Allan. He would never expand before he reached the workhouse in old age, provided he lived long enough, for which he saw no reason. He rose from the table, said it was the best meal he had eaten for a long time, she flushed with pleasure, and when she said she would wash up he volunteered to help her. 'You'll spoil all my fun,' she said. 'Let me do it alone.' In the sitting room he sat down in the armchair that faced Patsy's, stretched his legs, wondering where they were at that moment and what they were doing. It mattered little, and soon he would cease wondering, for they could be anywhere without it being his concern.

When Theresa had finished washing up she came in, asking him whether she should switch the television on. In a far too loud voice he told her not to. They heard a small owl, then a scooter taking a local boy and girl to a dance in Yeovil. After that the silence remained undisturbed.

'I think it's time to bed for you,' he said, and she wished him good night, and went obediently upstairs. 'Thank you again for my excellent meal,' he called after her. She turned round on the stairs, threw him a kiss, and a minute later he heard the water running in the bathroom. Perhaps Elisabeth was right.

Patsy's departure was further proof that money alone counted in this sordid world. Love like political convictions could thrive only on money. Were he a revolutionary who wanted to throw a stink bomb at the prime minister he would still need the wherewithal to buy the bomb and the bus ticket to travel to Downing Street. With love it was no different either. If he wanted to kill Patsy he would need money to fill the Land Rover's tank with petrol, or pay for a railway ticket. I'm too poor to kill her, he said to the night, and felt desperately bitter. She had left him because he had no money, and the distance would grow between them due to his lack of it. He imagined her somewhere in the South of France, sitting on a sunbaked terrace, drinking champagne with Hector at her side gloating over the grand bash they had had. He saw himself arriving on the terrace, Patsy trembling as she caught sight of him, then getting up, taking his hand and walking off with him, though not far because he would have to turn back to ask Hector for their fare to the village. 'So you can't even take me away.' He would leave empty-handed while Patsy lifted her skirt for Hector. He gave the television set a light kick.

Only money could save him, give him pride and self-confidence. He had had no professional training whatever, and except for his eye for cattle he possessed no talent, no gift whatever. Only a violent crooked action could help him, and even in such matters he was an utter ignoramus. It had been easy joking with Patsy about bank robberies, holding up cashiers or embezzling vast sums, but he hadn't a clue how to set about it. Well, he would have to learn. To stay on would ultimately crush him in this house without Patsy. He would go like the cuckoo in August, but only if he got hold of some money. It was as simple and as difficult as that. He remembered Lindsey, who had apparently taken his outburst seriously. Lindsey looked rotten to the core, so why not try him? He might have something really crooked to offer him. After another kick at the television set he locked the doors, went upstairs, lay down in the double bed and saw Patsy lying on it, her body waiting for a man, any man, and he alone excluded.

He dreamt of his ridiculous father, constantly out of work, running down every well-known actor, then forgetting to turn up in time at his agent's office. 'I'm not keen on such a small part.' In his dream his father was a stage carpenter, hammering nails into the head of every member of the cast, finishing by hammering a big rusty one into his own. Patsy was nowhere, and why shouldn't she be, with this boring hammering business going on on the stage? He woke up, thinking that Patsy made love in a vulgar fashion, no poetry, no lyricism, just a bitch on heat. And yet he would give an arm to be able to embrace her with the other. He dozed off, and there was his father again, sailing a toy boat in a lavatory basin. The old fool pulled the plug, and the boat floundered. 'Come with me,' his father said, pointing at the basin. Allan shook himself out of his dream, and saw to his astonishment that it was seven o'clock. He heard Theresa going downstairs.

7

Theresa came out of the house, dressed in white, carrying her bag. She hoped that Peggy would be pleased with her clean appearance. If you were a cook it was difficult to keep clean. If Aunt Patsy stayed away longer than was expected she would buy an apron or a kitchen overall. She calculated how much money she had left, concluding that it wasn't enough for all the things she intended to buy for the kitchen before Aunt Patsy's return. Being a man, Uncle Allan would neither be offended nor notice it. In the evening she would write to Mr. Weatherton, the second partner in her father's firm, to send her some money. Harold had told her to write or telephone Weatherton if she needed any. A loud guffaw behind her made her stop.

'Where are you going?' Horace asked.

'To the Court. Mrs. Latham invited me for the day.'

'She needs company,' Horace grinned.

'What do you mean?'

'Don't you know?' he asked, stopping, his face red with excitement.

'Know what?'

'Her husband left her with your aunt who isn't really your aunt.'

'How dare you lie like that? My aunt's gone to a sick relative in London.'

'That's what they told you because you're a child.'

'Because it's the truth,' she said fiercely, and Horace feared that she would start howling or do something equally obnoxious. 'You ought to be ashamed of yourself for telling such lies. I don't think I'll speak to you again.'

Horace regretted his words. His headmaster had often told him that if truth hurt it shouldn't be mentioned. But how could he know that this was the sort of truth that hurt? After all, Theresa hardly knew the woman, whom he couldn't stand, and had met Hector only a couple of times. 'All right,' he said. 'If you don't want to believe me then it's not true, but when you see that she is never coming back you'll see I didn't lie. My pa said he'll be better off without her, not that he knows much about things like that. He never goes near people, so he doesn't know what they do and what they think.' He looked at her sideways : she was walking fast, swinging her arms, trying hard to ignore him. 'When my ma died everybody said she'd gone to the seaside because she needed sea air. They made such faces. I asked my pa why she didn't write : he said she needed complete rest. Do you know the man they call Pig?'

'No, I don't,' she said, immediately regretting that she had spoken.

'Pig comes from Dorset. He's a plumber, but they call him Pig, not because he's a plumber but because he eats like a pig. They always know when he's in the village, I mean in the pub, because he spits out half what he eats. Well, he came to the vicarage a few weeks after my ma went to take the sea air, and when he saw me he said, "Oh, you poor orphan". I told you the truth so that you shouldn't be surprised or unhappy when someone else tells you. So you can't be angry with me. . . . Here you are.'

They were in front of the open gate, he stopped, she went through it. 'Oi,' he called, but ignoring him she began to run. He waited a brief while, shrugged his shoulders and moved away, whistling dismally. There was no justice or understanding in this world.

When Theresa rang the bell it was Peggy in person who rushed to open the front door. Though she had been expecting Theresa she looked at her disappointedly. She pulled herself together, switched on a broad smile, and said, 'I'm so glad you could come,' as though she were speaking to a grown-up person. 'Where is your uncle?'

'He'll come and fetch me in the evening. He can't come before as he's looking after the farm.'

As a matter of fact Allan was being bored almost to tears by Ted Coleman, who farmed on the other side of Thornford. He considered himself a scientific farmer, and in his opinion, which neither eyes nor tone of voice tried to hide, Allan knew nothing of agriculture. They stood before the bull calves, and Coleman was speaking. 'They're a pure waste of time. They don't come from a good milking strain, so you'll never get much for them.'

'My original idea was to breed Herefords. There's big money in them.'

'Herefords?' said Coleman, implying that Allan was too much of a tyro for Herefords. 'Herefords, they're a very different matter. Beef cattle.'

'I do know that,' said Allan, becoming irritated. 'That's why I wanted to breed them, but my brother wouldn't hear of it. Think of the money Argentines and people like that pay for a good bull.'

'But one must have a good bull, know how to breed a good bull.'

Before Allan could retort, Mrs. Bramm came out of the house, shouting that he was wanted on the telephone. He hurried indoors, lifted the receiver, saying 'Yes?' and was surprised by his weak voice. It was the insurance company, they needed some extra details about Justin's death. When he returned he found Coleman inspecting the pigs. 'You'll lose money on these,' he observed.

'I'm afraid I must go out,' said Allan. 'In fact, I must go at once.'

'I have a rule,' Coleman began, but Allan didn't listen. He got into the Land Rover, called to Bramm to see Mr. Coleman to the gate, and drove off as if he were late for an urgent appointment. Coleman and the telephone call had truly taxed his nerves. After leaving the village he slowed down to light a cigarette. The pack was still Patsy's. While smoking and driving aimlessly he told himself that the telephone would ring again, ring many times, today, tomorrow, the day after and in the weeks and months to come, yet he wouldn't hear Patsy's voice again. He had to accept that as the sea accepts the influence of the moon.

He tried to think of less burning matters. Like most successful men Harold was impressed by the success and know-how of other successful men. When he bought the farm he met Ted Coleman, and probably told him that his young brother knew mighty little of farming. He might even have asked him to keep an eye on him. Now Coleman was annoyed because of

89

the cavalier treatment he had received, and next time Harold condescended to travel down, which in all likelihood would happen when he and Elisabeth fetched Theresa, Coleman would complain. Let him, for he would be gone by then. Reaching a crossroads he turned round and drove back to the village. Coleman's car was no longer outside his door. He left the Land Rover in front of the house and walked to the pub. He didn't go to the parlour as Justin and Hector would have done, but to the public bar. It would be interesting and maybe edifying to find out how the village reacted to the grand elopement. Mrs. Bramm stared at him whenever she thought that he wasn't looking in her direction.

Pig stood at the counter, his mess tin beside his pint of rough cider, most of the food already on the floor. He touched his cap to Allan. The steeplejacks were having their lunch break, drinking rough cider too. Nelson's head rose above the counter, a bottle of ginger pop in each hand. 'The funny things people want,' he said, taking them to the parlour. On his return he asked Allan how he was keeping, adding that this was only the second occasion that he had seen Mr. Allan since Mr. Justin's death. 'It was a sad loss, came here every evening.'

'A very sad loss,' Allan said.

'Still you have your little niece to keep you company, sir. Must be a great comfort.'

His words didn't please Allan. The villagers hadn't cared for Patsy, and Nelson and the rest of them surely said to themselves and probably to one another that it was good riddance to bad rubbish. 'She looked in here the other evening to buy biscuits,' Nelson was saying. 'Quite a little lady.'

'Looked in here?' Allan asked.

'She rang the bell and waited till I came to the door.'

He nodded because he remembered the biscuits. Patsy had said that Theresa had made them a present of biscuits, or something to that effect. What mattered was the opportunity to conjure up Patsy on that night in that old dress that stuck to her body. Had she already been to bed with Hector then? The taxi driver appeared, and asked him how he was. The man looked embarrassed, which was natural enough, since not twenty-four hours had elapsed since he took Patsy to Yeovil station. Allan asked him to have a drink with him. He blushed, muttering, 'Half a pint of rough cider, if you don't mind.'

Mind? said Allan to himself, then smiled at the taxi driver.

He stayed for another twenty minutes, and when he departed he left the door open on purpose. Let them hold back their comments for a few more seconds. He saw the two old spinsters going towards their cottage, both pretending not to see him. You're doing me a service, he felt like calling. Mrs. Bramm rushed out of the house, saying, 'I bought you some cheese and sausages, and peeled some potatoes, so all you have to do is to boil them.' So Mrs. Bramm hadn't liked her either. 'There's someone waiting for you in the parlour.'

'Who's that?'

'Horace, the vicar's son. I told him you 'adn't time, but 'e's a stubborn one.'

'What could he want?'

'Just said 'e wanted to see you, I said you was out, 'e said 'e'll wait. As daft as 'is dad.' Then she called her husband, shouting, 'Big 'Ead.'

'Hullo, sir,' said Horace in his best man-of-the-world voice. 'Forgive me for intruding like this.' Word for word what the vicar had said to Patsy and Allan when he called on them the first time; and as Patsy had yawned several times in his face, that first visit turned out to be the last too. Ah, Patsy, who never failed to show her real feelings, where was she now? He smiled wryly, for she had been cunningly clever in not showing her feelings when he took Theresa to the fête. Horace thought that he was smiling at him. Emboldened by it he added, 'I won't keep you long.'

'There's no hurry,' said Allan. What did it matter if Horace or anyone else came to stand on the edge of his loneliness? 'Sit down.'

Horace stood beside the round table, his jeans dusty and a black toenail protruding from his decrepit tennis shoe with the certainty that the toe itself would follow in a day or two. It was the right shoe. A little jam was stuck to his chin. 'No thank you, sir. May I stand?' Allan nodded, and walked to the window, stared out, his eyes on a dying rose bush with only one rose blooming. In the middle of it a bee was busily at work. On their arrival in the village Patsy had informed him that she loved honey, so he bought a jar from Mrs. Boyle. She never touched it. Satisfied, the bee buzzed off, a small cloud hid the industrious sun for a second, and Allan jumped because he heard Horace saying, 'The lady who went away with Mr. Latham.'

'What did you say?' Allan nearly shouted as he turned round.

'I didn't know that your niece didn't know,' said Horace, who had been speaking for five long minutes, his doleful voice matched by the misery in his eyes.

'Didn't know what?' Allan snapped.

'That that lady went away with Mr. Latham. I thought she would know as she lives in this house because I, who don't live in this house, knew it too. It was easier for her to know it than for me.' Impressed by his logic Horace felt a little better. 'I promise you I wouldn't have mentioned it if I'd known that she didn't know.'

'So now she knows,' said Allan, almost sighing with relief because he wouldn't have to tell her.

'But she didn't believe it,' said Horace. 'She said I was lying and it wasn't true. If you want to, say to her that I lied. I swear I didn't want to do any mischief.'

Allan looked at the toenail, then at the boy's puckered face. 'Anyway, she would have found out sooner or later. Don't worry about it.'

'But my father,' cried Horace in an agonised voice.

'What has your father to do with it?' Surely it was too early for him to want to marry Patsy and Hector?

'My father,' Horace said, 'would be very harsh if you told him that I told your niece about it.'

'I hardly ever see your father.'

'But you might, sir. My pa . . . I mean my father isn't like other fathers. You see, I lost my mother very young.' The orphan act had often worked miracles. 'Since then he treats me like an enemy. If by chance you met him and told him that I . . .'

'Rest assured that if I meet him I won't say a word.'

'Thank you, sir, thank you very much,' Horace said, wondering whether he should add that Allan was a great Christian gentleman, one of his father's favourite expressions, though rarely applied to people he personally knew : he used it mostly when reading the obituary notices of outstanding members of the Conservative Party. On second thoughts Horace desisted. Allan couldn't be either a great or a small Christian gentleman considering that the untidy woman who left him wasn't his wife. With a third thank you he bolted from the house.

Before Allan had time to speculate on Theresa's possible reactions to Patsy's departure the telephone bell rang. He walked slowly across the room, no cause to hurry since it wasn't Patsy. An impersonal voice that tried to sound like flutes and lutes read out a cable addressed to him : his sister-in-law would ring her daughter Theresa from Houston, Texas, at sixteen hours, B.S.T. That meant that he would have to fetch Theresa soon after three. But why fetch her? She could walk back herself. Anyway, he wasn't keen to gaze at Peggy's misery-ridden face. To be wounded together helped neither party. Waiting for her mother to call her, speaking to her mother, then thinking of all her mother had said and discussing it with him would ease the situation, and perhaps he wouldn't have to mention Patsy to Theresa at all. Still, what would he do with the girl? To keep her here was out of the question. He wasn't made to be the nursery maid of an eleven-year-old girl, and she would become bored by an uncle who had no idea of behaving like one. Peggy was the best answer, and as he wanted to declare the problem solved he nearly groaned because if he sent her to Peggy the subject called Patsy would have to be broached. He rang Peggy, the Swiss parlour-maid answered, saying madame was taking coffee with her little guest in the orangerie. Allan begged her not to disturb her, just tell her that the little guest should come home at three as her mother was telephoning her from America at four o'clock. The Swiss said she would give the message at once.

'What a thrill,' Peggy said when it was delivered. Secretly she was glad that Theresa would leave at three. She had shown her the ornamental garden, the empty stables, the conifer plantation beyond the ha-ha, the two Stubbs horses in the library which had been her father's pride, and which Theresa connected with the empty stables. Peggy ran round the lawn with the two Great Danes while Theresa watched their romping with the slight condescension that girls who don't play any more with dolls have for those who do. When the dogs had enough of it and went to lie down panting under the cedar, in as casual a voice as she could muster Peggy said that Hector was called away on business. She had tears in her eyes as she mixed herself a dry Martini : Hector mixed them superbly. At lunch conversation languished. They had braised ox tongue, and Theresa plied her with questions. How was it braised? Was it an expensive dish? Did one put the carrots in at the beginning or only towards the end? Peggy, who knew nothing of cooking, called in the Austrian cook whose English was remarkably poor. Still, it gave Peggy a little respite. In the orangerie they had sat in silence before the message came. A mother telephoning from America being as good a subject as any, Peggy stuck to it till Theresa left. At the gate she made the girl promise her to come in whenever she felt like it.

Halfway back Theresa heard the loud guffaw. 'I'm not speaking to you again,' she called. 'Mr. Latham went away on business, you liar.'

'Liar?' said Horace, falling in beside her, speaking with a voice that Allan wouldn't have recognised. 'Don't you call me a liar. I saw your uncle in person, and he said it was true.'

Theresa stopped, her eyes taking up almost her whole face. In spite of her sunburn she looked pale and fierce. 'You're lying again,' she said, though this time with less conviction.

'I saw your uncle,' said Horace, putting his hand on her shoulder. She pushed it off. 'I told him I told you, and he said it was better that I told you because he knew that he could trust me because I never tell a lie. He spoke to me like one man to the other.'

'You a man? You're just a nasty boy,' was all Theresa could say.

'That's not what your uncle thinks. Do you know what Mrs. Simson said to me when I saw her at the post office? She said the bird has flown, and now your uncle will be better off. Did Mrs. Latham look very sad? She's a great chum of my pa, so don't ever speak of me to her.'

'Leave me. I must hurry, my mother is ringing me from America.'

'Your mother must be very rich,' Horace said.

Allan was having similar thoughts. Could he afford to ring anybody from such a distance? And he imagined Patsy in Nigeria with Hector, the black servant salaaming to her as he told her that a Mr. Ramshorn was on the line. 'From Lagos?' Bowing deeper the black man said, 'From the Imperialist British Isles.' Patsy laughed because it couldn't be Allan, for Allan had no money to ring even Yeovil. 'You're dreaming, steward.' That was funny indeed, for if he robbed a bank and had rolls and rolls of ten-pound notes he still couldn't impress her due to his past poverty. 'Who's the anonymous donor who sent me this diamond bracelet?' Laughing, Hector would suggest that it was Allan, and they would hee-haw together till their bellies ached.

From his sister-in-law his thoughts flitted to the Swiss parlour-maid, a redhead without a single remarkable feature. Even ugliness had considered her unworthy of attention. Yet he had heard her sing yodelling German-Swiss tunes as she drove in Peggy's runabout twice a week to the cinema in Yeovil. She hadn't a worry in the world, in a year or so she would go home to her fat Swiss father to help him with her knowledge of English to run a cheap guest house on a chamois-infested mountainside, listening to the cuckoo clock and to the cold wooing of a local mountaineer. Fundamentally everybody was as snug as a bug, he the one exception. He noticed Theresa's presence only after she had closed the door. He blushed. 'So you're back?'

'Hilde said you wanted me back at three.'

'That's right. Your mother's ringing you at four.' He expected her to grin with pleasure, yet she continued to look at him with a serious mien, her hands clasped behind her back. She probably stood like that in front of Mother Mary Philomena. 'It's a big surprise, isn't it?'

'She said she would ring me when she got to Texas. Before mother and father left I looked up Texas on the map. It's very big. Look what Mrs. Latham lent me.' She showed him Escoffier's cookery book. He laughed, saying it wouldn't help her much. 'It was given to her grandfather by Escoffier himself. He was the chef in some hotel called the Carlton, and her grandfather went there very very often.' She put the large book on the round table, then asked, 'Did Mrs. Bramm give you enough for lunch? She promised me that she would.'

Allan had forgotten the meal waiting for him in the kitchen. 'Oh, plenty,' he said.

'I'd better wash up,' she said, and started for the kitchen. 'Call me, Uncle Allan, when it rings.' She was back in a second. 'You haven't eaten a thing.'

'Didn't feel like it,' he said airily. 'Too hot.' She looked at him as though wanting to make some observation about the heat being no excuse to starve oneself, but instead her cheeks flushed, and she went back to the kitchen without uttering a word. Shortly after he smelt burning toast. She reappeared, bringing on a tray a pot of tea and three slices of only slightly burnt toast. The fourth, that is the black one, she had left in the kitchen in the hope that Mrs. Simson's chicken might eat it. The telephone bell rang. Before rushing up to it she deposited the tray on the round table. A cool customer, Allan thought.

'Oh, it's you, my darling mother,' Theresa cried, and Allan rose and left the room. The afternoon sun was roasting the neglected garden, the cattle were up on the hill in search of shade; only Doyle was visible, languidly hammering in a post. Ten minutes later Allan looked at his watch. So they were still at it : the rich knew how to waste their money. He became frightened as he asked himself, would Theresa tell Elisabeth about Patsy? What an idiot he had been for not thinking of it before. He would pay for his moral cowardice, and deservedly, since he could have broached the subject, even beseech the child to keep Patsy's departure to herself. She flew out of the house, calling, 'Come quick, Uncle Allan, Mother wants to speak to you.' He bit his lip as she took his hand to take him quicker to the telephone. Reaching the sitting room she whispered, 'I told mother that Aunt Patsy was out shopping in Yeovil.'

He hoped that the glance he gave her was grateful enough. 'Theresa seems in such excellent form,' said Elisabeth's metallic voice. 'Says she's very happy with you. Oh, Allan, we were so distressed about Justin. Harold is still utterly wretched. You must feel awful too, and it happening the day Theresa arrived and while we were flying to New York. Well, I'd better ring off, or we'll go on chatting for hours. Thanks awfully again for looking after Teresa so splendidly. My love to Patsy.'

'Thank you,' said Allan.

When he put down the receiver it occurred to him that he should have mentioned the farm, saying all was going well. 'Harold will be glad to hear . . .' or some rubbish like that, not that Harold cared one way or the other. 'What did mother say, if I may ask?'

'She said you seem to like it here.'

'I like very much being with you, Uncle Allan.'

He nodded. So Theresa didn't think highly of Patsy either.

She was speaking of her bicycle, which her mother had agreed should be sent to the village. She could bicycle to Yeovil and do the shopping without bothering him to take her in the Land Rover. Her parents would be on a ranch for some time before flying to Cambridge, Massachusetts, to stay with other friends. Allan saw a village girl who worked in a Yeovil factory coming up the street. She wore large trousers and a tunic, giving the impression that she was displaying pyjamas a pharaoh of the Third Dynasty would have envied. The trousers churned up a lot of dust, moreover the girl was knock-kneed and flat-footed. The sarcastic remarks Patsy would have made. Theresa, who was still chatting, suddenly rushed to the window. 'The butcher's van,' she cried excitedly. 'Shall I go out and buy meat? We must have meat, Uncle Allan.'

'Have you enough money?' he asked, pulling a pound note from his pocket.

'I've plenty,' she said, took her bag and ran out.

There was a queue near the van. It included Mrs. Simson, Mrs. Bramm, the postmistress and the Misses Cobb and Rawley, the two old maids. As Mrs. Simson saw Theresa she stepped aside to let her go in front of her, Mrs. Bramm did the same, the postmistress following suit, and Miss Cobb nudged Miss Rawley, then beckoned to Theresa to step before them. As Theresa politely protested Miss Rawley gently pushed her forward. Nobody would have done that to Patsy, Allan sighed. She came back with three lamb chops. 'Two for you, and one for me,' she said with a happy sigh. After making her purchase Mrs. Simson came to the window. 'If you want runner beans, Theresa, come up in about ten minutes.'

'Thank you so much,' called back Theresa. 'I'll be there in ten minutes.' She turned to Allan. 'Just what we need with the chops. The butcher swore they're English.'

'Clouds,' said Allan. 'I bet we'll have a thunderstorm.'

Old Fred, who had just arrived on his bicycle, thought the same, in fact it appeared as though the thunder clouds had sailed in with him. 'This,' he told his wife, 'is the end of the summer. Didn't I tell you? But you never believe I, bugger thee art.' But the thunderstorm kept him waiting.

It broke after Theresa had gone to bed, finding Allan in Justin's room. He didn't know the exact reason why he had come to the room. Mrs. Bramm had touched nothing; Justin could walk in any minute he wanted. The window was open, ominous stillness reigned on the other side. The sky looked threatening as if choosing the best moment to strike. Then it struck. The first thunderbolt cracked straight over the house, bringing a torrent of rain as if it had been the starter's pistol. The next flash lit up the village which dropped back into darkness before the thunderclap. Allan closed the window, left the room and stopped at Theresa's door. Was the child frightened? He knocked lightly on the door, she called 'Come in,' he opened it, lightning zigzagged past the window, and in the bed sat Theresa, reading Escoffier. 'I wondered whether lightning and thunder frightened you,' Allan said to apologise for his intrusion.

'It doesn't,' she smiled. 'Mother Mary Philomena says we're all in the hands of God, but that doesn't stop Mother Sainte-Agnès from getting very fidgety when there's a thunderstorm. I confess that I was frightened when we were on Lake Como, but there the thunder is so much louder, and one can see the lightning hitting the lake. Don't forget I was only seven at the time.' She laughed reminiscently.

'I don't want to disturb you. See you in the morning.'

'Sleep well, Uncle Allan.'

8

This can't go on, muttered the vicar to himself. That great oaf of a son of his was still in bed though it was eight-thirty. Was the Lord testing his patience? He burst into Horace's room, and at the sight of his father the oaf turned on his belly, pretending to be asleep. He would go on pretending come what may. 'Horace,' thundered the vicar, 'get up.' No answer. 'Get up, you evil boy. You're wasting my time, I know you are awake.' Horace let out a stentorian snore which might even have impressed a deaf person. 'Horace, stop fooling.' Horace turned round. 'I'm not fooling.'

'Get up. I've enough worries without you adding to them.'

'I'm on holiday.'

'That's no excuse.'

'No excuse,' Horace said bitterly, 'no excuse. Got to swot at school, then I come back and you say I'm not on holiday.'

'I never said that.'

'You said it just now.'

'I said . . .' A waste of time, the vicar sighed. 'I'll go and get the breakfast ready, so hurry up with your dressing, and don't forget to wash.'

'I washed yesterday.'

The vicar left the room.

This can't go on, he said to himself when they had finished breakfast, this time thinking of his parish and not of Horace who had bitterly complained of the scrambled eggs which, according to him, were more watery than at school. Peggy Latham and the two old maids didn't make a large congregation, but what could he do about it? He ought to go and commiserate with deserted Peggy, his Christian duty to that staunch upholder of the parish, yet he was too shy to broach such an unsavoury subject, and she might take it amiss. Duty and good intentions were one thing, to poke one's nose into other people's affairs was very much another. He looked at Horace who on second thoughts was ladling up the little strawberry jam left in the jam pot, then asked in as sarcastic a voice as he could muster, 'I take it we'll be terribly busy again today.'

'Can't you let me be?' complained Horace.

The sun was back, and only small, shrinking puddles were left behind by the thunderstorm. The old maids' roses and nasturtiums smelt heavenly, said the vicar to himself as he sallied forth with his daily resolution to do something to increase his flock. James Lindsey appeared from the direction of the post office. What about having a try? 'Good morning to you.'

'Hullo, vicar,' said Lindsey. 'That was a proper thunderstorm, will do my flowers all the good in the world. Couldn't have been better timed.' He waved to the vicar and hurried on. The vicar stared after him, shrugged his shoulders hopelessly, and went into the post office to have a chat with Mrs. Boyle, who was a chapel-goer.

Lindsey was truly busy, spending the whole morning in making a chocolate cake, for he had figured that with Patsy gone Allan was bound to bring Theresa along when he called in the evening. Allan was a lucky chap to have got rid of that obscene woman with the rippling body. Her breasts rippled and her arse rippled, and probably her belly too. The very idea of her gave him nausea, so he thought of Theresa whose little body looked and therefore was perfectly firm. He put down his cooking utensils, and went out, walked as far as the gate leading to the Court, then retraced his steps. Alas, there was no Theresa. Patience, he warned himself. One easily got into trouble without it. He didn't care to remind himself of past mishaps. As one wears a black patch over an injured or lost eye so he hid from his thoughts incidents that were better forgotten.

When with their ridiculous instinct the villagers began to look askance at him, and thought that his offerings of chocolate and sweets to little girls wasn't the normal thing to do for a balding man in his fifties, he drove if he felt the urge coming on to towns and large villages many miles away, where he was unknown and no prejudice surrounded him. Thus it happened that one afternoon he gave a lift to a schoolgirl

aged about ten, his favourite age because shapeless woman-
hood was still in the offing, and disregarding the girl's direc-
tions made straight for the country, saying she would enjoy
the ride. Already she was sucking a hard sweet he had given
her. The girl repeated that she wanted to go home, her mum
was expecting her and she mustn't be late. Laughing, he put
his arm round her waist. The girl began to shriek at the top
of her voice, then scratched his cheek. He pulled up, asking,
'What's wrong with you?'

'Let me get out or I'll call for help. We learnt at school . . .'

He wanted to hear no more, opened the door, pushed her
out, then drove off hell for leather. So they taught her at
school? What an abominable school where such matters were
mentioned. As his car roared past a wood he bitterly upbraided
himself for his impatience, for had he been less impetuous the
girl might have walked with him into the wood. He wouldn't
fail again; Theresa was too precious; he would be doubly
careful; he baked the best chocolate cake of his life.

After lunch he rang his friend Hickman, asking him to come
an hour earlier as he wanted a pow-wow with him before
Allan arrived. Hickman, who had nothing to do from sunrise
to sunset except visit his office for an hour or so, and had the
natural gift of being continuously bored, assented, in fact he
turned up before five.

'I want to put you into the picture,' Lindsey said.

'What picture?' asked Hickman, lighting his pipe.

'The fellow who's coming here this evening.'

'Oh, that fellow? Just looks like an ordinary average
Englishman.'

'I agree that he looks like one, but something could be done
with him precisely because of it.'

'I don't follow you, James,' said Hickman.

'I'll put you into the picture.'

'You've said that before.'

In Trieste Hickman had been Lindsey's chief, and neither
of them had forgotten. That only important period of their
lives was ever present in their minds, as though the world
around them still consisted of the tug-of-war and intrigues
between Italians and Yugoslavs. When the military government came to an end it was their own end, too, in as much as
all that followed was but a frail shadow reflected in a shallow

pool. Hickman and Lindsey hadn't the gift of friendship, yet if they were together they were wrapped in the warm cloak of comradeship because of the only epoch that had mattered to them; if they weren't together they didn't give each other a thought. 'Whisky?' Lindsey asked.

'Too early.'

'This fellow Ramshorn is embittered and desperate,' said Lindsey, sitting on the arm of a chair, dangling his legs till Hickman frowned. 'It's a long story. His brother, an accountant who's doing remarkably well and owns a farm here, has put him in charge of it, but he's bored and knows nothing of farming, a misfit.'

'Misfits can be very useful at times,' said Hickman, thinking of the misfits he had employed in the good old days when the pace was pretty hot.

'That's precisely what I was thinking,' Lindsey beamed. 'He came here one evening and told me he was at his wits' end, and he was ready to do anything. You heard me?'

'I'm not yet hard of hearing,' said Hickman, knocking out his pipe.

'I want to help him,' said Lindsey with deep insincerity, 'but I want your approval before I do anything.'

'You're thinking of using him?' asked Hickman, and Lindsey nodded, smiling contentedly, for it was like sitting in their office in Trieste, planning a job.

'I figure it this way,' said Lindsey, dropping his voice. A cow lowed, the only sound in the village. 'He could be used as a messenger. I see him arriving in any Iron Curtain country . . .'

'Warsaw Pact,' Hickman corrected.

'Warsaw Pact country with a group of tourists. He'll look the most average and commonplace of them. The ordinary quiet Englishman. He could be useful.'

'And how many times do you think one could do that without the other side sitting up and taking notice?' Hickman asked.

'Naturally it would be only temporary, but there are plenty of Iron . . . I mean Warsaw Pact countries, so he could be used for quite a while.'

'You think he'd play?'

'I'm certain. Told you the fellow's desperate.'

Hickman sucked his pipe, closed his eyes, his nose seemed

flatter than before, and Lindsey waited respectfully for his opinion. Suddenly they both craned their necks : it was only a tanker carrying skimmed milk. They relaxed.

'If he's that desperate,' said Hickman ponderously, 'he could be used to better purpose. Both sides always look out for desperate chaps. Remember Markovic?'

'Don't I? But he did come a cropper.' Lindsey saw Allan lying dead somewhere in the outskirts of Prague, a bullet wound in his temple and snow on the ground, while he sat with Theresa on his knees beside a cheerful fire. He sighed. 'He's not intelligent enough for really serious work.'

'Perhaps you're right, perhaps all he could be used for is to carry and bring messages. I hardly noticed him at the fête. To whom would you send him?'

'Seventy-Two is still in the Department.'

'I thought he retired.'

'Saw him in my club last time I was up. He's still with them.'

'Well, take him to him.'

Lindsey hadn't the slightest intention of absenting himself from the village the same time as Allan. That wasn't his plan. 'I'll go up in a day or two, speak to Seventy-Two, and if he's interested I'll send Ramshorn to him, and let them talk it over without witnesses.'

'Anyway, Seventy-Two wouldn't discuss it before you.'

Lindsey looked hurt. 'Why not?'

'You've forgotten the form,' said Hickman, filling his pipe. 'I could do with a tot.'

Lindsey went to fetch bottles and glasses, and Allan arrived while he was out of the room. Hickman gave him a professional glance. With that same glance he had summed up all the bogus agents and spies who were in need of a few thousand lire. Lindsey was right : nobody could look more ordinary, simple and average, the Englishman in the street as imagined by any foreigner. 'It was a decent thunderstorm last night,' he said.

'Made little difference.'

'You're a farmer?'

'I'm a farm manager.'

'Isn't that the same thing?'

'I wouldn't know as I never was a farmer,' said Allan whose mind was miles away. Peggy had telephoned to say that

Hector's solicitor had been in touch with hers. He and Patsy had no need of a solicitor to settle matters between them since with her walking out matters had come to an end. How sad to have no ties.

Lindsey skipped into the room. 'Oh, here you are. How nice of you to come.' He looked round like one who had lost something. 'Don't tell me that you left your little niece behind?'

'She's gone to Mrs. Simson.'

In order not to show his disappointment, which contained a good deal of anger, Lindsey said in a casual voice, 'We'll be able to chat more freely without such a young witness.' Inwardly he congratulated himself on his patience. 'Let me get you a drink.'

'Could do with a tot,' Hickman said, and lit his pipe.

When he had served his guests Lindsey pulled up a chair, bade Allan take a pew, and the plan was unfolded to Allan. Lindsey explained that he had given plenty of thought to their talk of the other night. He explained too that he and Hickman had been in intelligence and counter-espionage while they were members of the military government in Trieste. 'But keep it to yourself.'

'Anyway, he has to keep the lot to himself,' Hickman said.

Naturally, times had changed, but intelligence and counter-espionage were more needed today than ever before. He and Hickman knew the men who pulled the strings, and if Allan wanted a change and to break out of his bonds, here was his chance to serve the country and simultaneously have an exciting time, money and plenty of travel. 'Of course, all this is top secret.'

'It wasn't what I had in mind,' said Allan, staring from one to the other. 'When I spoke of wanting a change I thought of finding an opportunity of making big money, really big money, but I never wanted anything of that sort.'

Hickman and Lindsey exchanged a glance : the fellow had neither guts nor brains. 'Your answer astonishes me,' Lindsey said. 'You're young and young men are usually adventurous, and it could lead to bigger things. And what have you to lose?'

'Nothing, but that's not the point.'

Lindsey scribbled on a piece of paper, then handed it to Hickman, saying, 'The stuff for your fruit trees. Nearly forgot about it.' Hickman nodded, glanced at the paper and read,

'The woman he was living with has left him.'

'Thanks,' said Hickman, putting the scrap of paper into his pocket.

'It would give you an aim in life,' Lindsey said. 'I watched you, and, forgive me for saying so, I found that life hasn't treated you properly, and you were out of your element here. You deserve better.'

'Easy to say that,' said Allan.

'Could do with a tot,' Hickman said.

'You too,' said Lindsey, taking their glasses. 'We were both in it, and it's the most intense and most exciting life there is. Once you're in it they look after you as you've never been looked after before.'

'The telly, cinema and books say,' said Allan, 'that if you get into trouble you're dropped like a hot potato.' Dropped like a hot potato was his father's favourite expression. If a management no longer wanted him he informed all and sundry that he had dropped the bastards like a hot potato; the same went for agents, producers and directors.

'One more reason to be crafty and not get into trouble,' said Hickman.

Then Lindsey suggested that he would go up to London and see one of the great secret chiefs, arrange an interview for Allan, and once they had talked it over it was for Allan to take the next step.

'Why choose me?' he asked.

'Because you look like innocence incarnate,' Lindsey said.

He says that, thought Allan, because Patsy could carry on with Hector without my knowing about it. 'I don't feel innocent.'

'But you look it, and that's what matters,' Lindsey said.

'Anyway, nobody cares about your feelings,' Hickman said encouragingly.

'I tell you how it works,' said Lindsey. 'I'm going to see a chap who worked with us in Trieste and who listens to everything we tell him. Then he'll see you, form his own opinion, then he'll pass it up to his superiors, some of whom not even he knows, and then the wheel will start turning. Now if I fix you an appointment will you keep it?'

'He will,' said Hickman, knocking out his pipe.

'I'll go to the appointment,' Allan said. 'Why not?' He had

nothing to lose, and though he hadn't the vaguest idea of how to set about spying it was sure to be a fuller life than the one that had been allotted to him. And to feel a little money in his pocket, even if it was roubles, would be a change. Still, the conversation was so unreal that he was half convinced that they were pulling his leg. 'You let me know,' he said. 'Thanks for the drinks. I must go back, farm management, ha ha.'

Lindsey was wondering whether he should give him the chocolate cake, a present for Theresa. However, he decided against it. With their evil minds the Simsons and the Bramms and all the other yokels would smell brimstone and see the cloven hoof. Anyhow, he had got one thing out of Allan, a trip to London which would give him a clear day, good enough for a start. He would eat the chocolate cake himself without rancour. He saw Allan to the door.

'He'll play,' said Hickman.

'Will they want him?' asked Lindsey.

'They might. Looks stupid and greedy enough.' He heaved himself out of the armchair. 'Remember me to Seventy-Two.'

'Why don't you come with me?'

'I've been out of it too long.'

'Same here.'

'You're more adaptable,' said Hickman.

'Adaptable to what?'

'Change, I suppose.'

Lindsey grinned, taking it as a compliment. He watched Hickman driving off in his Daimler, then went out into the garden. In the distance he saw Doyle and Theresa ambling slowly towards the pigsties, deep in conversation; what could she have in common with a stupid, smelly farmhand? Doyle was speaking, Theresa listened intently, moving both arms when she answered him. Their voices didn't carry far enough for Lindsey to overhear them. They stopped, then went on without their pace quickening; for a brief instant he wanted to run after her with the chocolate cake. Steady, he warned himself. If Allan spent a day in London that day would be his. But would Allan go?

Allan was asking the same question. The last time he was up in London he had gone to see Harold, who had summoned him to discuss matters connected with the farm. Harold gave him lunch in the City, the day was warm, London was dusty, and as Allan alighted from a bus near Waterloo Station (Patsy needed the Land Rover, so he had travelled by train) a dove-grey Rolls-Royce pulled up, and a tall, long-haired fellow got out and came towards him with outstretched arms, as if wanting to throw them round his neck. He wore a lilac jacket, white trousers and shoes, his shirt had pink roses embroidered on it, and there was a gold rose in his buttonhole. He was Lennox Sherwood, an opulent dress designer, and had been at school with Allan, who now could hardly remember what he and Sherwood had said to each other in the shadow of Waterloo Station. However, he clearly saw the Rolls-Royce and the gold rose, and could still smell the heady scent of success. And here he was stuck to the village, wearing a pair of old corduroys, and even the Land Rover was in Harold's name. He decided to accept Lindsey's offer, if offer it was, and what did it matter if it entailed ending his life in Siberia? If he couldn't rise as high as Sherwood at least he would have a little travel and a kick out of life before permanent snow closed in on him. His long television sessions with Patsy had shown him many aspects of the lives of secret agents : each one preferable to hanging around a farm that wasn't his and which had only a taxation purpose for its owner. He was in half a mind to go back to Lindsey and tell him to get on with it.

He couldn't resist ringing up Peggy. 'Any news?' he asked. 'I telephoned my solicitor and told him I'm not divorcing.'

'You'll change your mind.'

'Never. I'm his wife.'

'You think they're still in London?' What did it matter? He waited eagerly for her answer, but she had no idea. She said that if Theresa was too much of a responsibility he should send her over tomorrow for the day. He said he would tell her, rang off, and when Theresa came in he clean forgot. 'Doyle,' Theresa said, 'has taught me so many interesting things about pigs. Did you know that pigs have an ear for music?'

'Frankly, I didn't, but how does Doyle know?'

'He saw a man on telly playing the violin to them, and they loved it. Mr. Weatherton phoned, my bicycle should arrive tomorrow. Mrs. Simson says there's a much better butcher in Yeovil. We'll get our meat from Yeovil when the bike arrives. And now pray for me, Uncle Allan.'

'What on earth for?'

'I'm going to roast the first chicken of my life.'

She ran to the kitchen, and he wished there was whisky in the house because the two drinks Lindsey gave him had roused his thirst. He hadn't bothered to buy any since Patsy had left. Not once did Theresa speak of her, though the whole day long he had been waiting for the inevitable torrent of questions. She had too much tact for her age, in fact for anybody's age, old or young. Patsy had said the girl gave her the creeps and was too weird for words. Admittedly, he hadn't met her like before. She was in every sense the opposite of Patsy. He had no idea what Patsy had been like when she was eleven; he couldn't imagine Theresa at Patsy's present age; yet he was certain that they could never have a trait in common. He began to dislike Theresa, wishing that he could find ways and means of getting rid of her. Anyway, if the spying business came off he would cable Harold that he was leaving the farm and he should send instructions about his daughter.

'I think it'll be all right,' said Theresa from the doorway. 'I'm basting it with its gravy.' She laughed. 'I'm not following Escoffier but Mrs. Simson.' She came nearer. 'You look upset, Uncle Allan.' She blushed, adding quickly, 'It's the heat, of course,' and ran back to the kitchen.

He went up to Justin's room, sat down on the bed and stared at the wardrobe. What would he do with Justin's suits, shoes, shirts, ties and the rest of the paraphernalia his so completely departed brother had left behind? Patsy had thought of selling them to a rag and bone man. In any case he must get rid of them because they brought back Justin without bringing him back. Why couldn't he leave his room as it was? However, it wasn't his room any more. Justin had been just a visitor, in the same way that he, Allan, was a temporary lodger in this house belonging to Harold. He wouldn't give it a last glance when he left. He heard pattering footsteps, followed by Theresa's appearance.

'I was looking for you,' she said. 'The chicken will soon be ready. It's quite brown.' She sat down beside him on the bed. 'I'm trying so hard to remember Uncle Justin, but when I think of him I see you. Was he so very much like you?' Her eyes were searching his face.

'Well, he hadn't my beautiful moustache,' said Allan, and couldn't help smiling.

'It is a beautiful moustache. Father is clean shaven, but I like your moustache. May I ask you a question?' It's coming, he said to himself. 'What are you going to do with Uncle Justin's suits and other things?'

'Don't know. Why do you ask me?'

'At the convent we collect clothes for poor old people, so if you don't want them and haven't any poor old people of your own, could I send them to the convent, and then the old people who get them will be so happy, and remember you in their prayers? I'd ask Mrs. Bramm to help me to pack them, and I'll take each parcel to the post office myself.' She stood up, waiting for his answer.

'You do that, Theresa,' he said, and she jumped on the bed, threw her arms round his neck and hugged him. 'God bless you, you're so kind . . . the chicken.' She jumped off the bed, and raced down the stairs. Shortly after he heard her voice. 'Dinner is ready.' He went straight to the dining room, the table was laid, and he thought how his habits were changing since Patsy had left. Or was it since Theresa's arrival? The meagre meals in the kitchen were as much a thing of the past as the glorious romps in the bedroom.

'The chicken's delicious,' he said, and Theresa blushed with pleasure. When she had washed up and came into the sitting room he asked, 'Do you want the telly on?' He had forgotten about it since Patsy's departure. 'I should have asked you before.'

'Do you want it on?'

'Not really.'

'Then I don't want it either.'

9

The bicycle arrived in the morning, and in the afternoon Horace stormed into his father's study. He was in a dreadful state.

'I must have a bike,' he shouted.

'You had one,' said the vicar, 'and smashed it up.'

'So you're holding that against me? So you still want to make my life miserable because three summers ago I had an accident?'

'You call that an accident? You wilfully pedalled down the hill after I warned you not to and knocked into the bridge, nearly killing yourself and smashing up the bike. I won't let you have another.'

'Then can I hire one?'

'It would be the same thing. Now leave me, Horace, I've a lot of work to do.'

'Work, work, work, that's all you think of.'

Horace knew his father, who like most weak men could be exceedingly stubborn. He had an idea, and walked out banging the study door. 'Come back and close the door properly,' the vicar called through the window. 'My foot,' said Horace in a low voice, then wished he had said it louder. The two spinsters were busy in their garden, Horace ignored them, and walked towards Allan's house. He had the gift of making himself invisible, that is, becoming part of the landscape, thus the few people who went by the house didn't notice the loitering youth. He could still remember the past owner of the house and his family that included a son he fought regularly. In their day there was a white nameplate on the door with blue letters proclaiming IVY HOUSE. However, when Allan and Patsy arrived they removed it, and their sole contribution to village life was getting the ivy off the walls, which the villagers called a shame. Since then the house had become faceless.

Theresa appeared, pushing her bicycle, and became aware of Horace only when he accosted her with his loud guffaw. 'I'm going to Yeovil,' she said, 'to buy steak.'

'All you do is to speak of food.'

'I'm looking after my uncle.'

'Mrs. Boyle said that when Mr. Latham gets tired of your so-called aunt she'll come back to your uncle.' He let out a cackle. 'Ha, ha, I frightened you. Like with the snakes.'

'I'm not frightened, I'm never frightened,' said Theresa with little conviction. 'If you want to be my friend you won't speak of her again. She's made my uncle very sad.'

'How do you know that?'

'I can see it.'

They were approaching the garage, the puppy slept beside the petrol pump, and the garage reminded Horace of his idea. 'So you want me to be your friend?'

'If you leave that subject alone.'

'I leave it alone, so I'm your friend.' He sighed, turning his eyes heavenward. 'We won't have a chance to be friends.' He let out another sigh.

'Why?' she asked. The bicycle was between them, she had practically to lean over it when she spoke to him.

'Because you have a bike and I haven't. I can't run behind your bike like a dog when you race to Yeovil.'

'Why haven't you a bike?'

'Because we're poor, my pa and me, so there's no money to buy a bike.'

'One can hire one. I hired one when we were in Lugano.'

'One can hire one in Somerset too,' he said in an exasperated voice. 'You think one can hire a bike only in places you go to.'

'Then why don't you hire one?'

'Because I don't have the money. One must leave a deposit, see?'

'If you weren't so big I'd lend you mine when I don't need it.'

'It isn't that,' said Horace, becoming irritated. 'I wanted a bike because then we could go riding together.'

'A pity that,' she said.

They were approaching the bridge as Horace decided to change tactics. 'Why do you carry your bag with you?' he asked. 'Looks stupid to me.'

'It's you who's stupid. I carry it because I've got my money in it, and you need money when you go to the butcher.'

'How much money have you got in it?'

'Twelve pounds eight shillings.'

Horace whistled. 'Twelve pounds eight shillings. Who gives you all that money?'

'Mr. Weatherton, Father's partner, sent it.'

'Why did he sent it?'

'Because I asked for it.'

'Asked for it,' cried Horace, 'asked for it. I can ask my pa till I'm blue in the face and all he'll give me is an old bone.'

Theresa laughed. 'You laugh at the poor.'

'Not true. I laughed because of the way you said old bone.'

He stopped, she stopped too, and leaning over the bicycle he said, 'If you don't laugh at the poor then you'll lend me enough to hire a bike and pay the deposit. You don't need twelve pound eight bob to buy two steaks.'

'How much?' she asked, opening her bag.

'About a quid for the bike, and three pounds deposit. You'll get the three pounds back when I give back the bike, and the other pound I'll pay you back myself some day.'

She gave him four pounds which he slipped into his pocket. 'Hire it here at the garage,' she said. 'I saw they hire bikes. Then we can ride to Yeovil together.' Since it was precisely the garage keeper who had told his father that the smashed-up bicycle couldn't be repaired, Horace had no intention of trying his luck with him. 'I'll hire it in Yeovil. You go in, I'll cadge a lift, and we'll meet at five outside the Wellington Hotel. Do you know where it is?' She didn't. 'Then ask, you're not a baby any more.'

She rode off, he crossed the bridge, picked up a handful of gravel, threw it into the stream, then leaned against the wooden fence, waiting for a lift, which came in the shape of an ancient family Austin driven by an old lady wearing a velvet hat. 'Going to Yeovil?' she asked.

'If you please, ma'am.'

Impressed by his politeness, so rare among present-day youths, the old lady bade him get in. Then to her surprise and pain she discovered that she had been helpful to an ordinary uncouth lout who hardly bothered to answer her friendly questions and alighted in Yeovil without saying thank you.

He went straight to a garage keeper he knew, a moonfaced man who had lived in the village when Horace was still a little boy with curly hair. 'What brings you to I?' asked the garage keeper. Horace explained his errand. 'I'll let you have one without a deposit if the vicar signs this paper 'ere.'

'But I have three pounds to pay the deposit.'

Moon-face became suspicious, and asked why the vicar wouldn't sign.

'He's against bikes,' said Horace.

'Then you can't have it. It's your dad that got to guarantee you. You get killed and I'm in trouble.'

'I'll be awfully careful. Look, Mr. Mare, it's like this. I've got a holiday job on a farm, but it's six miles from the village, so I need a bike to get there. My pa's too poor to give me money or clothes, that's why I took the job. I mean I must have a new suit, but my pa doesn't want me to have the job.'

'Why not? He ought to be proud of you for wanting to work.'

'But he's old-fashioned, says a vicar's son mustn't work. Proud, you know.'

'Bugger 'im. Listen, Horace. You take that bike, I want no deposit, you earn your honest penny, and pay I the hire when you've earned your money with the sweat of yer brow. Never 'eard the like of it. If I'd a son and he wanted to work to buy himself a suit I'd be proud of 'im.'

'You're very kind, Mr. Mare, and don't think too badly of my pa. He's been old-fashioned ever since my ma died.'

'She was a very good lady.'

Horace insisted on Mr. Mare taking ten shillings for the hire of the bicycle which he promised to bring back at the end of his holiday. He pedalled as fast as he could to the Wellington Hotel, where he had to wait, leaning against the wall, for a long hour. Twice a woman came out to ask him what he was doing there. At last Theresa arrived with her parcel fastened to her bicycle. 'How come I didn't see you on the road?' he asked. 'I got a lift.'

'I came through Snake Country. It's shorter.'

'Now look here you. Don't bicycle through Snake Country. There's never a bloomin' soul about. Haven't you read about all the little girls who disappear in lonely lanes and the police dogs find only their headless corpses?'

'You just want to frighten me,' she laughed.

'I'm dead serious.'

She continued to take it as a joke. He gave her back three pounds, saying the garage keeper trusted him because his reputation for honesty was a byword in Somerset. He kept the extra ten shillings to buy cigarettes that he would smoke in some quiet spot far from the vicarage. They rode back to the village, and before parting she said, 'Did Mrs. Boyle really say that or did you invent it?'

'I invented it,' said Horace out of sheer magnanimity.

'You ought to be ashamed of yourself.'

There was no justice in this world, thought Horace as he bicycled to the garage, where he left his mount for the night, for he wasn't in the mood to listen to his father's wearisome questions.

Theresa went into the house, which was empty, then out to the cowsheds, and Simson who saw her called out that Mr. Allan had gone to the Court and she should join him there. The sun had given an extra red coat to Simson's red face, and when he said 'the Court' he gave her a wink, for he and his wife had decided that once Peggy obtained her divorce she would marry Allan, which ought to do Allan all the good in the world. They had straightforward minds, and if one said two and the other said two they knew that they made four. Theresa jumped on her bicycle and pedalled to the Court. Her arrival stopped the conversation, in fact both Peggy and Allan looked a little guilty : they had been discussing her.

'I might be called away,' Allan had said. 'In that case could I leave the girl with you till her parents return from America?'

'I'd do anything to help you, Allan. You and I, we're in the same boat, but she frightens me a bit, so different from other girls of her age. Do you think she has some glandular trouble?'

'I think she's just precocious. Her parents spoil her, and apparently she's the apple of her mother superior's eye.' Peggy looked unconvinced. 'Patsy thought she was fey or something.'

'Don't speak of that woman to me. You shouldn't think of her any more. It was she who brought all the misery into our lives.'

'What about Hector?'

'She seduced him, the bitch.'

'Here she comes.'

Peggy jumped, thinking that he meant Patsy. The sight of Theresa relieved her till she remembered that she hadn't spoken kindly of her. She went out of her way to be effusive which the girl didn't seem to appreciate. She definitely had trouble with her glands.

Half an hour later Allan and Theresa walked back to the house, she pushing her bicycle, he deep in joyless thoughts. Had Patsy seduced an unwilling Hector? Was it really her fault? She was the first to admit that she was an animal. He had believed that all that she meant was her predilection for sex and her abandoning herself to it without reserve or after-thought. He had believed that it centred strictly round him, but apparently it centred round any man, and that must have been the true reason why she considered herself an animal. Was it she who made the opening moves? He saw her rubbing herself against Hector, a sight that made him wince, for if Patsy rubbed herself against a man the man had no will left. Theresa moved at his side with her eyes on the dusty ground. Did the weird girl guess his thoughts? 'What did you do in Yeovil?' he asked.

'I went to the butcher and got rump steak for dinner.'

'You're not here to act as my housekeeper, Theresa. You're here to amuse yourself like a nice healthy girl on holiday. You ought to see more of the kids of your age. What about asking in the Cran girls tomorrow?'

'Please don't. They're so childish. I'd rather talk to Bramm or Doyle, and I'm so happy to cook for you, Uncle Allan. Mother Mary Philomena always says that we must all have an aim in life. My aim is to do whatever I can for you, and it's such fun being in the kitchen and cooking and knowing that I'm not playing but doing something.'

'You're a strange child,' he said, patting her shoulder.

'Mother says that too . . . there's Mr. Lindsey.'

Lindsey was standing outside their gate, and came towards them as they approached. 'Theresa, you look sunburnt. I must congratulate you, my dear Allan, on your niece. She looks like health itself.' Pleased with herself Theresa laughed, raising her arm with which the sun had played havoc. Lindsey could have kissed it from shoulder to wrist. However, he saw Allan's brow darken, so he quickly added, 'I'm off tomorrow to London on our little business. All right with you if I fix the appointment for early next week?'

Allan said it was, Lindsey thought it wiser not to linger, and went off without glancing back, an effort. Allan and Theresa entered the house, he expected her to ask what the little business was, but she went straight to Mrs. Simson for fresh vegetables from her garden. He found a letter from Harold. It was short, and without any preamble told him to get rid of the bull calves, expressing his surprise that he hadn't done so before. Hadn't he been warned twice? Naturally, Theresa mentioned them in one of her letters, the damned, stupid girl. He must get rid of her. The bull calves were his only fun on the bloody farm, and now thanks to that little chatterbox he would lose them. The quicker he got away from her and this wretched place the happier he would be. Awful child, Patsy was right about her, and what would she tell in her next letter? Then Theresa flew into the room, a basket on her sunburnt arm, and proudly showed him the green peas and the freshly dug potatoes. 'For once you must help me, Uncle Allan, to shell the peas, otherwise we'll dine very late. But don't move, we can do it here. I'll spread a paper on the floor.'

She sat on the floor while they shelled the peas, his eyes on her dark hair, and feeling his gaze on her she looked up, giving him a radiant smile. He was unjust; he refused to admit it. 'The parcels have gone off to the convent,' she said. 'Mrs. Bramm was so very helpful. I hope I did nothing wrong, but she liked a pair of shoes so much that I said I was sure you wouldn't mind if she gave them to Bramm.'

'Of course not. How much did you pay?'

'I can't remember.'

'You can't remember?'

'It doesn't matter, that's why I can't remember,' she said, engrossed in shelling the peas as though shelling them alone mattered.

Sudden fury shook Allan. Yesterday he had asked her how much she had spent on food, and she pretended to have forgotten. Now it was the same with the parcels, and probably she wouldn't remember how much the steaks cost either. She must have heard from Harold and Elisabeth that he was a poor sap who lived by their charity and who should be treated like the pauper he was. One day in London he gave a match-selling beggar a shilling, the beggar held out the matchbox, he shook his head which made the beggar inordinately angry, exclaiming, 'Who do you take me for? I don't want alms.' Peggy had said that he and she were in the same boat; at the present moment he and the beggar were in the same one. His fury abated, and in a friendly voice he said, 'You must try to remember, Theresa, in fact write down every penny you spend here. Your father pays for your keep, so it's not your poor uncle who reimburses you but your own daddy. Got me?'

She jumped up, kissed him impulsively on the cheek, saying, 'You're the nicest uncle in the world.' And before she had time to reflect she blurted out, 'She wasn't so nice when I wanted to give her a present . . . oh, I apologise, I said nothing.'

The biscuits, thought Allan, seeing before him Theresa's red-rimmed eyes and the flush on Patsy's cheeks. 'Must speak to Bramm,' he muttered, leaving the room. Bramm had already left, so he chatted a while with Simson. 'We must get rid of the bull calves, Simson. My brother's order.'

'August's a bad month to sell them,' said Simson who knew how much Allan was attached to the three useless beasts. Then he spoke of other matters, to which Allan hardly listened, his thoughts having reverted to Patsy. 'She wasn't so nice,' Theresa had said. Undoubtedly Patsy was popular only with men. Perhaps far too popular for the good of their souls. He returned to the house, went to the kitchen, and Theresa, who was watching the simmering peas, turned towards him, her eyes full of apprehension. 'This smells delicious,' he said.

'This I learnt from Mother Sainte-Agnès,' she said, brightening. 'Four small onions, a few leaves of lettuce, a piece of butter, a coffee-spoonful of sugar, then simmer it slowly with very little water and with the lid on. Stir it a few times. Look, I'm just going to stir it.'

Lucky girl, he thought, who could play at being a cook and be one at the same time. 'Splendid,' he said.

At dinner he said, 'Tomorrow I'm writing to your father. I think I ought to tell him that you and I are alone now.' He waited for her reaction, but as she didn't look up from her steak and peas, he said in a louder voice, 'Or have you told him in one of your letters? You seem to write every day.'

'I said nothing, Uncle Allan. I only said "My aunt and uncle send their love".'

Poor child, how could she know that Harold didn't want the bull calves? 'Sooner or later they'll have to know.' To his surprise she stood up, and leaning over him she implored, 'Please don't tell them yet. Mother will think that with no aunt to look after me I'll be a nuisance to you all alone, and father will say, Theresa shouldn't stay on the farm with the aunt gone, and they'll send me to Mrs. Campbell who's an old friend of mother's and has three silly daughters, and I want to stay here with you. So please don't tell them. Promise, and if you don't tell them and I can stay here I'll cook you even better meals. I'm really useful to you, Uncle Allan. After lunch I sewed a button on your red shirt. I saw last night that one was missing. Don't tell them. If they ring we can say she's out shopping.'

'I won't breathe a word,' said Allan, thinking that she wanted to stay because she loved playing at being a housewife, yet he was curiously moved.

'You've made me so happy,' she said.

'Before you go to bed make your accounts, Theresa. Good housewives do them daily.'

That night as he went past her bedroom door on his way to bed he remembered how shocked Patsy had been when she found her praying beside her bed. And as he lay down and closed his eyes Patsy appeared before him, stark naked, lying in a field with her legs wide open, and a long queue of men in bowler hats, as one sees them on suburban railway platforms during the morning rush hour, was waiting patiently for her to make the sign. She made it, and the first trotted forward, then had her without taking off his bowler hat. Allan groaned in his sleep.

He was at the window soon after the sun rose, staring down the street leading to the bridge, watching the village awaken, and thinking of the men in bowler hats. Had Hector been among them? Towards eight o'clock Lindsey appeared, driving his Ford Cortina, dressed for London, and Allan regretted that he wasn't wearing a bowler hat. Every man under the sun should wear a bowler hat. 'Will have news for you tonight,' called Lindsey, who had hoped to get a glimpse of Theresa.

He left his car at Yeovil station, took a first-class ticket, and travelled up to Waterloo, taking breakfast in the breakfast car, where a sombre mother sat with two dark-haired daughters aged between ten and twelve, the right age, the darker of the two the more attractive. When they left the breakfast car he followed them to their compartment, and as he had no luggage he decided to remain. The mother sat in the window seat, scowling at the landscape, the girls beside her, the darker one dangling her legs while Lindsey pictured her on the yellow sofa beside the red brocade, her eyes full of fear and surprise as Marietta's had been on the first occasion. Once the girl looked at him, and he grinned at her like a dear old uncle. She couldn't help grinning back, but then he received the full blast of the sombre mother's eyes, so he lifted his paper, saying to himself that the girl wasn't a patch on Theresa.

To kill time till his appointment with Seventy-Two he strolled in the Park, looking at little girls. However, there were too many grown ups about to engage one, whom he rather fancied, in conversation. He met Seventy-Two in a large, un-distinguished club to which he would not have belonged for anything on earth. Still, that was the form, for in such a huge caravanserai no one would take any notice of them. It pained him to see how much Seventy-Two had aged since their last meeting. Instead of a neck he possessed a dewlap, his trim moustache had turned white as if he had had a shock in the night, and the pouches under the eyes nearly hid them. 'Nice to see you, Seventy-Two,' Lindsey whispered after he had sat down beside him in the enormous, crowded smoking room.

'Stop calling me Seventy-Two. Haven't been that for years.'

'Sorry, Colonel.'

'You can call me Philip. Stop living in the past,' said Philip Wace.

'But you're still . . .'

'One more year, and then, thank God, I retire. It's all becoming too technical, James, no time left to think or plot. What's your poison?'

Wace ordered two pink gins, then continued. 'It surprises me that they don't start using computers, but it'll come before long.' Lindsey laughed. 'I'm dead serious. And the people we employ now.' He dropped his voice. 'No dash, no courage, no brains. They want electronics engineers, radio experts, crack photographers, industrial designers and their like. No fun left.'

'A lot of stupid people, what?'

'Anyone who goes in for it must be damned stupid. But it always was like that, in our time too.'

'The master-minds sit in the dark background and pull the strings.'

'You live in the past, James. There are no master-minds left. Anyway, the computer will take their place.'

'But you're still interested in the East?' whispered Lindsey. The whisper was so low, and two obese men at the nearest table were discussing plastic shoe caps for export in such stentorian tones, that Wace told him to speak up. Lindsey pointed towards the bar. 'Why are you pointing?' Wace snapped.

'The bar is to the east,' said Lindsey.

'I don't care a damn. What's wrong with you?'

'I meant eastern matters.'

'Now I see. Can't you grow up? I'm still with eastern matters, the bear excepted.'

Lindsey smiled his delight, for the language hadn't changed, since Russia remained the bear. 'I told you on the buzzer that I've found someone for you. He's a stupid, ordinary chap who'd be taken for the ordinary stupid English tourist anywhere, and he's desperate and wants to get out of the humdrum, deadly life he leads as his brother's farm manager.'

'Sounds promising, but has he any guts?'

'I recommend him only for a menial job like bringing and taking back messages. He could be sent along with tourist groups. Would look more like the average tourist than any of the real tourists.' Lindsey looked up and glared suspiciously at a man who had stopped before the table. 'Ring me this afternoon,' Wace said to the man who nodded and moved on.

'Who was it?' Lindsey whispered.

'My nephew. Why does that chap want to risk a life sentence?'

'Because he's browned off and desperate, and his woman left him. Naturally, he can't be used too often. He can't arrive with a tourist group every second week.'

'He could if one wanted to get rid of him.' Lindsey nodded to show that he too knew the ropes. 'I'll pass him up, and if they're interested they'll be in touch with him through you.'

'The point is that I'm rather indebted to him, did me a

favour and that sort of thing, so I do very much urge you to get him up at least for one interview.'

'I'll do what I can. Can you bear to eat Pakistani horse curry?'

'I adore the stuff,' said Lindsey who wanted to stay in Wace's good graces.

They went to a dismal Indian restaurant, the tablecloth spotlessly white, the waiters obsequious, and hardly a customer. Here, thought Lindsey, one could talk without being overheard. 'You've got something on your mind,' he said.

'So would you be if you were in my boots . . . give me chicken curry and Bombay duck.' That was for the waiter. 'Something quite atrocious has happened, and I can't see how it can be hushed up. Nowadays the rule is that everybody who comes to us is photographed without him knowing it. Well, the chap who handled the hidden camera was on the payroll of the Ruskies. It broke yesterday. Busybody Special Branch caught him handing the photos to some contact. We'll be the laughing stock of the country when that chap appears in court.'

'As you're on your way out . . .'

'Still got to put up with it for another year.'

'Remember Markovic? He did us too.'

'But then he did himself. This is the worst muck I've ever eaten.'

'We talked of it the other day, Hickman and I.'

'About this curry?'

'About Marcovic.'

'What's Hickman doing?'

'He lives near me, he's a sort of sleeping partner in a firm of estate agents who operate in Crewkerne and Taunton.'

'He must be coining it,' said Wace enviously. 'And what about you? Keeping out of trouble? This country isn't like Trieste was.'

Lindsey wanted to say, you old bloody fool, senile idiot, I've been back in England nearly twenty years without ever having had trouble. But as he needed Wace to get nearer to Theresa, he said in an unctuous voice, 'I've grown out of it.'

'Glad to hear that. I never understood what you saw in . . .'

'It was sheer aesthetic pleasure. Grown women are like balloons with too much blubber sticking out.'

They could have no secrets from each other since it had been part of the form in Trieste to have each other trailed. 'Sheer aesthetic pleasure,' Lindsey repeated, though fully aware that he and Marietta had been followed every day.

'I like balloons,' said Wace dreamily. 'I remember a girl in Trieste. She danced in a cabaret-cum-knocking-shop, and her breasts came down to her belly. They said she could put her tits into her navel.'

Lindsey thought that he would be sick, so changed the subject, speaking of the photographer again. 'Don't spoil my meal,' Wace said. 'It's bad enough as it is.' When they rose Lindsey reminded him again of his protégé. Wace frowned as he inquired, 'Has your chap children?' Blushing scarlet Lindsey replied, 'Not that I know of.'

He travelled down in the company of a man who had two pairs of glasses: one to read with, the other to look at the landscape. He changed them at precise intervals, as though he knew in advance what he would see on the other side of the window and what he would read when he turned the page. He put both pairs into his breast pocket when he got off at Sherborne.

Now, thought Lindsey as he drove back to the village, he would be persona grata with Allan, and would have dozens of excuses to look in on him; that is, on sweet little Theresa. He stopped before the house, rang the door bell, and, as nobody came, he pushed the door open and went in. There wasn't a soul in the house. As a matter of fact Allan was in Yeovil to see a seed merchant. Before Allan left, Miss Cobb came in to ask Theresa to tea which Allan accepted in her name, thinking that the two old maids who kept away from Patsy considered the house less contaminated because she was gone, and they surely had said to each other, 'Oh, let us ask that nice little girl who must feel so lonely left on her own with that woman's cuckolded lover.' Theresa wasn't pleased with the invitation, for she had expected Allan to take her with him. 'It'll be a change for you,' he said.

Tea was served in the small garden at the back. The two old maids fell over each other in their effusiveness and went out of their way to please Theresa, who rather shrank in the glare of their artificial bonhomie. And she was bewildered too, for both answered to the name of Agatha. 'Bring the cake, Agatha.' 'It's on the table, Agatha.' It was truly confusing.

Towards six o'clock Theresa said she was to sorry but she had to leave to get the dinner cooked.

'A little mite like you doing the cooking?' said Miss Rawley, aghast. 'Did you hear that, Agatha?'

'I heard it, Agatha. I'm as amazed as you. Your uncle shouldn't use you as a beast of burden. It's no fault of yours that . . .' She stopped in time.

'But I love cooking,' said Theresa. 'Love every minute of it.'

'You poor child,' said Miss Cobb.

Since one didn't answer back to grown ups however stupid they were, Theresa made her swift convent curtsey, thanked them for the tea which, she said, had been lovely, got on her bicycle and rode off.

'What a beautifully well-mannered little girl she is,' said Miss Cobb.

'And he dares to turn her into an unpaid housekeeper.'

'I bet her wealthy parents pay handsomely for her keep.'

'I loved her,' said Miss Rawley, gazing at the brick wall against which their only peach tree stood forlorn. 'I wish I could have a daughter like her.'

'You and a daughter. Don't make me laugh.'

'I could have a daughter like any other woman,' said Miss Cobb, waxing angry. 'But why haven't I? The answer is simple. Because I met you, Agatha.'

'Is that so, Agatha?' Miss Rawley advanced threateningly. 'To whom, pray, did I give the best years of my life?'

'You could have kept them.'

'Is that any way to speak to me, Agatha?'

'I've got a lot more to tell you, Agatha, you who ruined . . .'

Red with fury the two women faced each other over the table, with the water-cress sandwiches shrinking in the sun. They heard the fast footsteps at the same second, so quickly put on their toothy smiles, and turned to Theresa who stopped before them. She had forgotten her parcel. They gave it to her, and as she went off Miss Rawley said, 'Probably contained food for that uncle of hers.'

'Child labour,' said Miss Cobb.

'What else can you expect from a man?' asked Miss Rawley, and once more united they moved the sandwiches out of the sun. They would have them for supper.

Hardly had Theresa entered the house when Lindsey

appeared in the doorway like one who was entitled to be at home, in fact had the run of the house. 'Where's your uncle?' he asked. He was in Yeovil; gone to see the seed merchant. She had tea with those two very old ladies.

'They're not so very old, Theresa,' Lindsey laughed. 'They're only quaint.'

'Why are they quaint? I thought they were just old.'

'You might have noticed that I'm not one of those idiotic grown ups who give children evasive answers. Children are far too intelligent to be bamboozled. You want to know why they are quaint. I'll tell you.' He stood near the window, a vantage point since he would see the Land Rover from the moment it crossed the bridge. 'They are quaint because they live as husband and wife.'

'But that's impossible,' she laughed. 'Two women can't have children, so they can't live like husband and wife.'

'How clever of you to spot that at once,' said Lindsey, coming nearer to her. 'How very clever. Of course they can't. They taught you about all this at your convent?'

'They taught us that men and women married to pro . . . procreate.'

'Quite. Now you see those two ladies are like children. They like playing and pretending. So they pretend they are married, ha ha.' He took another step forward, smiling down on Theresa while continuing to keep a watchful eye on the village street. 'You surely have at some moment pretended that you were somebody else. Come clean, dear Theresa.' Smirking, he waited for her to come clean.

'When I was much smaller I pretended, though only to myself, that I was St. Teresa of Avila.'

Lindsey was slightly discomfited; it didn't last long as time was too precious : any minute the Land Rover might appear. 'Speaking of Theresa, there was the great Empress Maria-Theresa. Ever heard of her?'

'The Seven Years War.'

'You're simply wonderful. Though she was called Theresa too she was enormously fat, not as thin as you. She was like this.' He opened his arms to show the girth of the empress. 'And look at you.' He took her by the waist. 'My two hands can meet round your waist. My arms wouldn't have met round hers.' His hands were still clasped round her waist. 'And she wasn't tall. You'll be tall. Look how tall I can make you.' He lifted her by the waist to the height of his face, their noses nearly touching. 'And perhaps you'll be even higher.' He lifted her higher, his nose almost between her legs. 'You'll grow as tall as this.'

'Please put me down,' she said. 'I don't like being lifted.'

Her voice was calm and friendly. He put her down, saying in a laughing voice, 'Now you saw how tall you'll be.' He took out his handkerchief to wipe his forehead.

'You're mistaken, Mr. Lindsey. I'll never be so tall. Mother is short and I've taken after her. Our doctor also said I won't be tall.'

'You mustn't believe him.'

'I ought to go to the kitchen and start cooking. Do you know what I'm going to cook?'

'You tell me, dear Theresa.'

She couldn't because she had caught sight of the Land Rover approaching in a cloud of dust. Flying out, she told Allan that Mr. Lindsey was in the sitting room, waiting for him. They went in together, and as she turned towards the kitchen Lindsey bowed to her. 'I think I fixed it,' he said.

'Fixed what?' Allan asked.

'Fixed the thing for you.'

'I see,' said Allan without enthusiasm.

'Aren't you pleased?'

'I don't believe a word of it. Why should they need me?'

'One mustn't look at life like that, Allan. If you look at it like that you'll end up considering yourself the most unwanted man in the world.'

'Aren't I?'

'Come, man, shake yourself out of it. I tell you it's fixed. You'll be called to be interviewed, the rest is up to you, but I know it'll work. They'll summon you through me.'

Allan wished that Lindsey would leave, and when he did go, he sat down in Patsy's armchair, surrendering to a sense of frustration mixed with irritation. The seed merchant had asked after Patsy, how was Mrs. Ramshorn keeping, and he smiled and said she was very well indeed. Did the hot weather not upset her? She loved the heat. The seed merchant's lady got spots from the heat; Allan assured him that Patsy was immune to spots. Why couldn't she have taken the lot with her, that is her memory, the impression she made on people, the likes and dislikes (mostly the latter) she had left behind?

Theresa was busy in the kitchen, preparing veau Marengo according to Escoffier. She had spoken of it to Mrs. Simson who observed, 'Why don't you give him a real fry-up instead of those fancy dishes?' One more reason, she thought, to study Escoffier. Allan had to make an effort to eat at all, but she watched him so anxiously and at the same time so hopefully that he slogged away at the veau Marengo till a smile of contentment appeared in her eyes; the loch kissed by the sun. She waited till the end of dinner to break her news. 'I had a letter from Mother Mary Philomena. She was in Belgium; the Order has a convent in Bruges. She asks me to thank you for your very kind and generous gift.'

'What sort of gift?'

'Uncle Justin's suits, raincoat and overcoat.'

'It's your gift really,' Allan said, and his brow darkened as he remembered that Patsy had wanted to sell the lot. Theresa's eyes were on him, and with the instinctive comprehension which the years to come might easily take from her, she decided to keep to herself the last sentence in her mother's letter which arrived at the same time as Mother Mary Philomena's. Elisabeth Ramshorn asked her sister-in-law to write to her. They were remaining on the Texan ranch another ten days. 'Mother wrote,' was all Theresa said. 'They seem to enjoy the ranch very much. Father rides horses. I can't picture him on a horse.'

'Nor can I.'

They laughed together and he felt slightly less bitter.

After dinner he went out and saw Simson who also felt in need of a little fresh air. 'The hottest summer I can remember,' Simson said. 'I was in the pub and the cider's as hot as tea. What the poor buggers who drink beer must suffer on a day like this. There's a lady staying in the pub.' He waited for the reaction, but as there was none he added, 'She's a Canadian from Winnipeg. Says she's staying for a week. Do you know why she's here?' Allan said he had no idea. 'She's 'ere because, she says, her granddad was born 'ere before he emigrated to Canada; Foster by name. I wouldn't know, my people are from Dorset. She talks to everybody, very friendly-like and puts it down like a sailor.'

'Big 'Ead, Big 'Ead,' Mrs. Simson called.

'No peace for the wicked,' said Simson, winked, and returned to his cottage.

Theresa was still in the kitchen. Allan looked in and offered to help with the washing up, which she refused. 'Rosario, our Spanish cook, always says that the kitchen is the cook's private territory. Of course, she doesn't use such words. She says, " 'Ere mio". As I'm your cook I say the same to you, Uncle Allan.' She craned her neck, and to his astonishment he kissed her on the cheek. He left the kitchen, climbed the stairs, everything an effort in the airless night, switched on the light in Justin's room, and, as he glanced round, decided that it was time to clear the drawers which were full of letters, old order books, and a large folder that contained his correspondence with the brewers. As the brewers had no claims against Justin, the best thing was to throw the lot into the incinerator next to the pigsty. Poor old Justin. What was their father's favourite expression which he used whether the occasion warranted it or not? *Sic transit*. Well, poor old Justin never had much *gloria,* so he wouldn't mind about the incinerator. He took the lot from the table drawer. Justin had been the kind of person who kept every letter, bill, and even slip of paper. A card announcing the change of management in a Weymouth Hotel lay on top of a scribbled note saying, *Sorry can't meet tonight. Ring you next week. Jack.* It was three years old. As Allan lifted a pile of letters out of the drawer one fell on the floor. He recognised Eric Hewitt's handwriting. He had been Justin's only close friend, who now lived in Ireland, and the two of them had written to each other once a week. When Allan sent him a telegram acquainting him with Justin's sudden death Hewitt rang up and cried into the receiver. Allan saw the words 'sister-in-law', so picked up the letter and couldn't resist reading it. The letter was two years old.

To fall in love with one's brother's wife, wrote Hewitt, *is as old as the hills. Usually it is the elder brother's wife, but, to judge by your description of your sister-in-law, I can appreciate that, in this case, it is the other way round.* How did Justin describe Patsy? *I agree with you that the only answer is not so much the conquest of yourself and your desire, as a complete eradication of the hopeless sentiment. I know you have it in you, and I am certain that . . .*

'Uncle Allan,' called Theresa from the landing, 'Mrs. Latham is here.'

'Coming.'

Going down the stairs Allan tore the letter into small bits. Would Justin be pleased to know that now he too harboured a hopeless sentiment? He entered the sitting room with Theresa on his heels. Peggy looked distressed; her double chin sagged, her scraggy neck seemed longer, and her eyes were those of a rabbit that had seen the ferret. 'Can I see you alone, Allan?' she asked. 'Excuse me, Theresa, but it's a very private business.'

'Most certainly,' said Theresa, thinking, she wants to speak of her husband and the woman. Probably she has heard from him. She went upstairs, and Peggy spoke only after hearing the girl closing her door. 'Read this,' she said. 'It's from Hector. They're at Saint-Tropez.'

Another letter, Allan groaned as he took it. Wasn't one sufficient unto the day? Hector was happy, and in his happiness his affection for Peggy grew daily. The affection coupled with his happiness would take perfect proportions if dearest Peggy gave him his liberty, which he was sure she would since they were such devoted friends. He knew her too well to doubt her loyalty. (That's a good one, Allan thought.) Patsy too was fond of Peggy, and in their delirious happiness they both asked their dearest Peggy to urge her lawyer to get the divorce proceedings going.

'What do you make of it?'

'He's a complete shit.'

'She's the one.'

Shouldn't he say, you're speaking of the woman I love? He said nothing.

'The cheek of it,' Peggy went on. 'The heartlessness of it, and all I did for him.'

'Well, now he wants you to do a little more for him.'

'I won't. I'm not going to help that adventuress.'

'She's not an adventuress,' said Allan, rapt in thought.

'So you defend her after the way she treated you?' said Peggy, wiping her eyes with a soaking handkerchief. Left in the stiflingly hot and airless car the two Great Danes first whimpered, then their whimpers turned into barks. Peggy didn't hear them. 'So you defend her.'

'The whole point is that she's no adventuress. I bet you that she doesn't care a damn whether he marries her or not.' Should he tell Peggy that Patsy was just an animal and proud of it? She wouldn't understand. 'Your dogs are barking.'

'I won't answer his letter. Anyway, my solicitor told his that I refuse to divorce him.'

He wished she looked a little less repulsive as he said, 'Do you think you'll get him back with that?'

'I won't help her to achieve her ends.'

'You don't know her as well as I.'

'Hector earns at least eight thousand a year.'

'I repeat you don't know her as well as I.'

'So you're hoping that she'll leave Hector and come back to this?'

He flushed. A luxury hotel in Saint-Tropez had certainly more amenities than the house that had been called after ivy. He wanted to be unforgivably rude to poor Peggy : Justin conquered himself, so could he. 'Theresa would be put out if she came back,' he said with a laugh.

'This isn't the time for joking.'

'Your dogs are still barking, Peggy.'

'Oh, Allan, you're of no help whatever,' sobbed Peggy. He patted her shoulder, said she shouldn't take it to heart, then slowly led her to the car. 'I won't sleep a wink tonight,' she said as she got in.

'You're not the only one.'

She shouldn't take it so to heart. Frankly, one did talk a lot of rubbish when one had nothing to say, and fundamentally he and Peggy had moved into the belt of silence, leaving gay words to Hector and Patsy. He saw Patsy lying in the sun in Saint-Tropez with millionaires and film stars ogling her while Hector impatiently waited for the next bang. And, looking at all the lusting males, he would congratulate himself on the valuable property he had pinched from Allan the pauper. The vision had such strength, the picture was so vivid, that he wanted to run. He went upstairs, listened at Theresa's door, and heard not a sound. Perhaps she was asleep. He opened the door a little : with her back to him Theresa was kneeling on the floor, her head bent. This is what Patsy saw, he said to himself as he tiptoed away, having closed the door.

He needed a drink. Only half past nine; the pub would still

be open. Dark clouds congregated above the village. Towards the bridge the sky was clear with the moon moving towards the clouds. In the distance a train hurried down to Cornwall, and there was a light in old Fred's window.

The bar was crowded; dart players were busy. He went round to the parlour with the one table in the middle, and a hatch for serving drinks. Before the open hatch stood a woman, staring into the public bar, a glass in her hand. This must be the woman from Winnipeg. She whisked round as she heard him close the door behind him. She wore the shortest skirt he had seen, the legs well shaped but the thighs too fat, the same fault as Patsy's. She had fair hair, a straight nose, grey eyes slightly dilated by drink, and a large mouth that would be generous with kisses. Probably, he thought, that was the origin of the cliché : a generous mouth. 'Hello,' she said. 'I haven't seen you before.'

'I don't often come here.'

'Well, I've been here two days. You know why I'm here in this picturesque English village?'

'I'm told your grandfather hailed from here.'

'Did you know him?'

'I came here three years ago.'

'Perhaps your dad knew him.'

Allan couldn't help laughing. His father simply wasn't the person who would have known anyone who had belonged to a small Somerset village. She asked him why he laughed. 'If you knew my father you'd understand. He was an actor, a bad and loud one for whom only the stage existed. Nothing off it had any right to be, and that included the audience.'

'You must be very intelligent.'

'You're the first person who ever said so.'

'Have a drink with me. My name is Penelope Stout.'

Nelson pushed his head in through the open hatch, and she ordered two large whiskies. Nelson served them effusively, giving Allan knowing looks, the meaning of which he comprehended only too well. Here was his chance to forget the bitch that treated him badly. He decided to keep his distance from Penelope Stout. However, that wasn't easy, in fact impossible, for the more she drank the more she showed a strong predilection for him. She showed it as much with her hands as with her eyes, then in words too. 'I can't keep my hands off you,' she said. And as he still tried to remain aloof she suggested they went up to her room, taking a bottle of whisky with them.

'You can't do that here,' he said. 'It'll be all over the village.'

She pushed herself against him, her right leg deep between his. 'I don't care. I'm here only for a week.' The dart players saw them stuck to each other, and, since one could play darts any night of the week, they stopped the game to stare better. 'We'd better go up,' Allan said. She laughed out loud, showing her fine North-American teeth. 'Because you've got a position to uphold in this God-dam village? Come on.' He wanted to tell her that as a matter of fact her embracing him in front of the villagers could only improve his position in as much as his reputation as a cuckold might be dimmed by his conquest of this desirable piece. Following her up the stairs he wondered whether there was a Mr. Stout or a constant lover whose heart would break if he saw them together on their way to her bed. It made no difference to him, he frankly admitted to himself. So why should his existence have made any difference to Hector whom he labelled as a rotter, a blackguard and a thief?

Penelope was a woman of few words. Anyway, this would be beautifully anonymous with nobody way back in Winnipeg ever being the wiser. She closed the door, drew the curtain, undressed, lay down on the bed, as an afterthought put the second pillow under her behind, then called to Allan, 'Don't stand there, come here.'

She had larger breasts than Patsy, but the lower part of her body was like hers. He undressed slowly, savouring her impatience, asking himself if Patsy was as impatient when Hector had undressed for the first time before her. And what did Hector feel as she lay like that waiting for him to penetrate her?

As he penetrated Penelope he became Hector, and of course she was Patsy, just as warm, just as randy, just the same gasping animal. Where was Allan? What did Allan matter? This was the thing; this alone. 'You're the best lover I ever had,' cried Penelope. He pushed harder because he, Hector, was the best lover Patsy ever had. When it was over he felt strangely comforted; when Penelope praised his virility he wanted to thank her in Hector's name.

'If my husband could do it like you,' she sighed.

'Where is he?'

'I'll join him in London next week. He's flying across on Sunday.'

Allan nodded. Allan is in the cowshed, I'll join him in an hour's time if we've finished.

'We've five days,' Penelope said.

'Who?'

'Well, you and me, you ass,' she laughed, pulling him against her shoulder. 'We'll make hay while the sun shines.'

He left at midnight. Nelson had already gone to bed, and he let himself out through the back door, nearly falling over a dustbin. The clouds had dispersed and the moon was lording it in the sky. The village slept, there wasn't a light even behind Penelope's curtain. Not a dog was awake. He lit a cigarette as he approached the house. Before he reached the front door a voice spoke from above. 'I was so worried about you, Uncle Allan.' He looked up at Theresa leaning out of her bedroom window.

'You shouldn't be up at this time,' he said.

'I'm coming down,' she called.

They met in the sitting room; Theresa in a white night-dress, the whiteness of which was accentuated by her sunburnt shoulders and arms. She looks like a sort of elf, he said to himself; perhaps Patsy was right, but she looks too anxious for an elf. 'I went to the bathroom,' she said, 'and saw that your bedroom door was open. So I knew that you went out.'

'Why? I could have been down here.'

'I came to look and you weren't. I went back to bed, but you never came.'

'Look here, Theresa, I'm a grown-up person. I can come and go as I choose.' He spoke in a bantering tone as he had no desire to hurt the solemn, worried little face.

'It isn't that, Uncle Allan, but you always tell me when you go out. You told me this afternoon that you were going to Yeovil, didn't you?'

'If you must know, I went to the pub and had a drink with some of the local people. Now are you satisfied?'

'Yes, but please tell me next time when you go out. It's not that I am afraid alone in the house . . .'

'The Simsons live hardly a hundred yards away.'

'I said it isn't that, but I was just afraid that something

132

happened to you. Being taken ill or something. Perhaps I was stupid.'

'You're never stupid, Theresa. You're an awfully nice girl. Now we'll both go to bed.'

They mounted the stairs side by side, he gave her shoulder a pat, she went to her room, he to his. Towards three o'clock the barking of a dog woke him. The barking was drowned by the spluttering of a motor-cycle, then the village was silent again. Did the girl think that he had gone out to commit suicide because he couldn't live without Patsy? She could have read of dozens of such cases in the newspapers which nowadays were no longer kept from children. He sat up. Wasn't his going with Penelope a form of suicide?

In the evening Theresa asked whether he was going out.

'No,' he answered.

IO

'I hear,' said the vicar to Horace, 'you went last Sunday to Mass at the Catholic church in Yeovil.'

'It was for purely ecumenical reasons,' Horace said. It was after breakfast and he was in a vile temper. He knew all his father's tricks : namely to sit in sullen silence at breakfast, then attack, choosing the moment when, considering himself free, he was on the brink of leaving the vicarage till lunch. He looked at his decrepit tennis shoes, waiting for the outburst. None came, so he quickly added, 'It's you who always speaks of it.'

'This coming from you,' the vicar exploded. 'You who never listen to a sermon of mine.'

'You preach to me from the moment I wake. I know all your sermons by heart.' He knew he had gone too far; high time he did.

'There's one member of our family who's lucky,' said the vicar.

'My poor ma because she hasn't got to see or hear me.'

'Get out,' said the vicar, but as Horace reached the door he called him back. 'Why did you go to the R.C. church? In order to upset your mother even more when she looks down on us? Do you intend to become a Catholic?'

'I haven't thought of it,' Horace said candidly.

'Then why did you go?'

'If you must know everything,' Horace sighed. 'You know Ramshorn's niece? He's the fellow whose woman left him.'

'Can't you speak with more respect of people who are much older than you?'

'I've nothing against him. Well, on Sunday I saw her pushing off on her bike, see? I asked her where she was going. Said to Yeovil. As I've nothing in the world to do during hols, no friends, no fun, I said I'll ride in with her. When we got before the R.C. church, she said she was going in for Mass. I said that was all right with me, but she said come in too, then we can ride back together. So I went in, and then we rode back. Can I go now, pa?'

The day before the vicar had lunched at the Court. Peggy poured out her heart, her words inundating him, the Swiss parlour-maid joining in, and in the course of the meal Peggy mentioned Theresa, saying the girl had second sight, was a zombie and not really right in the head. The vicar had smiled non-committally which he could do convincingly, then expressed the opinion that being an only child the girl was probably spoilt, though on the two occasions he spoke to her he found her civil and bright. Now that girl had taken Horace, who never went near his father's church, to the Catholic one. Perhaps Peggy didn't exaggerate.

'And what has that to do with the ecumenical movement?' he asked.

'Don't go on badgering me with questions,' complained Horace. 'Look, there goes Mr. Lindsey. Can't stand his guts.'

Lindsey's cheeks were blown out with self-importance, his eyes shone as he thought of tomorrow. The interview was for eleven-thirty, thus Allan couldn't be back before the evening. As luck would have it, Theresa was alone in the sitting room, writing a letter. She rose to receive Lindsey who said, 'Dear Theresa, you look ravishing in trousers. The first time I've seen you in trousers.'

'I've a pair of shorts too.'

Tomorrow she would wear shorts. It was on the tip of his tongue to ask her to wear shorts tomorrow so that he should be able to judge whether shorts suited her better than slacks, when he remembered that a skirt was the easiest to deal with. 'But you look far more ravishing in a skirt.'

Allan appeared from the office, Lindsey pranced up to him, hit him on the shoulder which Allan disliked, then declared, 'The interview is tomorrow at eleven-thirty. My friend just rang through to tell me. From now on, everything will be plain sailing.'

Allan saw that Theresa was listening intently, her eyes wide with curiosity, so he took Lindsey into the office. 'I don't want the child to know anything about it.'

'Naturally not, it's top secret, in fact even more than that.

Believe me, that I myself refuse to know about it, and if you are taken on I'll forget the whole business. I've been trained for that.'

'Where do I go and whom do I see?'

'I don't know whom you'll see,' said Lindsey, speaking in a whisper. 'I'll explain the form. You go up to London, then be at eleven-thirty at this number in Shaftesbury Avenue.' He wrote down the number, his voice becoming almost inaudible. 'You go up to the top floor, and you'll see an office with a brass plate. Hilcock & Flack, Exporters. Go in and say to the girl, "I've an appointment at eleven-thirty". That's all, don't give your name. Then somebody will see you. I've no idea who.'

'Sounds like a spy film on telly.'

'It's the form. Going up by car?'

'I think so,' said Allan.

'That's the best,' said Lindsey. He would be away longer if he went in the Land Rover. 'Not a word to anybody.'

Lindsey had to restrain himself from dancing back to his cottage, and when he woke next morning on the yellow sofa, his eyes immediately focussed on the red brocade, congratulating himself on his cunning and tactics which would bear juicy fruit today. He must tread carefully, for there were too many enemies. He would wait till Theresa left on her bicycle, then follow her in his car. He shook his head. No, he wouldn't do that as too many eyes would see him. The girl usually left at ten, and ten was the hour when most of the village women were either in the post-office-cum-grocers or on their way to it. Therefore, it was better to forget the car. He would go to the house shortly after she returned from Yeovil with her shopping bag tied to the handlebars, dear child. That was usually around noon when the villagers were back in their kitchens cooking their dinner; and that included Simson, Bramm and Doyle, not that they did any cooking, but their wives expected them home to eat the filthy mess they prepared for them. Thus none would be about when he entered the house. Theresa would be getting ready to make herself a meal. He would say, dear Theresa, I want to save you from the trouble of cooking a meal. You cook enough when your uncle is at home, so come to my cottage and feed with me. Even Allan couldn't object.

He became tense in his excitement as he pictured them together. The other evening when he had lifted her he felt the taut, lithe body, the chest still flat, surely no hairs yet, and no fat or bulge anywhere. They would have romps after lunch. With Marietta, rum had worked wonders, hence he would give her a pudding with the raspberry jam chock-a-block with rum. Eventually they would find themselves on the sofa, and he would say, let's play. I'm a doctor and you're the patient, and I'm sure you've appendicitis, now let me see. Later on he would say, this is the doctor's stethoscope . . . He rushed up to the bathroom to have a cold shower.

From the bathroom window he saw Allan driving away, waving with his right hand, presumably to darling Theresa. He would start preparing the lunch straight after breakfast. Plenty of rum in the jam, plenty of rum.

However, the moment Allan was out of sight, Horace detached himself from a hedge, looked right, then left, making sure his pa was nowhere, shot across the street, and, without ringing or knocking, went into the sitting room, where Theresa had started to clear away the breakfast, which was unnecessary since Mrs. Bramm would be in in a moment, but to clear away the breakfast was part and parcel of her life with Uncle Allan, and now that he was gone for the day she considered it her special duty to do so. 'My uncle has just left for London,' she said in an important voice. 'He's gone up on business.'

'I knew,' Horace said.

'How did you know?'

'Things get around in a village like this one. Now I want to put a straight question to you, Theresa. Can you pedal for a couple of hours this morning, then for a couple of hours back in the afternoon?

'Of course I can.'

'In that case I'll take you to Sherborne, and there we'll lunch with Mrs. Weightman, the only person I like in this world.'

'I thought it was me,' said Theresa, hurt.

'Next to you,' said Horace generously. 'So get ready and off we go.'

'I'm not going.'

'Why not?'

'I didn't tell my uncle, and I must think of dinner.'

'You can do your shopping in Sherborne.' She shook her head. 'I know why you don't want to go. You haven't the guts to bicycle twenty miles. I forgot that you were just a poor, weak little girl.'

'I'm not.'

'Then show it.'

'I'll show it,' she said fiercely. 'I'm coming, but first I must leave a note in case my uncle is back before me, though I don't think he will.'

'Tell Simson.'

'I'll tell him, but even so I'll leave a note.'

'What did you say in your note?' he asked as they rode away. (Since they took a short cut past the Court, Lindsey couldn't see them.)

'That's none of your business.'

'They say in the village that you're a very funny girl, playing the part of a cook-housekeeper.'

'Why is that funny?'

'I don't say it's funny. People say it's funny.'

'I'm doing it because he's my only uncle. The other one, as you know, died.'

'In a way you're lucky,' he guffawed. 'If the other hadn't died you'd be cooking for the two of them.'

'You are nasty. I'd do anything for Uncle Allan because he's a very kind man and next to Mother Mary Philomena and my parents I like him most in the world.'

'What about me?'

'I like you too, but I wouldn't cook for you.'

'You're not really nice.'

'If you say that I turn back.'

'Don't be a kid. We'll take this lane here.'

'You know the way well?'

'Sherborne is my school, but don't think my pa pays for it. It comes out of a trust my maternal grandfather left.'

They rode along a lane, where they met no traffic and saw not a soul. They crossed a main road, entered another lane, and suddenly came to a halt. A small herd of cattle was before them, a compact mass which nothing would move. 'Now what do you think I'm going to do?' Horace asked.

'Turn round?'

'Not on your life.' He bent down and picked up a large pebble. 'I'll throw it at them. That'll make them move.' He threw the pebble which hit a bullock between the horns. None the less, neither the bullock nor his companions moved. 'A farmer explained that if they don't move then they're a nasty lot, and the best thing is to keep away from them. Mind you, I'm not afraid of them, but as you're with me I think we'd better turn round and take the road.' Having uttered those words he jumped back on his bicycle, she followed suit, and the distance quickly grew between them and the unfriendly cattle.

'I wasn't afraid of them at all,' Theresa said as they reached the road.

'It's easy to say that now.'

For a while they pedalled in silence because traffic was dense. Three crammed holiday coaches roared past them in convoy with some of the passengers wearing paper hats in anticipation of candyfloss, winkles and bingo on the sea shore. Lorries abounded. 'We'll try this little road here,' Horace said. They met no bullocks this time. 'Does the lady know that we're coming?' she asked.

'She's always happy to see me.'

'But will she have enough food for us if she doesn't know that we're coming?'

'You cook-housekeeper. All right, I'll ring her from the next filling station.'

He rang, then told Theresa that Mrs. Weightman was delighted to have them for lunch. The filling station was at the edge of a village, and as they rode through the village Theresa said she felt thirsty. 'I could do with a coke myself,' Horace said, 'but I spent my last sixpence on phoning Mrs. Weightman.' Since Theresa didn't react at once he added in a reproachful voice, 'It was you who wanted me to phone her.' Still she said nothing. 'It wasn't necessary. I told you she'll be glad to see me and any friend I bring.'

By then the village was behind them. Shortly after they reached a garage which also sold soft drinks. Theresa got off her bicycle. Horace, whose thoughts were full of her lack of understanding and meanness, had pedalled on. She called him back. 'Why did you stop?' he asked.

'Because I want you to have a coke with me.'

Horace had had a long chat with Mrs. Bramm only the other day. She confessed that she had never seen the like of Theresa. 'That just goes to show that you don't poke your nose enough out of this village,' he replied, but now he admitted that Mrs. Bramm was probably right.

Refreshed by coca-cola they bicycled on, reaching Sherborne soon after twelve. 'There's my school,' he pointed out. 'Now we'll push our bikes up the hill. She lives near the castle.'

Mrs. Weightman's red brick early Victorian house was surrounded by a large garden in which sat a stout woman with dyed red hair who was all wrinkles and sagging flesh. 'Is that Mrs. Weightman?' Theresa asked in a low voice.

'Don't be stupid, that's her old mother, stone deaf and you don't have to take any notice of her.'

Anyway, the old woman took no notice of them. Theresa's next question was, 'Is Mr. Weightman at home?' He explained that first it wasn't Mr. Weightman but Colonel Weightman, and secondly he was dead. 'So she's a widow.'

'The nicest widow in the world. They lived in the village when I was a kid. Nobody's been as kind to me as she. When he died she moved here and got her old ma to live with her. When I can get away from school I come right here and she gives me everything I want, even whisky.' He hoped that the whisky impressed her. He pushed open the gate; the garden smelt of roses. He said in a loud voice that Theresa need not look in the old woman's direction, then before they reached the front door it burst open, and a coarse-looking fat woman with lilac hair and an imposing bosom appeared. Theresa made an involuntary movement of repulsion. Mrs. Weightman was perspiring, the perspiration running down her cheeks with the mascara.

'My honey lamb,' she shouted in a strong Liverpool-Irish accent. 'Here you are, and this is your little girl friend. Hullo, little one.'

'How do you do?' said Theresa.

'Oh, you look sweet and what a grown-up face you have. You'll have this same sweet intelligent face when you're fifty. And the success you'll have. Better marry her, my honey lamb, before she's old enough to look at other fellers.'

Theresa blushed scarlet, and felt grateful to Horace when he said he would never marry. Mrs. Weightman took Theresa by the hand, pulled her indoors, observing that it was too hot in the garden. They were in the drawing room, the blinds were down, but even so Theresa marvelled at the quantity of furniture it contained. 'Do you want to pee?' Mrs. Weightman asked. Theresa blushed again, and said, no, thank you. 'After your long ride? Bad for the bladder, my little one.' Theresa thought it more polite and expedient to ask where the loo was. 'I'll show you to the toilet meself, dearie.'

When she came back she let up the blinds, the sun inundated the furniture which was imitation Adam, the Danish porcelain cows that were Mrs. Weightman's pride, and picked out the late colonel's portrait painted after a photograph six years after his death. On the portrait he was a serious-looking captain of the Royal Army Veterinary Corps. Mrs. Weightman had been furious with the painter who had forgotten her instruction to paint a crown and a pip instead of the three pips on the photograph. 'What'll you drink, my honey lamb?' Horace asked for ginger pop. As she was having gin and It she poured a drop of gin into Horace's glass. 'She's a funny little thing,' she said. 'I bet she's brought up in a convent.'

'She is, but she's all right.'

'Of course, she's all right. Don't forget I'm a Papist myself.' With glass in hand she stood at the window. 'Look at that,' she exclaimed. 'Come here and look.' Horace got out of the chair, and lumbered to the window. 'Just look at her, me boy. Do you know that my mum never speaks to nobody?'

Horace knew that, since old Mrs. O'Shea, the mother, invariably ignored him. Theresa stood near the old woman who had sat up, was speaking fast, and with a sudden impulse took Theresa's hand. Though Theresa had to shout they were too far to hear her infrequent answers, but they could make out her features lit up by her luminous smile. 'Who is she really?' Mrs. Weightman asked.

'She's Theresa Ramshorn.'

'You can be dense at times. I asked you, who is she?'

'Theresa Ramshorn. Her uncle lives in Ivy House, you remember it. She's spending her hols with him.'

'Who are her people?'

'They're in America, but they'll come back to fetch her. I went to Mass with her the other Sunday simply because she went into the R.C. church. You ought to have seen the fuss my pa kicked up. Probably thought I wanted to become the Pope or something. Anyway, he'll never be even a canon.' Mrs. Weightman sighed, for boys were so inarticulate.

Theresa was leaning over the old woman who was still holding her hand. With the other Theresa pointed at the house. Mrs. O'Shea nodded vigorously, pulled Theresa down to kiss her on the forehead, then the girl came running into the drawing room. Mrs. Weightman was mixing herself a second gin and It. 'Please, Mrs. Weightman,' Theresa said, 'your mother asked me to tell you that she wants to lunch with us.'

'Well, I never,' exclaimed Mrs. Weightman, and beads of perspiration dropped into her glass. 'She never wants to eat with me when I have company, especially not with my honey lamb here, the naughty boy. It's you dearie she's taken to. All right, I'll tell Maisie to lay the table for four, but I warn you, dearie, she's a very dirty feeder. Spits her food all over the place.'

'That must be because of her age,' said Theresa, and raced back to the old woman.

'A smash hit,' said Mrs. Weightman. 'Now don't wriggle like that, Horace. Go and piss. You'll never be a gentleman if you just sit and wriggle like that. A gentleman empties his bladder without ladies having to ask him.'

'Don't preach at me like my pa. I'm going.'

Lunch was announced by Maisie who was a round grey-haired woman with a strong smell and a low giggle. Truly Mrs. O'Shea was a dirty feeder, continuously upbraided by her daughter when not busy firing questions at Theresa. How old was she? Where was her convent? What did her father do? How old was her mother? What did she do with herself the whole day long in that small village which she, Mrs. Weightman, had left when the colonel died because without him it was suicidal?

'My uncle is alone, so I cook for him and help Mrs. Bramm with the housework.'

'Well, I never,' said Mrs. Weightman. Then she shouted to her mother, 'Mum, did you hear that?'

'What?'

'This tiny little girl of eleven cooks for her uncle. She's a kind of housekeeper.'

'She's a lovely little girl,' said Mrs. O'Shea, wiping her mouth with her hand, then taking Theresa's. 'She'll be lovely, too, when she grows up.'

Horace nearly choked, which was partly due to the great

quantities of steak and kidney pudding he had conveyed to his mouth.

'But how can your parents send you to a bachelor uncle to do his cooking and cleaning and all?' asked Mrs. Weightman. 'That's not a holiday.'

'You'd better tell the truth,' said Horace with his mouth full.

'When I arrived,' said Theresa, looking at her plate, 'my aunt was still there. Then she had to go away, so there was nobody to look after my uncle.' She raised her head and shot an imploring glance in Horace's direction which was intercepted by Mrs. Weightman who was a kindly woman, saw the agony in the girl's eyes, and decided to ask different questions. In honour of Horace, Maisie had baked an enormous cake. Mrs. O'Shea guzzled till her temples throbbed. It ended with a loud belch, after which she fell asleep.

'We'll leave her here,' said Mrs. Weightman. 'Go into my drawing room, dearie. I want to show something to Horace.'

She had nothing to show him, only to ask him why the aunt had left. Under the seal of secrecy Horace told her. 'A miracle,' she said. 'She's a real genuine miracle, what?' On their return to the drawing room she sat down, watched Theresa, and hardly spoke, a rare occurrence with her. The grandfather clock chimed three o'clock, Theresa jumped up and said, 'Please forgive me, but I must go. My uncle said he would be back in the course of the afternoon, and I must do my shopping first. Could you tell me who's the best butcher in Sherborne?'

Mrs. Weightman gave the name of her butcher. Theresa wished to say goodbye to Mrs. O'Shea; however Mrs. Weightman thought it was best to let her sleep the excitement and joy off. She asked Theresa to come and see her whenever she could. She stood at the gate waving to them, and shook her head as she went back to the house.

'They're very common people,' Horace said as they freewheeled down the street, 'but she's my best friend . . . next to you.'

'They're very kind, especially the grandmother.'

'The mother, you silly.'

When they reached the garage that sold soft drinks she went in, then came out with two bottles of coca-cola. 'You 'shouldn't have done it a second time,' Horace said.

'It's to thank you for having said nothing about her.'

I'm a Judas, thought Horace, but anyway she's having one too.

They were overtaken on the bridge by old Fred who was going home earlier because he felt seedy. 'Shirking work, Fred?' Horace called.

'I won't 'ave any of your cheek, Horace,' Fred called back. Horace guffawed. As they approached the garage he said, 'I leave you here.'

'Thanks awfully for the outing,' said Theresa.

Not a bad kid, Horace said to himself.

She rushed into the house : her uncle wasn't back. Why was he late? Quickly she recited three Hail Marys that he should meet no accident, then went to the kitchen to examine the kidneys she had bought in Sherborne.

As a matter of fact, Allan was already approaching Yeovil. He drove slowly, his mind full of the interview in Shaftesbury Avenue and all it might lead to. He had mounted the stairs in the liftless house at eleven-thirty sharp. On the top floor were two offices facing each other, Hilcock & Flack to the left. The landing badly needed scrubbing. A notice said, 'Don't knock, walk in.' He walked in; the waiting room looked dismal; however the tall girl who received him was pretty, and he liked her smile. 'I've an appointment at eleven-thirty,' he said, his voice sounding foolish to him, as if his were a badly learnt part in a school play. 'This way, please,' said the girl, taking him into a room with a large writing table in the middle and two empty bookcases side by side against the wall. There were two chairs before the table and an armchair behind it. Through a second door a tall, bearded man appeared. A false beard of course, Allan said to himself, but when the man began to speak in an intense voice he changed his opinion. The beard was a real one; the man the crusader type. To Allan's astonishment the man took an immediate liking to him. Before Harold had given him the job on the farm he drifted from one employer to another, usually finding them unimpressed by him. Here was the great exception; moreover, the man took him seriously. After the preliminaries such as asking how old he was, where he was at school, was he married and so on, the man made a long speech during which Allan repeated to himself that this was the true crusader type.

'I understand you, and I appreciate it. I'll go even farther : I admire you. You are fed up by the humdrum life your generation is forced to lead. There is no danger, no noble outlet. Think of it; if you'd been born at the beginning of the century you could have had a choice. Now there is none. Your spirit of adventure could have been satisfied in many splendid ways. You could have been on the Afghan Frontier, in British Borneo, in East Africa, the globe your choice.' The man, thought Allan, was reared on Kipling. 'You could have fought the Fuzzy-wuzzies, the hillmen, the Zulus, in short your sense of adventure and lust for danger could have been amply and nobly satisfied. Today all there seems to be left is to break fixtures in the L.S.E.'

Allan let out a little laugh, expecting the interviewer to laugh with him. He remained serious and intense.

'When we abdicated from the Empire,' he went on, 'we gave away the future of the generations to come. Gave away? We betrayed them. And who were the we? Satiated old men who had got tired of the glory of Empire building because they'd had it too good. They had lorded it in India, in the Sudan, on the Gold Coast, in fact everywhere and led a dangerous, exciting life, but in their decrepitude they sold the Empire down the river, the same way as an impotent old man sees no beauty left in women. Your decision to risk your life for your country is a generous one, and an intelligent one in so far as there is no other outlet. Our service alone can provide it. Can you think of any other?'

Allan admitted that he couldn't.

'It is dangerous and ungrateful. I want to be frank with you. I was given the impression that all you could be used for was taking and bringing messages, but I can see in your eyes that you can be used much better, and thus you will have all the danger and excitement and perhaps even the martyrdom you crave for.' Allan swallowed. 'You'll need intensive training, but you have a formidable asset : there is nothing shifty about you, your honesty sticks out a mile. You are the last person anybody will suspect, an immense asset that. When can you start?'

'By the middle of September.'

'I don't have to tell you that mum's the word. Anyway,

you'll only risk your life if you talk to anyone, including your nearest and dearest.'

Allan said he understood that. The man then told him that by the middle of September he should tell his brother Harold that he was leaving the farm because he wanted to take a job that gave him the chance to travel.

'Would I be joining this firm?' Allan asked, thinking of the tall girl.

'I don't think so. We have plenty of other firms.' He gave him a telephone number where he could ring him, though not to ring before he was ready to come. As he accompanied Allan to the door he said, 'If James Lindsey—I believe that's his name, the one who lives next door to you—asks you what took place in this office, tell him that the conditions didn't suit you, and you said no.'

'By the way, what are the conditions?'

'You'll be looked after, you'll live well and dangerously. Besides, you are not the man who wants to do it for gain.'

The girl was no longer in the outer office.

Possibly, thought Allan driving through Yeovil, the man was right. He had never bothered about gain, only about Patsy. There was no earthly reason why he shouldn't live dangerously, and if he came a cropper no one would really miss him because none cared for him. Harold would look his manly self, declare he was distressed, then continue to coin money. His father wasn't worth speaking of. With Patsy gone, no tie was left since ties were strings of affection. He had reached the village, and as he drove past the garage he saw Theresa's small figure shooting out of the house, then running towards the Land Rover. He suddenly felt tears he wouldn't shed pricking his eyes, for the little thing running towards him did care. Still, she would outgrow it in time. 'Jump in, Theresa, and we'll drive hell for leather to the garage.'

'I was in Sherborne,' she said, her shoulder against his arm. 'Rode twenty miles on the bike. Horace was with me, and . . . oh, how selfish I am. I never asked you whether you enjoyed yourself in London.'

Lindsey saw the Land Rover, and in the mood he was in, he hoped that both uncle and niece blew up. He had spent the whole morning cooking, the cottage smelt of rum, and when he went to the house and his ringing and knocking was unanswered he realised that he had cooked in vain. In his temper he went to Simson's cottage, the Simsons were eating, he wished they choked, asked them where Allan was, and was told that Allan had gone to London and Theresa to Sherborne. He returned to the cottage, convinced that Theresa would stay away for days, so didn't bother to watch the two streets, and now when he saw her running out of the house which meant that she had come back and for a time must have been alone in the house, he felt like murder. He lifted the cake off the table, rushed with it to the lavatory, carrying it as if he had caught it after long pursuit, threw it into the basin, then pulled the plug. (Next day he had to call Pig, the plumber.)

However, appearances had to be kept up, therefore he called on Allan towards seven. He found him and Theresa seated in the two armchairs before the empty grate. When he saw her his anger evaporated, and he wished her well, that is to be lying under him. 'You're back, Allan?'

'As you can see. I said no, so that's the end of the matter.'

Lindsey perceived that he would have to use different tactics.

II

Theresa came out of the confessional, and burst into tears. They were hot and desperate tears, and the priest who came out after her stopped and patted her cheek, saying, 'One mustn't look back on one's sins once Our Lord has forgiven them.'

'I'm thinking of him, not of me,' she sobbed.

'You write that letter and your conscience will be clear, my child.'

A grim old woman appeared in the church, the priest sighed, went back to the confessional, and patiently waited for her to confess that she still hated the neighbour whose garden adjoined hers.

Theresa knelt in front of the Sacred Heart, remembered Horace waiting for her outside, crossed herself, then joined him. 'I thought they whisked you away to the dungeon of the Vatican,' he said.

'Leave me alone.'

'Is that the way to speak to me?'

'Leave me alone. Can't you see how unhappy I am?'

'What's wrong, you silly?'

'I can't tell you,' she said, and burst into tears again. She rode straight on to the pavement nearly hitting a lamp post. 'You can't see for your tears,' Horace announced. She took her handkerchief from her bag, wiped her eyes, then said, 'Horace, I'm awfully miserable.'

'Tell me why. I might help.'

'You can't. I have to do it. Come on, I won't cry again.'

'You'd better not or you'll find yourself under a lorry. Tears give no visibility.'

She mounted her bicycle and they rode side by side, Horace falling behind when meeting traffic. They took the narrow lane running through Snake Country. With him, she was allowed to take that short cut as he would defend her; without him he didn't allow her. However, he was unaware, since she kept it to herself, that when alone she invariably rode through Snake Country where all she had seen to date were only a few grass snakes. As they reached the derelict farm house she got off her bicycle. 'Do you want to pee, as Mrs. Weightman would say?' he asked.

'Certainly not,' she said angrily. 'If you use such words . . .'

'I said, as Mrs. Weightman would say, didn't I? That doesn't mean that I would say that, does it?'

'I'll tell you what happened,' she said in a tragic voice. 'It is the end.'

They sat down among the weeds, and she told him. In the course of her confession the priest asked her whether she had been telling any lies. She said only one but that one repeatedly. In her letters to her parents she made them believe that her aunt was still on the premises, whereas she had gone away weeks ago. The priest exhorted her to write at once to her parents and tell the truth. When she got as far in her narrative she began to cry again.

'Is that all?' Horace asked.

'Isn't that enough?' she sobbed.

'If you don't want to, don't tell them. Do you think I ever tell my pa anything?'

'But I must tell them.'

A jay flew overhead; they both stared at it till it vanished from sight, then Horace asked, 'Why must you?'

'Because if I don't then I remain in sin, and can't go to Communion tomorrow.'

'You're a queer lot of people,' Horace sighed, 'and my pa in his deep wisdom thought I wanted to be one of you.'

'So tonight I'm writing to father and mother.'

'Honestly, what does it matter? Everyone knows that it was Mr. Latham's doing, not your uncle's.'

'It isn't that,' she sobbed. 'If they know that I'm alone with him they'll think that a child like me needs a woman's care. A man alone can't look after me, so they'll tell him to take me to Mrs. Campbell, but I want to remain with him, I don't want to leave him . . . oh my God !'

'Stop howling,' said Horace not unkindly.

'And who will cook for him?' she sobbed on. 'Mrs. Bramm will give him such awful food.'

'Cook-housekeeper.'

'I am, I am.'

'If you go on howling like that all the vipers will come here.'

'Let them.' She buried her face in her hands. 'You understand nothing. He'll be so alone when I go. He's still thinking of her, and when I'm gone he'll think only of her because there will be nobody with him. Do you know that every time the phone rings he rushes to it because he thinks it's she?'

'I think the people in the village are right when they say you're not a girl of eleven but a wise woman. I ought to tremble with fright because you might turn me into a werewolf.' He hoped that would make her laugh.

She didn't laugh. 'Let's get back and let me get it over.'

'Don't write it.'

'It's my duty before God to write it for the salvation of my soul.'

'Oh, you convent girl. Your Mother Mary Philomena speaks like that, what?'

She nodded. They got on their bicycles, and he pointed out a cock pheasant that hurried into a hedge; she didn't look at it. When they reached the garage he asked in a small voice, 'I'll see you before you go, eh?' She nodded again, and when she arrived she ran up to the bathroom to bathe her eyes. She was already in the kitchen as Allan came in.

'What's wrong with you?' he asked.

'Nothing, Uncle Allan.'

'You cried. No bad news from your parents, I hope?' She shook her head, afraid to speak. 'Then what is it, Theresa? We're friends enough to tell me.'

She burst into tears, he bent over her, put his arms round her shoulder which made her cry louder. 'It's nothing, nothing.'

'Something you didn't like in Sherborne?'

'I liked everything in Sherborne,' she sobbed. 'There was such a nice deaf old lady.'

'The phone,' he said, and went to answer it.

He thinks it's she, she wept; and if it really were, and she wanted to come back? What would she do if she came back? She wouldn't stay a moment longer even if she came at night.

She would walk out into the darkness and never be seen again. She heard Allan repeating words, so it couldn't be Patsy, then saying, 'Yes, I want a copy Monday morning.' He put down the receiver, came into the kitchen with a slip of paper. 'A cable from your parents. "Flying to Boston tomorrow in our friends' private aircraft, will telephone Tuesday 18 hours B.S.T. Ramshorn." '

Theresa's tears dried, and her smile returned, for Boston wasn't on her parents' original itinerary, therefore she hadn't the address, which meant there was no need to write before they rang up, and that would take her as far as Tuesday. She would say nothing on the telephone since the priest had said she should write but didn't mention the telephone. In short a whole week would be gained. 'You're a funny girl,' he said. 'By the way, I promised Peggy to lunch at the Court tomorrow.'

'I'll bicycle straight there from church,' she said, and slept well that night.

Peggy was lying in a deck chair near the cedar when she arrived. Allan hadn't yet appeared and she sat up as Theresa approached, saying to herself, here comes the little witch. The Great Danes lazily wagged their tails. 'I thought you'd come together.'

'I came from Yeovil.'

'What were you doing there?'

'I went to Mass.'

'I always forget you're an R.C. Why are you one?'

'My mother is.'

'Yes, of course, you people have some funny rules . . . here's your uncle.' Now she took the trouble to get up. 'I'd a post-card from him,' she said in an aggrieved voice. 'A picture post-card, a coloured one with a lot of dark blue sea, sailing boats and white houses . . . the cheek of it.'

'What does he say?'

' "We wish you were here with us." The monster.' She remembered that the little witch was standing beside them. 'We'll have drinks in the library.' She turned to Theresa, 'Would you like to play with the dogs?'

'If you want me to.'

'Yes, please. I've one or two things to say to your uncle.' The dogs weren't in the mood to play, preferring peace under the cedar. Theresa lay down in the deck chair, waiting to be summoned.

'Is he doing this to put salt into the wound?' Peggy asked.

'He's doing it because he wants you on his side,' Allan said, 'that is, he wants to get the divorce quickly.'

'And that's why he torments me?'

'He doesn't think he's tormenting you,' said Allan. 'Don't forget that Hector is a high-geared salesman. I know a lot about salesmen because Justin was one. He said the whole secret of being a successful salesman is to have no sense of psychology and no understanding of the human soul and intelligence whatever. But you must have seen that for yourself, Peggy. The salesman comes in while you're crying over your dead baby and offers you a washing machine or a do-it-yourself kit. I'm not being funny. Simson had a collie puppy which died, and there we were, Patsy and I, trying to console him and Mrs. Simson who still rocked the dead puppy in her arms, and suddenly a man with a thick moustache entered without knocking, and started to badger Mrs. Simson, almost succeeding in forcing her into buying washable plastic curtains for her kitchen. If we hadn't been there she'd have fallen for them. Well, in his salesman's mentality, Hector is trying to sell you Hector married to Patsy.'

'Your ex-mistress,' said Peggy whose cheeks had turned red with anger when he had said, '. . . and there we were, Patsy and I . . .'

'My ex-mistress whom he took from me. Can Theresa come in? The dogs don't seem willing to play.' He pointed at the three of them under the cedar.

'You think only of that child.'

'I'm in charge of her.'

'Call her if you want to.'

It was a dreary meal. Peggy was sullen and silent, wishing Theresa elsewhere so that she would be able to go on and on about Hector and the postcard. The Simsons had a far gayer meal in the course of which Simson said to Gus, his brother-in-law, a grocer in Yetminster, 'Since that bitch has left our Allan is taking a little more interest in the farm.'

'It's since Theresa has come,' said Mrs. Simson.

'So that she tells her dad how hard he works,' said Gus.

'You don't know our Allan,' said Simson.

Their Allan and Theresa were on their way back to the house while the Simsons still sat at table, drinking Merrydown. 'What will you do this afternoon?' Allan asked.

'I'm going to read the life of St. Theresa which Mother Mary Philomena sent me. Wasn't that sweet of her?'

'Very sweet. There are less than three weeks left before you're off to Morocco and then back to the convent.'

'I wish I didn't have to go to Morocco,' she sighed.

'Why? Don't you like the idea?'

'I'd like to stay here till the end of my hols.' He had sat down beside the fireplace, she was standing before him. 'Could I come here for all my hols?'

'But your parents will want you to spend them with them.'

'I could spend half of them here. Would you want me to?'

'Very much so.'

'Oh, I'm glad. I'll persuade them to let me. I'm going upstairs to fetch the book.'

She rushed upstairs, and he smiled at the fast mounting little legs. Then his mind reverted to the postcard. The rich life in Saint-Tropez was so unsuited to the Patsy he had known; to be impatient to marry Hector didn't fit into the conception he had of her. They had gone to bed together the evening he met her; if he hadn't insisted she wouldn't have bothered to see him again; and now she was stamping with impatience, hardly able to wait for the day when she could marry her Hector. It wasn't in keeping with Patsy. Or had Hector's buoyant personality influenced, hence changed, her? He couldn't imagine her different from the Patsy he had known, the one who precisely at this hour would have said, come upstairs, I want it. He would have followed; she would have thrown her dressing gown dress on the floor, then hurled herself on the bed, waiting for him, her mouth half open, the legs wide apart. He didn't hear Theresa coming down the stairs, and remained unaware of her presence till she pulled her chair near to his. What did Peggy understand of the physical despair that still gripped him whenever he conjured up Patsy? Peggy had lost a husband to another woman : he had lost Patsy to insufferable Hector.

In the Sunday quiet the telephone bell began to ring, an intruder choosing the wrong moment. 'Shall I answer it?' Theresa asked. He nodded. However, before he could return to Patsy lying on the bed, Theresa called, 'It's Mr. Weatherton. He wants to speak to you.'

What could Weatherton want? Probably Harold had written to him to find out whether the bull calves were sold, no excuse for Weatherton to ring him Sunday afternoon. He lifted the receiver. 'Hullo,' he said.

'Theresa is of course in the room with you?' Weatherton asked.

'Yes.'

'Then don't answer me but just listen to me. She mustn't guess. It'll be your duty to tell her, Allan. I don't envy you.'

'Go ahead,' said Allan who couldn't resist glancing at Theresa. The girl had returned to her chair and book.

'Howard Table, our American associate,' said Weatherton, speaking in a low voice, 'just rang me from Houston. Harold and Elisabeth were killed in a plane crash . . . are you there?'

'Yes,' said Allan, no longer looking at Theresa.

'When the Finsters' private plane took off it literally exploded. There were five in it. There aren't even charred remains left.'

'Yes . . . wait, I want to light a cigarette.'

The packet was on the chimneypiece, so he had to go twice past Theresa. He kept his eyes averted. 'Go on,' he said.

'I think you ought to come up to London first thing in the morning. I take it you'll bring Theresa with you.'

'That's right.'

'Both of you come straight to the office. A terrible calamity. I repeat I don't envy you having to tell the child. But tell her today. It'll be in the papers in the morning. Reuters were on the phone. Finster is very well known in America, and Harold was an outstanding figure in the City. See you in the morning. My wife is in tears.'

As Allan didn't know his wife he cared little about her tears. 'Thanks for ringing,' he said.

'A terrible calamity, a real catastrophe. I'm all shaken up.'

Allan put down the receiver, stamped out his cigarette, then asked himself why he had done that since there was a good five minutes' smoke left. 'May I ask,' he heard Theresa's voice saying, 'what Mr. Weatherton wanted?'

'A farm matter,' he heard himself saying. He lit another

cigarette. 'I must go out for a quarter of an hour or so, but wait for me here.'

'I'll wait. Do you know what we're going to have for dinner?' He made a little movement with his head, and no one could have guessed whether he meant yes or no. 'Caneton aux navets. Do you know what that is?'

'I think I do.'

'I bet you don't, Uncle Allan,' she laughed. 'That's duckling with white turnips. Do you know how that dish is cooked?'

'You'll tell me when I come back.'

He hurried out. Doyle's bicycle leaned against the low brick wall. He jumped on it and pedalled as fast as he could to the Court. Peggy lay in a deck chair near the cedar, and in their boredom the Great Danes barked at him. 'Have you the London telephone directory?' he asked, his voice harsh and loud.

'I haven't. What's wrong, Allan? You look as though you'd seen a ghost.'

'I've seen two. I'll get through to Inquiries.'

He ran into the library, where he dialled Inquiries, and while he was waiting to be given the telephone number of the Convent of Our Lady of the Seven Sorrows, Peggy swept into the room. 'What is it, Allan? Did you hear from her?'

'I haven't heard from her. My brother Harold and his wife were killed in a plane accident.'

'How ghastly!' exclaimed Peggy. 'Poor Allan, losing two brothers under a month.'

For the first time since Weatherton had rung, Allan realised that Harold hadn't been only Theresa's father, but his own brother too. He hadn't time to give it any thought. 'I'm thinking of Theresa.'

'Have you told her?'

'Not yet.'

'Children don't feel as deep as we.'

He could have strangled Peggy. That scraggy neck simply asked for it. 'Are you there?' said Inquiries' rather bored voice. 'The number is . . .' He wrote it down on the blue sea of Hector's postcard which still lay on the writing table. Peggy moved closer to him. 'My poor Allan. I am so, so sorry for you.' He said nothing as he was already dialling the convent's number. 'How does one address a mother superior?'

'I've no idea; never met one.'

'You're not very helpful,' he said irritably. 'Oh, hullo, could I speak to the mother superior?' Oh God, he prayed, let her be in. 'Mr. Allan Ramshorn speaking, Theresa Ramshorn's uncle. It's rather urgent.'

'I'll fetch her,' said a voice.

'Very clever of you,' said Peggy. 'In your place I'd do the same. Drive her up and let her nuns deal with her.'

As he wanted to give her a murderous look Mother Mary Philomena's voice asked, 'Mr. Ramshorn? I hope there's nothing wrong.'

'Please, Mother Superior,' said Allan, 'I need your help. I just heard that both her parents were killed in a plane crash.'

'My poor Theresa.'

'I want you to do something for her,' said Allan, his eyes on Peggy who had seated herself on the edge of the writing table. 'Theresa has real veneration for you, and she's very religious. I've seen her praying and she goes regularly to Mass, so, you see, you are the one person to tell her, to console her. I'm not funking it, but coming from you it'll be easier for her. Please ring her up and tell her the ghastly news.'

'I will, Mr. Ramshorn. Is she in the house? Can she overhear you?'

'I'm ringing from a friend's house precisely because I don't want her to overhear me. Please ring her.'

'But you must go back. You have to be with her when I speak to her. She will need you to comfort her. In all her letters she speaks with deep affection of you.'

'I'm going back right now. Ring her in about forty minutes.'

'Rely on me. I'm going immediately to the chapel to pray for her parents and ask God to give Theresa courage in her ordeal.'

'I'm taking her to London tomorrow morning. May we come to see you, Mother Superior, in the course of the day?'

'By all means.'

Peggy was following her own thoughts. Justin died the day Theresa arrived; in less than a month her parents were killed; therefore the next to go would be Allan. The girl was a witch, or, if not a witch, a harbinger of death. She had faith in her Swiss parlour-maid who only that morning had observed, 'That Theresa has strange eyes. They make me shudder. She looks at you like an old, old woman.' Then she told a Swiss story of an old, old woman who lived in a village perched on the edge of a precipice, died at the age of a hundred, then appeared in the village before every avalanche. The story impressed Peggy, for hadn't Theresa appeared in her village before Hector went off with that bitch?

'I'm going back right now,' said Allan.

'Won't you have a drink first? You need one, my poor Allan.'

'Haven't time,' he said.

As he approached the house he caught sight of Horace chatting with a young man who was the local darts champion. Allan beckoned to him. Horace turned his back on the champion and approached Allan, moving cautiously, waiting for harsh words, expecting to be told that he shouldn't take Theresa for long rides, or something to that effect. 'Horace,' said Allan, 'I'll be needing you.' Horace's eyes lit up. Nobody had ever needed him before.

'I'll do whatever you want me to, sir.'

'Theresa's parents have been killed in an accident.'

'In that private plane? She told me they were flying to Boston.'

'She doesn't know yet. I rang the mother superior . . .'

'. . . Mother Mary Philomena,' said Horace, shifting his weight from the right foot to the left. 'There's also Mother Sainte-Agnès who's French.'

'Quite,' said Allan impatiently, 'but that has nothing to do with it. I asked the mother superior to ring her and give her the awful news. Naturally, I'll be there when she rings. What I want from you is to come in in about an hour and a half. You might help me to console her.' Horace shifted his weight from the left foot to the right, then pulled his right ear lobe. 'She likes you, I think. I count on you.'

'I'll come, sir. Will it be in the papers?'

'I guess so. You lost your mother, didn't you?' Horace nodded twice. 'What were your reactions? What did you feel?'

'Can't really remember any more. I was such a small kid, but I think I howled.'

'I want her to howl as little as possible,' Allan said drily. 'That's precisely why I want you to come in.'

You ought to have seen her yesterday afternoon, Horace said to himself.

The wall had risen between him and Theresa, thought Allan as he mounted the three steps to the front door, for he knew that they were dead, whereas for her they were still alive. If he had the courage he could knock down the wall by the simple means of telling her, but perhaps it was better in the long run that her parents should live for her half an hour longer, time gained, since after that they would never live again. He looked at his wrist watch : only twenty-five minutes were left.

He switched on a large smile, and it didn't waver as he entered the sitting room. Theresa put down her book, stood up, and he received her sincere smile. 'I forgot to ask you,' she said, 'is a private plane much smaller than the ones father, mother and I usually take?'

'Much smaller.'

'Were they alone in it or did they have the friends they were staying with in the plane too?'

'My guess is as good as yours,' he lied.

'Mother will tell me when she rings on Tuesday. Now I'm going to explain to you how the caneton aux navets is made.'

'Don't explain it, I'll watch you cooking it.'

'Marvellous,' she exclaimed. 'You are the nicest uncle that ever lived. I really don't want to go to Morocco.'

'We'll see about that,' he said, glancing at his watch : nineteen minutes left. 'Let me look at the paper. I haven't had a chance yet.'

Behind the Sunday paper he tried to think hard, that is look into the future that Weatherton's telephone call had brought into being. He had no idea who would be Theresa's guardian; maybe Weatherton or maybe the unknown Mrs. Campbell whom Theresa didn't much like. Of course she would remain at the convent which would make it easier for the orphan. What would be the fate of the farm? He remembered that he was leaving in the middle of September bound for his dangerous adventure. Imagine if the Russians or the Bulgarians, in short, whoever he would spy on, were to kill him. Theresa would be left without a single relation as her mother had been an only child. He couldn't help looking at her; their eyes met, and she quickly asked, 'At what time would you like me to start cooking?'

'Whenever you feel like it.'

'I'll begin at six o'clock.'

His watch said there were another fourteen minutes to wait. He buried his face in the newspaper. There was her grandfather, Allan groaned inwardly, who happened also to be his, Harold's and Justin's father. He would send him a telegram because he hadn't a telephone. How would he take it? King Lear or Saturnus? One never knew with him, and what would become of the allowance Harold paid him? They were, he mused, a centrifugal family because the centre had been too soft and weak, in fact practically non-existent; Harold alone retaining a family feeling, giving his father an allowance, finding Justin a job and employing him. Now there was nothing left of him. He must control himself and not start sniffing, which wouldn't do.

'I got the duck through Mrs. Simson,' Theresa said. (Unnoticed by him he had put down the paper.) 'It's a young one, so it ought to be tender. Still, it's a shame that it had to die.'

Only ten minutes were left. 'If we felt like that we'd all be vegetarians,' he heard himself say. His father indulged in that kind of verbal reverie, boring his three sons stiff.

'That wouldn't be right either,' Theresa said. 'We don't know if vegetables feel, do we?'

'We don't.' His eyes were on the telephone.

'I wrote a little story last term for which Mother Mary Philomena praised me. It was about a rose that lay on a grave. Shall I tell you the story?'

'Tell it while you cook.'

'I can tell it in one sentence. The rose didn't understand why it wasn't treated with the same love and respect as all the other dead in the cemetery. After all, it was dead too. What do you think of it, Uncle Allan?'

'A very moving story,' he said. The forty minutes were nearly up. 'A very moving story indeed.'

'One of the girls who's called Pam Morton wrote a story about a puppy being run over.'

'You are a morbid lot at your convent,' Allan nearly exploded. Why hasn't she rung yet?

'Oh no,' smiled Theresa, 'but we all wanted to write about death. It was really a competition.'

159

'Did you see Mrs. Simson today?' he asked in order to change the subject.

'I told you I did. I went to fetch the duck. I tell you something about Mrs. Simson. She's really a very kind woman, but she always gives me some sticky fudge, and I don't like fudge. I've the same taste as mother. She doesn't like fudge either. Mother...'

The telephone bell rang. Though he had expected it, it caught him unawares and he nearly jumped. It rang too loud, too sure of itself. 'You answer it,' he said.

'It'll be for you,' she said. 'Father and mother won't ring before Tuesday.'

'Go and answer it,' he nearly shouted.

She went to the round table, lifted the receiver, said 'Hullo,' and then her whole face lit up; hers the happiest smile he had ever seen. 'Oh, it's you, Reverend Mother. How kind of you to ring me.' She couldn't resist turning to Allan, 'It's Mother Mary Philomena.' Her voice was ecstatic. 'Yes, I am very well, thank you,' she said into the receiver. 'How are you, Mother? Did you enjoy your visit to Belgium?' She was leaning forward, listening intently, and Mother Mary Philomena must have made some jocular observation about her trip because she laughed gaily and dutifully. Allan shifted in his chair.

'How is Mother Sainte-Agnès? Is Sister Mary-Rita back?' Allan half expected her to curtsey. Mother Mary Philomena was speaking now, and she listened respectfully, still smiling, nodding her head several times. Suddenly her expression changed. 'From the bottom of my heart,' she said, putting her free hand on her chest. 'Always,' she said a few seconds later. Then, 'I never forget my prayers. I never miss Mass here though I must bicycle to Yeovil.'

Allan stood up.

'I know He watches over us,' Theresa was saying. She was gripping hard the receiver. 'We must submit to His will. I know that, Mother.' Allan could almost hear the mother superior telling her that her parents were killed. He was standing beside Theresa who, he was convinced, had shrunk. In a small voice she asked, 'When?', and her hand dropped from her chest. He wished he could hear what Mother Mary Philomena was saying. 'I am not,' Theresa called out. 'I promise I won't.' Allan pulled up a chair for her which she ignored. She was listening so hard that she must have forgotten his presence in this world in general and in the sitting room in particular. Then she cried out, 'All my life. I promise you and promise them. All my life, Mother, all my life.' Mother Mary Philomena spoke again, and Theresa nearly bent double to catch every word she was saying.

'My dear child,' said Allan only a few inches from her, yet somehow afraid to touch her.

'Tomorrow,' Theresa said. 'I understand . . . yes, immediately.'

She put down the receiver, shot past Allan and rushed up to her room. He stared at the stairs as if expecting her to be still climbing them though he had heard her door close. What should he do? He would give her a few minutes, then go up. However, a few seconds later he found himself on the stairs, then tiptoeing along the passage. He listened outside her door and, as the silence in there was complete, in fact so complete that he thought that she must have flown through the window as Mrs. Simson's budgies would if their cage were opened, he entered the room. She was kneeling before the bedside table on which stood a photograph of Harold and Elisabeth in a leather frame, holding the small Crucifix that usually lay next to the photograph. She saw him but didn't move. What a fervent yet surprisingly calm little face, he said to himself. Now Harold, who had never bothered to give God a single thought, was sucked in by this fervour and brought before the Divine throne. Theresa kissed the Crucifix, rose, said, 'I won't be a moment,' and ran out. He approached the photograph, lifted it, and gazed at his late brother and sister-in-law. She looked every inch the successful man's wife, dressed expensively and soberly, her teeth looked after by the best possible dentist money can buy. Harold was the dry Harold he had known all his life. Death gave that face no fresh importance, not the face to move one. He heard Theresa coming up, so he stepped back. She laid a rose before the photograph, which she had picked from the dying rose bush near the kitchen door; one that would never open. He wished he knew what to say.

'I haven't cried,' she said, turning to him. 'I promised Mother Mary Philomena not to. She explained why I mustn't cry. There is no need to cry because, if I deserve it, I will see them again after my own death. She said that we have that on authority. Tomorrow you can tell her that I didn't cry. She also said that if I cried that would only cause them pain.'

'Theresa, I can't tell you how sorry I am, my dear child,' he said, bending down and kissing her on the forehead. She threw her arms round his neck, and it was he who dropped a few tears. After all, he had promised nothing to Mother Mary Philomena. 'Let's go down,' he said. 'You go first.' She preceded him which gave him the chance to wipe his eyes.

He passed Justin's door. Poor old Justin, events have overtaken you. Theresa gave him her smile, as spontaneous and radiant as ever. 'Was it Mr. Weatherton who told you on the phone?' she asked. He nodded. 'And then you went at once to ring Mother Mary Philomena?' He nodded again. 'You're so good, Uncle Allan. You're my only relation left, so now I can always come here for my hols, can't I?'

'Always,' said Allan, and decided to ring the crusader to tell him that it was off. But supposing her guardian, whoever he would be, wanted to sell the farm? In that case he would take some job in London and take her out once a week. 'Don't forget you're my only relation left, Theresa.'

'I'll be a very good relation. Shall I make tea?'

'You do that. I told Horace to look in.'

'He's funny, isn't he?'

What faith can do to a person, he thought as he walked towards Simson's cottage. Simson, Mrs. Simson and the brother-in-law came out of the cottage, their faces solemn, their heads slightly bent. 'Let me tender my most sincere sympathy, Mr. Allan,' said Mrs. Simson.

'Me too,' said Simson.

'And me,' said Gus.

'How on earth did you find out?' Allan asked.

'It's that boy Horace who came to tell us,' said Mrs. Simson. 'Does Theresa know, the poor little mite?'

'She knows. She took it wonderfully. There's something to be said for those Papists.'

'She'd have taken it the same way if she'd been one of us,' said Mrs. Simson who was a Methodist. This wasn't the moment for discussing the merits of different religions, Allan said to himself. 'First Mr. Justin went,' said Simson, 'and now it's Mr. Ramshorn himself.'

'Now she'll be all alone,' said Mrs. Simson. 'All she'll have is you, a responsibility you can't shirk, Mr. Allan.' She means Patsy, thought Allan. 'Shall I go and see her? It might do her good.'

'I'll tell her to come here after tea.'

'The farm now belongs to her,' said Gus.

'Our boss,' said Simson.

'I haven't thought of that,' said Allan.

'You ought to buy her a couple of budgies,' said Mrs. Simson. 'They'll cheer her up no end.'

The conversation became desultory, and, his duty done, Allan escaped back to the house. A thrush sat on the dying rose bush near the kitchen door. 'Tea is ready,' said Theresa. He looked at her : no, she hadn't cried. Anyway, her eyes betrayed nothing.

'I've been reckoning,' she said a little later. 'If I live a very long time then it'll be a very long time before I see father and mother.'

'It'll be a very long time, in fact, I hope a very, very long time.'

'One isn't allowed to pray for death to come quickly, Uncle Allan. If it's God's will that we live long . . . that must be Horace.'

She rose, went to open the door, and Horace shuffled in, his left holed tennis shoe covered in cow dung, part of which he lost as he came across the room. 'Look how dirty you are,' Theresa said.

'I'm very sorry, sir,' Horace said, 'but as I was coming here I walked behind Jenkins's cow, and she dropped it straight at my feet. I'll take my shoes off, and leave them outside the door.'

'Too late,' said Theresa. 'I'll get you a cup.'

'Wait,' said Horace. 'You haven't heard the latest. Old Fred's had a heart attack and was taken to hospital in Yeovil.'

'Poor old Fred,' said Theresa, who had spoken to him only once.

'You ought to have said something to Theresa,' said Allan after she had gone to the kitchen.

'It's so difficult on such occasions,' said Horace. 'When Mrs. Bury died, my pa told me to see him, and say how sorry I was. He was the sexton. I went in and said, "Mr. Bury, I am very sorry indeed." Do you know what he answered? He said, "A relief, Horace, a relief." So you see. When I told my pa, he said I invented it because I was wicked, and now my ma had definite proof that I was wicked. There's no justice, is there?' Theresa came in with a cup and saucer. He turned to her. 'I am very sorry indeed to hear that you've become an orphan.'

'Don't call me an orphan,' she said angrily. 'I'm not one. My parents are still alive. They've eternal life. They are with God.'

Horace looked at Allan, his eyes asking, was there any justice? 'All right, I won't call you an orphan.'

'There's a girl at the convent,' Theresa said. 'She lost her parents, and when we see her we say to each other, "Let's be specially nice to Ludmilla because she's an orphan." I don't want them to say the same about me.'

'You tell them not to,' said Horace.

'I'll leave you,' said Allan. 'I've got some work to do in the office.'

'At what time are we leaving for London?' Theresa asked, and Horace said to himself, the orphan is showing off.

'We'll take the eight-twenty,' Allan said.

He had the vague intention of bringing the farm books up to date in case Weatherton asked for figures, but instead of settling down to it he listened to Horace and Theresa, their voices floating in through the open window.

'They didn't suffer,' Horace was saying. 'It's too sudden. You're dead before you know where you are. There was a man in Sherborne who drank twenty pints of cider in the pub, then wanted to light his pipe and blew up.'

'I don't believe a word of it,' Theresa said.

'You're like my pa, but it happens to be true. He blew up, and the other men in the pub all said he'd a smile on his face, so, you see, he didn't suffer.'

'One can't blow up smiling.'

'How do you know? You never blew up. Now don't come telling me that you blew up. I know you were in Spain, in Switzerland, in Italy, but you never blew up, Theresa.'

'That man didn't either.'

'You always get round it.'

'I respect truth.'

'You're a prig; a real one.'

'I'm not a prig.'

It was a good idea, Allan thought, to have asked Horace in.

A little later she appeared in the doorway. 'Do you know when father and mother will be buried?'

'Don't know yet,' he said, thinking that there was probably nothing left to bury. 'They might be buried in America.'

'Will we go to their funeral? I mean, will we fly out?'

'I don't think that there will be time.'

'But later on we can visit their graves.'

'That's it, and now go back and entertain Horace.'

She gave him a conspiratorial smile before returning to the sitting room; a strange girl whom often he couldn't make out. He ought to telegraph his father, however he didn't want to do it in front of Theresa, and had no desire to do it from the Court. Let it wait till he got to London. He was beginning to have second thoughts about the crusader. He had exaggerated when he decided not to take on the job. Fundamentally, he had nothing to offer Theresa who needed the care of a woman far more than that of a bachelor uncle. The mother superior was the right person for her, and surely in his will Harold had appointed some female to act as her guardian. Their relations were based on Patsy having decamped. Had Patsy remained, they wouldn't have hit it off. He would take the job, and in any case the farm had, as it were, lost its importance through Harold's death. Horace and Theresa seemed silent indeed, so he went to investigate.

She sat on the floor in front of the fireplace while on all fours Horace was drawing on a sheet of paper. Horace jumped up when he caught sight of Allan. He blushed as he said, 'I was just drawing a dog for her.'

'A dog?'

'We always see the same dog when we cycle through Snake Country.'

'A small, round dog,' Theresa said.

'Get on with your drawing,' Allan said. 'I still have work to do.'

The very young, he thought, needed no help from their elders; one more reason to take the job with the crusader. Never did he fear danger less than today. Justin dead, Harold dead, the world unchanged, so what difference could his own death make? Suddenly he thought of the pub: from the pub he could telephone the telegram through. He walked across in the Sunday calm. The pub was not yet open, but Nelson let him in, and he sent off the telegram feeling at that moment sorry for his father who had lost two of his sons without being able to care about their deaths. Nelson condoled with him, saying he never considered aeroplanes safe. 'Has the lady from Winnipeg left?' Allan asked.

'Two days after the night you came here. She was a funny one, she was.'

'We're all funny if we come to think of it,' Allan said, then asked himself what he had meant by that. Nothing. Nelson offered him a drink which he accepted, then Nelson inquired what would become of his little niece. He would know tomorrow. Nelson said it was time the weather changed, the farmers were complaining of the drought. Allan thanked him for the drink, and as he went back to the house, he saw Lindsey from a distance, his deportment showing that he hadn't yet been told of Harold's and Elisabeth's death. Apparently Horace had thought only of the Simsons who must have told Nelson. He heard loud voices as he approached the front door.

'You can't,' Theresa was saying.

'Only for a few minutes,' Horace begged.

'You shouldn't even think of it on a day like this,' she said angrily.

'What is it all about?' Allan asked, coming in.

'Horace wants to look at the telly,' Theresa said.

'There isn't one at the vicarage, sir,' said Horace.

'Today he can't, isn't that so, Uncle Allan?'

'You can't, Horace,' said Allan, thinking that it might be on the news.

'All right, sir,' said Horace, disappointed.

A few minutes later he left and Theresa went to the kitchen. Allan hurried after her. 'No cooking tonight. We'll go to Yeovil and dine there.'

'Oh, Uncle Allan, please let me cook the duck.'

'You prefer that?'

'I do so want to cook it.'

'Have it your own way, but first go and see Mrs. Simson who wants to see you.'

When she returned her eyes evaded his. Had she been crying? Better to leave her alone; and he sat down in the sitting room, his mind void of thought, lacking even the strength to light a cigarette. All of a sudden an awful smell burst into the room, like a warehouse on fire. The next moment Theresa rushed in, sobbing loudly, 'I burnt the duck. What am I to do? I burnt the duck.'

'Don't take it to heart, happens to the best cook.'

She buried her face in her hands, her body shook, and she continued to cry in an agonised voice, 'I burnt the duck, I burnt the duck.'

12

'You could have told me last night,' said the vicar in an aggrieved voice. 'Then I could have gone and condoled with them.'

'They only wanted to see me,' said Horace.

Father and son were having early breakfast because the vicar had to go to Salisbury to see a canon, an old friend of his. It was cloudy outside, and not a breath of air.

'I can't believe that they chose you alone to share their grief,' said the vicar, 'but the fact remains that I am the vicar, and it is my duty . . .'

'Why? He believes in nothing and she's an R.C.'

The vicar felt like hurling his cup at his son. 'Don't speak with your mouth full,' he said, then picked up yesterday's paper, and pretended to read while he cooled off. 'It'll be in today's papers,' Horace said, munching toast.

'Don't gloat,' said his father, 'over other people's misfortune . . .'

'It isn't that. Anyway, she told me that she never looked at papers.'

'Who is she?'

'The girl. She said her mother said papers are full of crime and disaster and only depress one.'

'An intelligent lady.'

'Who?'

'The mother.'

'She's dead, so one can't say she is an intelligent lady.'

'I think I've enjoyed sufficiently your company,' said the vicar, rising from the table.

'May I go now?' Horace asked.

'Yes, you may. At lunch time Mrs. Bramm will come in and give you some ham and lettuce. At your age you should be able to prepare yourself a meal, but, alas, you're incapable of fending for yourself.'

Horace hurried down to the garage, jumped on his bicycle, and cycled to Yeovil station, taking the short cut through Snake Country. It wasn't yet eight o'clock. He strolled up and down the platform till Allan and Theresa appeared. 'There's Horace,' she said.

'I've come here for a parcel,' said Horace, 'but it's too early to collect it.'

'I thought you came to see us off,' said Theresa.

'You think a lot,' he muttered.

He stayed with them till their train came in, and remained on the platform till it pulled out, then rode back to the village.

Allan took Theresa into the breakfast car. At the same table sat an aged man, drinking whisky, and the countryside looked tired out by the sun of the summer. During the night Allan had twice opened her door, trying to make as little noise as possible. She slept, lying on her side, a hand against her cheek. She hadn't moved either when he looked in the second time. As they were leaving early he decided to rise at six, so as to wake her since he didn't want her to face the day unsupported. She was downstairs when he woke up.

The whisky-drinking old man seemed to amuse her. He got off at Salisbury, a fat, perspiring woman taking his place. Theresa wasn't interested in her. After Basingstoke she said, 'I'm ashamed about last night.'

'Why?'

'I behaved like a baby. I shouldn't have cried, but, of course, you know it was only because of the duck, so you don't have to say anything to Mother Mary Philomena.'

'Rest assured,' he smiled. When the steward came with the bill he asked for a large whisky. 'Like the old gentleman, Theresa.' He felt he needed it.

They drove to the City with Theresa chatting all the time. She had been twice before to her father's office, and on the second occasion he had given her lunch nearby. 'When I think of it I forget that father is dead. We had mutton chops.'

The office was in a new building lacking the aura of the City. Harold, Allan remembered, had been a great one for things that were new, thinking that they were part and parcel of his dynamic personality. Allan and Theresa went up in a lift that stopped only on every second floor. The front door of the office opened automatically, a light went up in the waiting room, and a round woman in her fifties came in to receive them. She wore a necklace made of red and green beads. Allan asked for Mr. Weatherton, the woman said, 'Your name, please.' Allan said, 'Mr. Ramshorn and Miss Ramshorn.' The woman didn't bat an eyelid as she inquired whether they had an appointment. She too, Allan thought, belonged to Harold's new world, her roundness notwithstanding.

Weatherton came out, looking embarrassed. 'Hullo, Theresa,' he said, grinning sheepishly.

'How are you, Mr. Weatherton?' Theresa said, bowing.

'Come in both of you,' said Weatherton.

He must have lost no time in moving into Harold's room because there was a framed photograph of Elisabeth on the writing table. 'There's mother,' Theresa said.

'It's more convenient in here,' said Weatherton, a tall man, all legs and hardly any body. He became more sure of himself once he was seated, for he could treat them as if they were regular clients. 'Words fail me,' he said with eyes raised to the ceiling. 'Your daddy and I worked together for twelve years. My loss is as great as yours, so I don't have to tell you how desperately unhappy I am, poor little Theresa.'

'Father and mother are with God,' she said, 'so we mustn't be unhappy.'

'Oh yes, quite so,' said Weatherton. 'That's the way to look at it.'

'When will they be buried?' Theresa asked.

'I'm sure to get a cable today,' Weatherton said, playing with Harold's paperweight which had the shape of a cradle. 'I've arranged for you, Allan, to meet Lockburn, Harold's solicitor, at twelve. I hope the hour suits you. I'll be there myself. The will is with him. I take it that Theresa would like to see the mother superior of her convent. Harold told me, Theresa, that she is devoted to you.'

'I am to her,' Theresa said.

'Do you need any money for Theresa?' Weatherton asked, rising. 'I mean cash.'

'Not this moment,' said Allan, disliking him.

'Anyway, we'll settle all this with Lockburn,' said Weatherton, and saw them to the door. 'Twelve sharp,' he called after Allan.

Allan turned back. 'I haven't his address.'

'I thought you knew him.'

'Never met him.'

Weatherton wrote down the address, then escaped back to Harold's room. They went down in the lift, came out into the bustle and the sunshine, Allan hailed a cab, gave it the convent's address, and as they got in Theresa said, 'Mr. Weatherton speaks very little. Mother always said, "He's as silent as the grave." But father said, "That's because he's a very wise person." Mother said, in that case she preferred silly persons.'

Her eyes shone while she spoke as though by repeating their words they were brought back to her as alive as they had been when she heard her mother say that Weatherton was as silent as the grave, and her father that Weatherton was a very wise person.

'Will they give you lunch at the convent?' Allan asked. 'I might be delayed in the solicitor's office.'

'I'm sure,' she said with a broad smile. 'Mother Sainte-Agnès wouldn't let me go hungry.'

He dropped her outside the convent. She was disappointed because he wouldn't come in, but he promised to return immediately after lunch. He rang the bell for her, and got back into the taxi before the door was opened. He dismissed the cab at the next street corner, and walked off, saying to himself that this was worse than a hangover.

With Harold's death an era had ended. Since his teens Harold had been his only background even if a seldom pleasant one, for Harold had been a nagger. However, nobody else had ever taken the trouble to nag him. Harold had provided him with a job, and made it as empty and frustrating as possible. None the less, Harold had been the sole person who had bothered about him. In Weatherton's presence he had felt how little he was connected with Harold's real world, he the younger brother to whom a few crumbs had been thrown; no fresh crumbs would be thrown, since the loaf had passed out of Harold's possession. It would be picked up by Weatherton and whoever was appointed Theresa's guardian, and what a fool he was when he thought that Theresa could remain in his life. Well, her holiday would end in less than three weeks, and it was the natural course of events for him to lose her. What had a girl of eleven to do with a lone man approaching thirty-one? The crusader was his salvation; nobody and nothing else. He went into a pub, and had a small whisky.

Of course, Weatherton didn't know that Patsy had left him and that he and Theresa had fended alone for themselves. At the solicitor's he was bound to find out, one more weighty reason to take the girl away, that is not to entrust her to him. But why bother when the crusader was waiting? He left the pub, and took a cab to the solicitor's office. He was being generous with himself today, one cab after the other. Weatherton had arrived before him.

Lockburn was short, and his grey moustache seemed to weigh him down. He was portly, and wore a double-breasted dark blue suit and a pearl-grey tie. A man, said Allan to himself, from whom one expected little. His office was a wide room, the armchairs large, and a Soutine on the wall. 'Sit down,' he said, 'sit down both of you. This is a sad occasion. I liked Ramshorn so much, such a gay man.' Allan looked startled. 'An efficient one too. His will is straight to the point.'

'Naturally, I know its contents,' said Weatherton.

'Do you?' Lockburn asked Allan, who shook his head. 'Let us go through it. You're both interested parties.'

He liked his voice, read slowly, stopping after every second sentence, then starting again as though doing his audience a favour. Allan listened as from a distance. Harold left all he possessed to his wife Elisabeth, and a better and more devoted wife no man ever had. To save her of all the difficulties and annoyance the management of an estate entailed, he appointed his friend and partner Ronald Weatherton as sole executor of his will. (For a moment Allan thought that by estate he meant the farm.) In case his wife Elisabeth predeceased him his daughter Theresa would become his universal legatee. In the event of both he and his wife Elisabeth dying during Theresa's minority his estate would be turned into a trust till her majority, with Ronald Weatherton acting as the sole trustee and his own brother Allan as her guardian . . .

'What?' Allan nearly shouted.

Weatherton gave him a knowing smile, and Lockburn read on. Harold had the greatest confidence in his brother Allan who, he knew, would loyally and devotedly fulfil his obligations as guardian of his daughter Theresa. His appointing Allan wasn't meant as an offence to his brother Justin, but simply was proof of his complete faith in Allan. Besides,

172

Justin, in case he married, might move away from the farm, and it was his definite wish that, if left an orphan, Theresa should spend her school holidays on the farm and make her home there till her majority. (Of course, he thought I was married to Patsy, Allan said to himself.) It was also Harold's definite wish that Theresa remained at the convent till she finished her schooling. In case of any unforeseen difficulties, his brother Allan should invariably consult with Ronald Weatherton.

'You accept the charge?' Lockburn asked.

'I do,' said Allan, thinking : all this is under false pretences. Harold wouldn't have appointed me if he had known that Patsy and I weren't married.

'We should face straightway the unforeseen difficulties,' said Weatherton.

'So there's a catch to it,' said Allan.

'Lockburn knows it as well as I,' said Weatherton, rising. 'What it all amounts to is that Harold wasn't as well off as he believed he was.' He strode up and down while he spoke, his hands clasped over his waistcoat. 'He earned a vast amount, but that ceases with his death. Of course, his partnership is worth a goodish amount, then there is the lease of his house which I intend to sell, but the picture isn't as rosy as you, Allan, might imagine. Harold and Elisabeth were inveterate spenders. Moreover, his own private investments weren't fortunate. They might have been in the long run, but there is no more question of that.' Allan nodded. 'What I'm trying to get at is that the farm can't be considered any more a rich man's plaything, and since you are the farm manager I'll have to count on you to turn it into a going concern.'

'Harold never wanted me to do anything with it,' said Allan.

'He knew nothing about farming,' said Weatherton, 'and it suited him not to earn money with it. But that has to cease. The whole point is, can I count on you to make it earn real money? For Theresa's sake I am prepared to put in an assistant manager, perhaps get rid of Simson, and let the assistant advise you, or if you don't feel up to the task . . .'

'He has left a thousand pounds to each of his two brothers,' interjected Lockburn, 'so if you choose not to run the farm you won't be in immediate straits.'

'As Theresa's guardian,' said Weatherton, sitting down on

a narrow chair near the bookcase crammed with legal books, 'the trust would provide you with money you might need for expenses connected with your duties. The important thing is that the farm must earn money.'

Never before had Allan possessed a thousand pounds, and to run the farm at a profit would mean hard work. He appreciated what hard work meant since he had kept generally aloof from it. 'I'm going to run the farm with Simson,' he said, 'and make it earn money for Theresa, but it'll need some money spent on it first.'

'We'll talk that over,' said Weatherton. 'The farm will have to be Theresa's main source of income.'

'You can count on me,' Allan said grandly.

When they left, Weatherton asked him to lunch with him. Allan said he couldn't because Theresa was expecting him. 'I hope,' said Weatherton, 'that your wife will be like a mother to Theresa. Why didn't she come up today?'

'For the simple reason that she has left me. Besides, she wasn't my wife.'

They had reached the street, Weatherton stopped, then turned on Allan, his pale face white with anger. 'If Harold had known that he wouldn't have made you her guardian.'

'I thought of that myself, but, believe me, it's better like this.'

Yes, he sighed, it was better like this.

'I hope you'll consider it your duty to be loyal to Harold's intentions.'

'We've been alone for three weeks now, and I don't think Theresa missed her aunt when she left me. I must leave you, Theresa is expecting me.'

'I'll come down to see over the farm,' said Weatherton as rudely as he could. 'I want to see what's going on there.'

'Come after Theresa's gone back to school. Anyway, I'll send you a list of the things I need for improving the farm.'

He went away, thinking that a new life always started with enemies. Yet Weatherton was right in a sense. If it hadn't been for Theresa, life would have been impossible after Patsy left. Or would it have been more impossible if Patsy had stayed? Theresa hadn't taken to her, but how could a man like Weatherton understand? Anyhow, tonight he would ring the crusader since now it was definitely off. He felt exceedingly bitter. It hadn't been his wish that Patsy should leave him, their parting wasn't of his making, none the less he appeared before Weatherton as an impostor. But wasn't one an impostor if one was weak and stupid enough to lose a woman?

He went into a pub which was crowded with lunch-time customers; a world of pork-pies, sausages and egg and tomato sandwiches. He had no desire for food, so he ordered a large whisky. Weatherton had been lying when he said that Harold had left no real fortune. He said that to spur him on, or rather to force him to throw his hand in. Probably he wanted some nominee of his to run the farm. And what did it matter? He could be Theresa's guardian without remaining on the farm. With the thousand pounds he would receive he could start another life elsewhere. If necessary he could spend a few weeks in the house during Theresa's holidays. He shrugged his shoulders, for that wasn't necessary either since he could be her guardian without living under the same roof with her. Perhaps the crusader remained the answer. Anyway, when his father died the capital of the income Harold had made over to him would revert to Theresa, so the will said. Definitely Weatherton was lying. Weatherton would turn his life into hell, and he'd had enough hell without needing a new one. He desired no responsibility, no difficulties, and he wished that the bearded man with a bit of pastry in his beard pushed less. He glared at him, and left the pub.

He took another taxi. London was too large after the T-shaped village. The driver was loquacious, drying up only when he noticed that his fare wasn't listening. The convent was a large late Victorian building with a mock-Gothic front door. Funny that he hadn't noticed that door in the morning. Patsy would have made scathing remarks about that door; the sort of door that a nun with downcast eyes would open. He rang the bell, and a rubicund woman with grey hair and wearing a white overall appeared in the doorway. For an instant he thought he had come to the wrong address. 'Is this the convent?' he asked.

'Whom do you want to see?'

'The mother superior.'

'You're Theresa's uncle?' He said he was. 'Come in, sir.'

He entered a long passage with a Crucifix on his right, and a statue of the Virgin at the end of it. The stone-flagged floor was wet. 'Careful,' the woman said, 'it's wet. General autumn cleaning.' There was a second rubicund woman in the passage. 'I'll announce you to the mother superior.' The other woman had stopped scrubbing, lit a cigarette, and said to Allan, 'In three weeks' time it starts, and then one must go out to smoke.' The first woman came back, and said in as refined a voice as she could muster, 'This way, sir.'

He was ushered into a room almost as long as the passage. It looked like the office of a busy executive but for the Crucifix and a painting of the Virgin. Beside a table stood two nuns, one tall with an aquiline nose and a parchment-like skin, the second small, fat and red-faced. Allan approached the tall nun who, he was certain, was the mother superior. It was the small one who stepped forward. 'How do you do, Mr. Ramshorn?' she said in a deep voice. 'We spoke on the telephone yesterday. This is Mother Sainte-Agnès to whom Theresa is deeply devoted. She is to me too, the dear little girl, such a brave soul. May I tell you how I grieve over your brother's and sister-in-law's death?'

Mother Sainte-Agnès bowed and left the room. Mother Mary Philomena asked Allan to sit down, then seated herself in an armchair next to his. 'Where is Theresa, Reverend Mother?' (Hadn't Theresa called her reverend mother on the telephone?)

'She's gone with one of the lay sisters to her home. The servants are away on holiday, but there's a housekeeper in the basement, so she can get in. They promised not to tarry. Anyway, Theresa knows that you are coming here, and I can assure you she has great affection for you.'

'I am very fond of her.'

'It's her love for you that gives her the strength she needs in this tragic hour.'

'And your inspiration,' said Allan, thinking, what a tiny woman yet what strength.

'You have, Mr. Ramshorn, an enormous burden on your shoulders. One can't let down children, especially not a sensitive child like Theresa.'

'I'll never let her down, you may rest assured of that.' Again the crusader was on the way out.

'I'm certain you won't, but still it is a great responsibility. A Mr. Weatherton, who will look after her financial interests, rang me a little while ago. He told me you are her guardian; an immense task, Mr. Ramshorn.' Busybody Weatherton, Allan said to himself. 'I know it'll be only a matter of her holidays since she'll be with us the rest of the time. Even so your responsibility will be a lasting one. In the short time she spent with you down on the farm she has come to love you, and I know you return her love. You will be her entire and only family, but you are young, and my only fear is this : What will happen if you ever marry? Your future wife might not take to her, and she's a very possessive girl. We know that here in the convent. Forgive me for speaking so frankly, but you and I will be the two pivots of her existence till she grows up.'

What did she know, and what had Theresa told her? She surely knew at the time that Theresa was going to her uncle and aunt. 'I'll do nothing against her peace and happiness,' he said in a manly voice.

'If it ever happens,' said Mother Mary Philomena, 'that you marry and your future wife doesn't get on with her then come to me and tell me. We can always arrange for her to spend her holidays with the families of other girls we have here. What I am trying to say is that you shouldn't make either yourself or her unhappy, but be frank with yourself, her and me, and then we can save her and you from unhappiness. As a grown-up person you can cope better with complications than a girl of her age, and with the simplicity of heart one still has at that age. Our Lord loved children.'

He had the sudden urge to tell her about Patsy, to assure her that it was over, and there was no cause for fear on that count. The urge didn't turn into words, and all he said was, 'Theresa's interests will always come first. You may rely on that, Reverend Mother.'

Then Mother Mary Philomena chatted about the next term, Theresa's gifts, and her aptitude for learning, asked questions about the village, was delighted to hear of her housekeeping and cooking, and Allan knew that he had disappointed her, yet couldn't bring himself to do anything about it. 'They ought to be here by now,' she said after a while. Sure enough Theresa arrived with the lay sister, bringing a suitcase with her. When she came in she rushed up to Allan, grabbed his shoulder, saying, 'Such a long time since I've seen you. Did

Reverend Mother tell you that Father Bull, our chaplain, has said a Mass for father and mother?'

Harold sucked into Glory, said Allan to himself. Perhaps he deserved it after all, or was it the gift of a thousand pounds that made him think that, or Mother Mary Philomena's presence? 'I was going to tell your uncle,' said Mother Mary Philomena; and before he left with Theresa she said to him, 'I am not worried any more. I'll pray for you, Mr. Ramshorn.' He still wished he had told her about Patsy.

'What have you in that suitcase?' he asked Theresa in the taxi that took them to Waterloo station.

'Mostly photos,' she said, 'and Mother's big Crucifix. We bought it in Venice.'

'Venice,' he said. 'You'll miss your travels.'

'I won't, Uncle Allan.'

'You know I'm now your guardian.'

'What's a guardian?'

'I'll have to look after you.'

'You did that since I arrived in the village. Won't it be good to be back tonight? Mother Sainte-Agnès has explained how not to burn food.'

But what did she say about Patsy to Mother Mary Philomena?

In the train his qualms returned. The cheek of Weatherton to announce to Mother Mary Philomena that he was the girl's guardian. Couldn't he have left it to him to tell her in person? And the farm? Weatherton would give him hell, make life impossible, therefore wasn't it the best solution to take Mother Mary Philomena's advice and let Theresa spend her holidays with her chums? He looked across to her, she was asleep, her face pale as though the harsh sun of this summer had missed her out. Suddenly, a few tears coursed down her cheeks, a sob followed, and she woke up, giving him a bewildered glance. Then back came the smile. 'When I was in the house I didn't go into their bedroom,' she said in a low voice, 'but now I dreamt that I did.' She blinked, and he thought, in her dream they were in the bedroom, poor girl.

'There it is,' she cried with pleasure as they came out of Yeovil station, pointing at the Land Rover. The sun was a round red ball, blinding their eyes. 'So nice after London,' she said. 'And the trees.'

In the letter-box he found a letter addressed to Theresa by the late Elisabeth. It had been mailed before the final flight. As Theresa was still busy with her suitcase he swiftly put the letter into his pocket. He would give it to her perhaps in six months' or a year's time. Simson came into the house to say that Mrs. Latham had looked in, and would Mr. Allan ring her the moment they got back? She also left a letter for Theresa. 'Here's a letter for you,' he said when she appeared, handing her the one Peggy had written.

'It's very kind of her,' said Theresa, showing it to him. It was cliché-filled, and it could just as well have been written and sent to a woman who in ripe middle age had lost her doddering parents, both taken away in extreme old age. He decided not to ring Peggy before the morning. 'I'll go and ask Mrs. Simson to give us eggs, vegetables and fruit, will that be enough?' He said it would be plenty. 'But tomorrow I'll give you a very good meal. Mother Sainte-Agnès explained how to make pot-au-feu.'

Taking advantage of the cheap evening rate, his father telephoned. In an unctuous voice he informed Allan that he was heartbroken. 'Will this never end?' he called into the receiver, then waited for the answer. 'If it doesn't end,' said Allan, 'I'll be the next one.' His father declared that he disliked jokes in bad taste, forgot to ask after Theresa, and rang off when the three minutes were up.

Allan walked to the cowshed, the light was fading, the pigs were asleep, and the three bull calves were in the old stable which had become their home. Turn this into a going concern, he said to himself, shrugging his shoulders. It would mean starting from scratch, and would that fool of a Weatherton let him rear Herefords for export? Simson appeared in the twilight, smoking a pipe. 'We'll have to mind our steps,' Allan said. 'A Mr. Weatherton, who was my brother's partner, will hold the purse strings.'

'We'll deal with him,' said Simson. 'Town people know nought of nothing, the buggers.'

'The point is that my brother left less than we thought, so the farm can't be run any more at a loss.'

The bowl of Simson's pipe was burning red with the effort he was making. He scratched his head before observing,

'That'll cost money, Mr. Allan. If this farm wants to prosper we'll need a lot of money sunk into it.'

'And plenty of work.'

Simson felt less enthusiastic about work. 'A lot of money,' he repeated.

'If we put Theresa's money into it,' said Allan, 'our responsibility will be greater, mine at any rate.'

Simson wanted to get back to his wife to ask her what had come over their Allan. 'I can hear a man in the house,' he said, 'a nasty man, Lindsey by name.' Thus having got rid of Allan he hurried to his wife. No wind of change from the compost, could have been his motto.

Lindsey was commiserating with Theresa. They stood near the round table, he bending over her, she gazing up at him. 'You must see them as stars watching over you,' he said, his nose nearly touching her hair.

'I see them with God,' said Theresa. 'His Mother is smiling at them, and that's exactly what Mother Sainte-Agnès said today. La Sainte-Vierge leur sourit. You speak French, Mr. Lindsey?'

Lindsey said, a little, then straightened himself because Allan had come into the room. Lindsey left after a few minutes' desultory chat. 'You look tired out, Theresa,' Allan said.

'Could we have only boiled eggs tonight?'

They had boiled eggs, and he sent her to bed. He called the number the crusader had given him. The telephone bell rang, and while he waited impatience seized him, for he wanted it to be finished and done with. At last a voice. 'This is Allan Ramshorn speaking.'

'Yes,' said the voice. 'When are you coming up for your business appointment?'

'I'm afraid it's off.'

'That happens,' said the crusader with no astonishment or anger in his voice.

'My brother died, and I'm now his daughter's guardian.'

'Less strenuous, thanks for ringing.'

Well, that was over. Was it Theresa who had saved him from torture by the Ruskies? He yawned, and thought he too ought to go to bed. Before falling asleep he said to himself that if anybody saved him it was Harold and Elisabeth. Not even they : the aeroplane that exploded. He woke up in the middle of the night, convinced that he had heard Theresa weeping. He tiptoed to her door, but there was total silence.

In the morning came the vicar and the Misses Rawley and Cobb to express their heartfelt sympathies to uncle and niece. After they left, Theresa took Allan to her room. The Crucifix hung on the wall; on the table stood photographs of her parents, about a dozen of them, all framed, and among them one of her as a baby.

13

Hickman came to have a drink with Lindsey. They sat, as it were, under the aegis of the red brocade. 'That fellow Ramshorn ratted on me,' complained Lindsey. 'I got the whole machine working, he was called for an interview and said no.'

'I never quite understood why you wanted to help him,' said Hickman.

'Out of the kindness of my heart.' Hickman laughed. 'Don't laugh, I am made that way. The fellow was fed up with life, so I wanted to give him a helping hand.'

'He might have had second thoughts. It might not have looked attractive to him.'

'Because he's a yellow-bellied bastard,' said Lindsey vehemently.

'You don't seem to like him,' laughed Hickman. 'Our trouble really is that we still see ourselves as brave young men in Trieste. But that was part of the game. This fellow probably dislikes games.'

Hickman departed in an excellent mood as befits one who had put youth and the game behind him, who lived only for his own comfort and filling the old oak chest. He had left half of his second whisky : Lindsey finished it. He sat down on the yellow sofa and thought of Theresa. He felt more sure of the future. The game, he sneered, the game, yet it was due to the game that he had done some useful intelligence work. That oaf of a Horace had asked him the other day why he had bought a bicycle. After all, he had a car. 'I like exercise,' he had answered. Now the village had become accustomed to his riding round the countryside on his bicycle. In every sense a bicycle was a better proposition. Stupid little girls were beginning to be frightened by men in cars offering them lifts. To see a cyclist following them into a wood or a meadow was almost natural to them. The man gets off the bike, chats with them, and then it is up to the man to find the plausible excuse. Anyway, with Theresa there was no need to find an excuse. She was sexy : he had felt that the day he lifted her. The sweet little body trembled; it only needed awakening. And they were friends, therefore it wouldn't be a case of having to strike up an acquaintance. It would be plain sailing.

He had gone the day before to see old Fred who was leaving hospital today. It was clever of him to see him while he was still there. At home that tiresome wife of his would have been present, and old women were vicious spies. In the course of the conversation he inquired from Fred whether there were short cuts between the village and Yeovil, for while he patrolled the road he had never run into Theresa, though he knew she rode to Yeovil at least once a day. Fred said there was one through Snake Country which he didn't use as it was too bumpy. Today Lindsey had taken up his position in the vicinity of the giant sycamore, hiding cleverly, and she came, but with Horace. They returned together too. Still, she wasn't glued to that oaf, and there must come a morning or an afternoon when she would be cycling through Snake Country alone. He would do something about Horace if he continued sticking to her. Perhaps ask the vicar whether Horace could run some errand for him. He could start with offering a donation for his empty church.

He lay back on the sofa, savouring the vision of Theresa with her flat chest, hairless body and little backside which was really no backside at all. He had lightly touched it the evening he condoled with her. He turned on his belly better to savour the vision. He savoured it to the full.

When he sat up exhausted, a nasty picture appeared before him. It was three years old. He had driven to the Midlands, far more people up there. Besides, down here in Somerset one was more conspicuous. Outside a small industrial town, dark and dreary, he saw a girl of about ten waiting for a bus. She had red hair and red cheeks, and was too fat for his liking. None the less, he offered her a lift. She jumped into the car, he had to drive her through the town because she lived on the other side of it. It was getting dark, and when they were rid of the town, as it were, he said he had to get out to look at his rear light which he thought wasn't working. She was munching a sticky bit of chocolate he had given her. Cunningly he stayed beside the rear light on the lonely road, and, naturally, the girl followed him, out of sheer curiosity, as he had expected. She joined him, and with her hands pressed against her knees she bent over the light which, needless to say, he had switched off before alighting. Then he lost his head, if that was the right expression. One hand grabbed her neck, the other ripped off her thick panties; mesmerised by fear the girl didn't let out a sound. The hand gripped her neck hard, and he raped her there and then. She must have banged her nose against the boot because next day he found blood marks on it. When it was done he got into his car, she hadn't the strength left to move or shout, and he drove away as fast as he could. He had frightened himself, but days went by, and he saw nothing in the papers. Anyway, he was back in the village on the same night. He resolved never to let himself be taken in again. (In retrospect he had decided that it was the girl who seduced him.) He was a normal human being, no fault of his that love of beauty was more developed in him than in most people. At odd moments he still felt panicky, for he knew perfectly well that a little more pressure on the fat girl's neck could have, if caught, put him in an extraordinarily awkward position.

That night Theresa visited him in his sleep, lay down beside him, and begged him to love her. 'That's all I want to do,' he said repeatedly, yet did nothing about it. Eventually she left, deeply disappointed. He grinned when he awoke, whispering, let her come and she won't go away disappointed. He could promise her that and plenty more.

The day was hot and golden coloured, autumn far away, probably non-existent; only an unconfirmed rumour spread by old, embittered folks. Lindsey decided to venture farther today than the sycamore, since the tree was too near to the main road. He felt hopeful, convincing himself that she would come alone. He rode as far as the derelict barn, hid the bicycle inside, then disappeared behind a clump of bushes only a few yards from the bumpy lane. The humming of a distant tractor was a sort of background music to the silence around him. A little later he nearly jumped as two pigeons flopped out of a tree. He saw the bobbing tail of a rabbit, the tail ceased bobbing which meant that the rabbit had sat down and was listening. Suddenly a bicycle appeared ridden by a man who looked like a gypsy. Lindsey had a horror of gypsies. The man got off the bicycle, let it fall over while he made water against a tree, then picked it up, and rode on. Dirty fellow, Lindsey said to himself. He sat down, but soon jumped up because of the ants swarming under his seat. How long would he have to wait? Patience being the finest virtue he would wait till noon since it was pretty certain that she would go shopping in Yeovil. The day before yesterday had been Sunday, hence the shops were closed. Yesterday she and Allan were in London, so it stood to reason that today she would go to Yeovil. If only that oaf of a Horace didn't accompany her.

He heard the voice of the oaf. He became rigid, stepped back a little, an involuntary movement, unnecessary since the bushes hid him completely. 'Look,' said Theresa's voice, 'there's a dead bird here, poor thing.'

'A jay,' said Horace in a disgusted voice. 'Horrible birds, jays.'

'But it's dead,' said Theresa, getting off her bicycle. She leaned over the dead jay to examine it. 'Poor jay.'

'What do you want to do with it?' guffawed Horace as she picked up the dead bird. 'Bury it?'

'It ought to be buried.'

'If you want to bury it you'll bury it alone.'

'I'm going back to get a spade and bury the poor jay.'

'Don't be daft,' laughed Horace. 'The countryside is chock-a-block with dead birds. If you start burying them you won't have time to do anything else.'

'I am going to bury it. Wait for me, I won't be long.'

It was an awful vista for Lindsey. Remaining with Horace all alone near the barn was a prospect he didn't care for. The fidgety big oaf might even poke his head into the clump of bushes and discover his presence, or look into the barn and find his bicycle. Then to his relief Horace said, 'I'm not going to wait here. I'll meet you beside the car park when you've finished this stupid nonsense.'

'A burial isn't stupid nonsense, and how can you say that to me of all people?'

'Oh, my God,' groaned Horace, 'now don't start.'

It was Lindsey's turn to groan. The oaf would stay, and his one great chance would be lost. 'You go on,' Theresa said, 'and I'll get the spade. Doyle has a very small one, like a toy.'

'I won't wait in Yeovil till the evening,' Horace said.

'I'll give this poor bird a proper burial, then I'll come at once.'

She got on her bicycle, and pedalled off, leaving Horace contemplating the dead bird which lay near the clump of bushes. Tired of contemplating it, Horace gave a kick which sent it to the edge of Lindsey's hiding place. Lindsey could easily have touched it with his toecap, but he didn't move till Horace was gone. He gave it a few more seconds before he emerged. He shot across the lane, and went into the barn. There would be nothing suspicious about it if he came out of the barn, saying he had been exploring it, and would she like to go in with him as it was such an interesting old barn. Once they were inside . . .

He couldn't believe his luck, in fact it almost frightened him. He saw her entering the barn with him, he gently suggesting they sat down on the straw. He heard an approaching sound, the sound came nearer, undoubtedly a bicycle, and to his utter disgust he saw Miss Rawley, looking dishevelled, her face covered in perspiration, riding past on an old-fashioned lady's bicycle. Horrible old lesbian, he muttered to himself. Shortly after, two children, a boy and a girl, appeared. His heart sank, for they were surely the offspring of the local farmer, and would remain here to play hide and seek or something of that kind. However, the two solemn children marched on without saying a word to one another. Who would come next?

Theresa too was perspiring as she entered his ken, the sweet, desirable thing with her determined features. She pushed her bicycle against a tree, untied the string that held the small spade, then picked up the jay, pressed it to her cheek, and in the darkness inside the barn Lindsey thought that she was exaggerating. The tractor was now humming nearer which he welcomed since the noise would drown any little shrieks of surprise from adorable Theresa. She was walking round in a small circle, the bird still pressed to her cheek, her eyes on the ground, looking for an appropriate burial place. Lindsey expected her to bury it near the clump of bushes or under the elm on the other side of the lane. She was talking to the bird, but he couldn't catch her words. She approached the barn, and he stepped back, for he had no intention of revealing his presence before the bird was under ground. If he did she might ask him to help. Moreover, he knew that children hated being disturbed while they performed a task they set as their aim.

She wasn't six feet from the barn when she said to the jay, 'I'll bury you here so that nobody can run you over.' She put the jay on a stone, and went to fetch the spade. Suddenly she changed her mind, took the jay and the spade to the clump of bushes, and started digging in front of it. She dug with her back to Lindsey who licked his lips as emotion mounted in him. Those sweet legs, the thighs as thin as the legs, and the exciting white knickers she wore. He wished she would stay like that for a long time. To his surprise she lifted the jay again, took the spade, and started on a new hole nearer to the barn. If she went on like that, undecided as she seemed, she would spend the whole morning digging, and the neighbourhood would become a sieve. 'This is where you'll lie,' said Theresa.

Digging the new hole she was again with her back to him, therefore he didn't feel in any hurry. When she considered the grave deep enough she put the jay into it, but perceiving that it was too small for the tail feathers she took the bird out, and widened the hole. She was satisfied only when the tail feathers had plenty of room, as if she expected the jay to spread its wings before rising and flying off to Bird Paradise. She lifted out the jay, returned to the bushes, and picked many small leaves. Her mien, Lindsey observed, was more and more solemn. She made a bed of leaves inside the hole, put the jay on top of it, then moved her right hand as though she were sprinkling the grave with holy water. Definitely she exaggerates, said Lindsey to himself. 'Now I am your gravedigger,' Theresa said, and filled the hole with earth. She made the sign of the Cross over the jay's grave, now practically facing Lindsey who moved farther back. He wouldn't start before she finished with her nonsense.

'You died, poor jay,' Theresa said, her voice rising above the din of the tractor, 'and eternity is before you. You were a decent and good bird, so you deserve eternity. You will go unhindered to your rightful home which will be everlasting. By the mercy of Our Lord Jesus Christ you will rise from this grave and fly to Heaven, and you'll meet no accident and you won't blow up during your flight. You will sit in branches

187

from which you can't fall, and if you feel like flying round and see father and mother, tell them that they are always in my prayers, and I know that some day we'll be reunited in Our Lord Jesus Christ, and I want you to be with us too. If I don't recognise you, because that'll be in many years' time, then you tell me that it's you.'

She sang the *Circumdederunt me* in a squeaky voice, moved her hands as if holding a censer, then ran to a tree, tore off a twig which she planted in the middle of the jay's fresh grave. She made the sign of the Cross again, and before Lindsey, who was staring open-mouthed, could make a movement she jumped on her bicycle and rode away, forgetting the spade beside the twig.

Before he had time to think or move he heard the horrible oaf's voice. 'I've come back to look for you,' Horace said.

'You didn't have to,' said Theresa.

'I told you that a kid like you shouldn't bicycle alone in Snake Country. There might be horrible tramps lurking under bushes, waiting to cut your throat.'

'Nobody wants to harm you if you bury a poor bird out of sheer charity.'

'The balls you talk,' said Horace, 'and where's the spade?'

'I forgot it; left it on the grave,' Theresa exclaimed. 'I'm going back to fetch it.'

'You start pedalling to Yeovil, we're late as we are. I'll fetch it and catch up with you.'

Theresa pedalled for all she was worth in the hope of reaching Yeovil before Horace could catch up with her.

Lindsey drew farther back in the darkness as Horace appeared. Horace picked up the spade without giving the grave a glance, and went in pursuit of Theresa. Lindsey looked right and left to see if the coast was clear. Suddenly his eyes focussed on the grass near the jay's hole. The grass was trembling, almost mesmerised he watched the trembling approaching, and when it ceased he beheld a snake coiling itself round the twig.

14

Silver fog covered the village, the bridge and the stream. It hadn't lifted for two days, and the villagers stoutly called it mist, pretending that it was blown in from the sea, though they recognised it as the fog that came as a yearly visitation shortly before Christmas. It was a murky, damp fog, and hands and cheeks became wet if one hazarded out. Allan stood before the window through which he saw nothing. Today she's coming back for her Christmas hols, he said to the fog. He put on a leather coat which Patsy had bought him last year, and went to the milking. They had ten new cows. However, the Friesian bull calves were sold, and the idea of breeding Herefords for export had been dropped, for when Weatherton came down after Allan had taken Theresa to the convent and told him even more bluntly than at the solicitor's how unsatisfactory Harold's finances had turned out to be after an inventory was made of all his assets, it was he who decided to bury the idea. 'If this farm makes no money,' Weatherton had said, 'Theresa will have mighty little when she comes of age.' Simson overheard them, and the next day suggested to Allan that they go in for more intensive dairy farming, and start market gardening which, Simson confessed, was the one thing he knew about.

Raising shibboleths, Allan said to himself, pushing his way through the fog, had been one of his main pastimes. Harold, the hard and cold rich man, had been one of them, and Weatherton's beastliness another. Yet Harold didn't die as a rich man, therefore couldn't have been hard and cold, and Weatherton seemed to be doing all he could to safeguard Theresa's future. There were moments when he felt pretty empty without his pet hatreds. He shrugged his shoulders because one could accustom oneself even to being void of anger. He entered the cowshed, and there were Bramm, Doyle and Simson, his red cheeks shining through the fog. 'Today,' said Doyle, 'Miss Theresa is coming back.'

'That was the first thing the wife said when she got me out of bed,' Simson said.

'My wife she said the same,' said Bramm, not to be left out.

'Funny,' said Simson, 'that she never asks any more where Mr. Ramshorn and his lady are buried.' He was much impressed when Allan had told him that there practically wasn't a bone or any other bit of charred remains left of Harold and Elisabeth. 'Better like that,' Allan said.

'Will you be going to the funeral?' Simson asked.

'I won't be able to,' said Allan. 'I've got to fetch Theresa. She's coming by an early train.'

'She'll cheer us up in this bugger of a fog,' said Doyle.

'I must go,' said Simson.

'Poor old Fred,' said Bramm.

When old Fred came out of hospital he had shrunk to half his size. He explained to all and sundry that losing weight was good for one's health. He was too weak to go back to work, walked painfully about, stopping anybody who approached him to declare that he was feeling so much better. In the evenings he looked into the pub, not to drink his pint of rough cider which the doctors had forbidden him, but to inform the dart players that he would start working after Christmas, and had never felt better in his life. They were burying him today.

'I 'ear the phone ringing,' said Bramm.

Perhaps, thought Allan, it was Theresa announcing that she was taking a later train. The voice was Peggy's. 'Do me a great favour,' she said, 'and come to breakfast.'

'In this fog?'

'In this fog. You won't regret it, Allan.'

He couldn't plead Theresa's coming as an excuse because Peggy, so to speak, knew every train by heart. He said he would come.

As far as he was aware Peggy hadn't had news of Hector for a long time, and he didn't mind that, for news from them only lifted his particular kind of fog in which he enveloped Patsy's memory. On the round table lay half a dozen books on dairy farming and market gardening. He spent his evenings reading them, seldom looking at television. He went back to the cowshed, then on to the pigsties, and at half past eight

he got the Land Rover out of the garage. He put on the head-
lights and the fog reflected them, forcing him to move at a
snail's pace. On reaching the Court he found the fog so dense
that he couldn't make out the shape of the cedar. He rang the
bell, and the Swiss girl appeared with a mysterious expression.
'Mrs. Latham wants first to speak to you,' she said. She was
going home to Switzerland in the spring, going for good, and
not a single memory would she take with her. One could sense
that. 'Here,' she said, pointing to the morning room which
was rarely used. In a tweed skirt of brownish hue and a blue-
grey pullover Peggy pounced on him.

'Before I tell you anything,' she said, 'I want you to give me
your word of honour that you'll never speak of or mention our
awful mistake.'

'What mistake?'

'That night in October,' she said, dropping her voice. Her
pinkish eyelashes fluttered.

Allan stared at her because he hadn't imagined that she
would bring that up again. An awful mistake? It hadn't even
been that.

It was a rainy October evening, and an agitated Peggy
summoned him to the Court, for Hector had written. That
admirable salesman declared that if she remained hard-
hearted he and Patsy would fly to Reno and get a divorce
there. It would be better for her to give in gracefully, and thus
keep his and Patsy's friendship. 'What it amounts to,' Allan
said, 'is that he's not too keen on going to Reno.'

'But he might do it,' she said in a desperate voice.

'If he married her after a Reno divorce he could be pro-
secuted in this country for bigamy.'

'Is that so?' she asked, her eyes lighting up.

'Definitely.'

'I'll tell my solicitor.'

She was pleased, visualising Hector begging her on his
bended knees not to send him to prison and promising to leave
Patsy and return to her. In her high spirits she insisted on his
staying for dinner. Hector had a good cellar, and they
polished off two bottles of Volnay '62. As neither of them was
accustomed to such a quantity of wine they left the table with
flushed faces, Peggy's double chin glistening with perspiration.
She sat down on the sofa in the library, lay back, and asked

in a strangely vibrating voice whether Patsy held her men by carnal attraction.

'Carnal attraction?' said Allan. 'It was more than that.'

'Was she one of those insatiable women who live only for sex?'

'I should say so.'

'Wanting it all the time?'

'All the time, and made no bones about it.'

'And you liked that?' He nodded. 'And now Hector likes it.' He nodded again, a brief silence followed, ending by her jumping up and saying in an embarrassingly matter-of-fact tone, 'Take me, Allan.' He stared at her, hardly trusting his ears, and was on the verge of saying, I beg your pardon? or What did you say? when she repeated, 'Take me, Allan,' adding, 'I want you to take me.' As he was still staring at her, she exclaimed in an impatient voice, 'If you don't, I'll never speak to you again.'

'You must undress first,' was all he could say.

'I don't want to. Take me like this. I wear nothing under my dress. Indoors I never do.'

She lay down while she spoke, her head against a velvet cushion, and eyes fixed hard on him, as she waited for him to come to her. 'Don't have to,' she said when he wanted to take his trousers off. 'Hurry.' There was more romance between a bull and a cow, he thought. It was an uncomfortable performance, her fixed expression like that of a statue, and he remembered the woman from Winnipeg and he pretending to himself that he was Hector and she Patsy. Did Peggy think that she was Patsy and he Hector or was she just trying to get nearer to Patsy and through her to Hector? Neither, he decided. A log dropped out of the fireplace and Peggy's fixed gaze turned into an interested one as her eyes focussed on the log. Not a sigh or a word escaped her; he had no idea whether that rigid body felt anything; and when it was over and he had risen, she sat up, saying in her normal voice, 'We won't mention this again, Allan.' He was all for it. Only after he had driven away did he recollect that they hadn't even exchanged a kiss. In the morning, she looked in on him to talk of Hector and Reno, and now two months later she was asking him to give her his word of honour concerning something he had chased from his memory.

'You may rest assured that I've forgotten it,' he said. 'Such momentary after-dinner impulses . . .' He didn't bother to finish the sentence.

'Come to the breakfast room,' she said, but before they reached it Hector pranced out of it, spruce and freshly shaven, smelling of some after-shave lotion which, thought Allan, was probably called *Pour Gentlemans*. Hector wore a homespun jacket and corduroy trousers, the countryman back in his element.

'I am delighted to see you, my dear Allan,' he said, holding out his hand.

Allan's first reaction was to ignore it. However it was a domineering hand, so he let his slip into it. 'I can't say I'm not astonished,' he said. 'When did you come back?'

'Last night,' said Hector, still holding his hand.

'How long are you staying?' asked Allan, freeing his hand.

'Back for good, of course. I'm very good at learning my lesson . . . Oh good.' That was for the Swiss girl who brought in the bacon and eggs. 'We'll speak of it later.' They sat down, Hector enjoying his breakfast, observing between two mouthfuls, 'Peggy is wonderful at choosing bacon, has a perfect flair. Grilled to my taste, my darling.' He took her hand, patted it, then turned to Allan. 'When your brother was killed in the air crash I wanted to write to you, but was too shy. What's going to become of his daughter?'

'I'm her guardian,' said Allan, amazed by Hector and Peggy not having yet reached the subject of Theresa. Wasn't she the cuckold's ward?

'I don't suppose that'll be an onerous task,' said Hector. 'You can always pack her off to friends or relations during her hols.'

'I won't pack her off anywhere,' said Allan.

'Allan takes his guardianship far too seriously,' said Peggy. 'Isn't it marvellous, Allan, to have him back? He rang me from Yeovil station. He said, "Say you forgive me and I'm taking a taxi right away to the Court."'

'And what did Peggy do?' said Hector, beaming on her. 'She fetched me at the station . . . I say, this bacon is uncommonly good; the best I've had for ages. Did your brother leave a lot?'

'Far less than one expected.'

'It's always like that,' said Hector. 'Only on dead scrap-merchants does one find wads of ten-pound notes.' He let out a cheery laugh. 'But, I trust, he did leave you something. After all, a child's guardian deserves to be paid for his hard work.'

'A moment ago you said it wasn't an onerous task,' said Allan.

'You do harp on words,' said Hector in a reproving yet friendly voice.

Out of the fog came loud baritone barking. Hector jumped up, and with an expression that plainly asked What would you do without me? he went to the French window to let in the two Great Danes as wet as if it had been raining. 'They ought to be rubbed down,' he said.

'I'll fetch a towel,' said Peggy, rising from the table.

'The most admirable woman in the world,' said Hector, smearing butter and marmalade on a piece of toast. 'I can't say the same of the lady whose favours we shared.' Allan blushed with anger; however before he could express it in words the door opened, Hector put his forefinger to his lips, and Peggy started to rub down the dogs. 'I'll have to go to Libreville in January,' Hector observed. 'A big deal, I hope, a railway and a motor road, but plenty of competitors, both French and German. I'm taking Peggy with me.'

'Isn't that marvellous?' said Peggy to the Great Danes.

'Peggy needs sunshine,' said Hector. 'She'll get plenty out there, but I've explained to her that as the equatorial sun is treacherous, she'll have to keep away from it. Believe me, Allan, there's nothing like sunshine as long as one is careful. My chest is still sunburnt by the sun of Saint-Tropez. Now Saint-Tropez is the ideal place for a summer holiday. Know what we'll do next summer, darling? We'll go for a few weeks to Saint-Tropez.'

Allan expected Peggy to throw the wet towel at Hector. 'I'd love that, darling,' she said.

The Swiss girl appeared, the gardener wanted to have a word with madam, and as Peggy rose from her knees Hector said most chivalrously, 'Leave it to me, darling,' and left the room.

'How could you take him back?' Allan said.

'You'd take her back if she wanted it,' said Peggy, 'and she wasn't even your wife. Hector is my husband. It is my duty to take him back, and I can assure you he has bitterly repented.'

'I wouldn't take her back.'

'Why?' laughed Peggy who on that foggy winter morning was as happy as a lark in summer. 'Because Theresa doesn't like her?'

'Who told you that Theresa didn't like her?'

'Mrs. Simson or Mrs. Bramm, I can't remember.'

'He wanted to know about his Christmas holiday,' said Hector, like one who had fulfilled an important mission. 'I told him to discuss it with you later in the day. Now, Allan, Peggy has her household chores to attend to here, we're only in her way. Come, old boy, to the library, and we'll have a long chat.'

'It can't be long,' said Allan. 'I've got to fetch Theresa in Yeovil.'

'Always Theresa,' laughed Peggy.

Wet wood smoked and hissed in the fireplace in the library, and with his eyes on them Allan idly wondered whether a log would drop out. Hector invited him to sit on the sofa, then sat down beside him. 'I owe you an explanation,' he said.

'You don't. Honestly, you don't.'

'My dear fellow, I know how you feel, but bear with me. We must clear the air.'

Hector, thought Allan, was selling Hector to him. The Hector he was selling was a generous soul, a staunch friend and a straightforward chap, and while Hector talked he remembered a story his father was wont to tell about another actor whose wife had left him for a merchant banker. One day the actor ran into them. He didn't want to show them his hurt heart, so when they asked him to join them for a drink he went with them to the bar of a large hotel; the sort of bar the actor seldom could afford. 'We're civilised people after all,' said the lover, and since he didn't want to seem uncivilised the actor agreed. He paid his round which cost more than he could afford. After the fourth the merchant banker invited him to lunch with them in the grill room of the hotel. Were they or weren't they civilised people? They were, and the lunch ended with champagne. It was the champagne that brought back the actor's wrongs. When they left together the merchant banker held out his hand. 'I'm not going to shake the hand of the foul fiend who stole my wife,' the actor said with great dignity. He must, Allan warned himself, try not to imitate the actor. But suddenly he was listening intently.

'We were in Saint-Tropez,' Hector was saying, 'for four weeks. There's no place like it in the world. On one side cinema stars and every woman looking like Brigitte Bardot and probably is, on the other the scum of the earth. I mean long-haired dope fiends and guitar players, many of them just tramps. We stayed at the best hotel, fed in the best restaurants, in short I gave her the time of her life. You should have seen her bathing suits.' Allan nodded, for he could see her bathing suits, her body too.

'One night while we were dining, a hirsute fellow practically in rags came up to our table,' continued Hector. 'Naturally, he had a guitar. He was English, I'm afraid to say. He said, "You're English," and literally begged me to give him a few francs. I shooed him away. He was rather rude to me. You know this newfangled language those bums use, called me a bourgeois and the rest of it. I called the nearest waiter to speed him on his way. Afterwards the waiter said what a pity it was that the gendarmes didn't arrest him and his like. I couldn't have agreed more with him. What about a shot of brandy on this cold and murky morning, Allan?'

Before Allan could answer he fetched a bottle of brandy and two tumblers. 'Neat or with Perrier water?' Allan didn't mind one way or the other.

'It's nice to be home,' said Hector, stretching his legs. 'Let me go on. She made no comment. She went every morning to swim, I joined her only much later. One morning I thought that I saw that bum not far from her, but I wasn't sure, as there were so many of his kind about. If in Saint-Tropez you're not the Bardot, you're just one of those hippies. I think I've said that before. We left for Paris at the end of August, there, too, we stayed in the lap of luxury. You must appreciate, Allan, and I'm saying this without wanting to be the slightest bit offensive, that when she came to me she hardly had a dress to wear.'

'She had three.'

'My dear fellow,' said Hector, patting his arm. Allan thought of the actor. 'Three. Well, I wanted her to have many more. In every man who desires a woman there lives a Father Christmas, don't you agree?'

'I wouldn't know,' said Allan without envy or bitterness.

'I see what you mean,' said Hector. 'Have more brandy.'

'No, thank you. I've got to drive in this bloody fog.'

'You're a wise man. I'll have a little more. Don't forget we're celebrating my home-coming. Well, there we were in Paris, living on the fat of the land. I took her to the best dressmakers, dressed her up as she was never dressed before, in short I gave her the time of her life. Don't forget she's never been abroad before.'

'She told me that she went once to Spain.'

'On the cheap. That doesn't count. She wanted, so she told me, to see all the famous buildings and churches of Paris. I thought that reasonable since she hadn't travelled before. I didn't accompany her on those sightseeing tours. If you don't look at the famous buildings on your first visit to a town you don't seem to find time for them on subsequent ones. So I let her go alone.' He put his hand on Allan's shoulder. 'At times she stayed away for hours but I found nothing suspicious about that.' He grabbed Allan's shoulder. 'Not with a word, not with a gesture did she give me any inkling that she was contemplating leaving me. I wanted to get a divorce and marry her, the fool that I was. I talked of nothing else. I admit that she often said, "Why bother? Aren't we all right as we are?" One morning she did say I was spending too much on her, and it wasn't good for her to have so much money spent on her. I laughed that off.'

She had declared to Allan that they were a bad influence on one another, and his answer was to make love with her. His own way of laughing it off, he supposed.

'We came back in October,' Hector went on, 'and in my infatuation I threatened my darling wife to divorce her in Reno.'

The night on this same sofa, thought Allan, looking at the damp logs.

'We took a very expensive furnished flat in Knightsbridge. She spent her mornings shopping, I mean buying food and things like that. Often she remembered in the afternoon that she had forgotten something or other, and out she rushed, and I congratulated myself on having found such a conscientious housewife, ha ha.' He laughed indulgently.

'Here it used to be shopping in Yeovil,' Allan said.

'Don't bring that up, my dear fellow. We're past that.'

'You're right there.'

'Allan, you're a great chap. Have a little tot, come on, have one.'

Allan accepted, and why shouldn't he? Was he or wasn't he civilised? Accepting a second brandy proved that he was. Peggy looked in, they both jumped up, Peggy said, 'I won't disturb, I can see you have still a lot to say to each other,' and practically tiptoed out of the library. There was a draught, and as she closed the door a log fell out of the fireplace. Hector ran to kick it back while Allan watched him unsmilingly.

'Then one day in November,' Hector said, 'I came back to the flat. It was late afternoon, I had been lunching with two big noises, discussing the Libreville scheme. We had a Spanish maid, young and stupid, and she gave me a letter which I thought had come by the second post. You see, I went out quite early. I opened the envelope, three lines from Patsy, and my first reaction was to tick off the Spanish girl for not telling me that it wasn't really a letter but just a chit from the señora. In those three lines Patsy told me that she had left me, regretted she couldn't tell it in person but that would only have caused a lot of unnecessary discussion. She added a post-script, saying she left all dresses and presents behind because it wasn't fair on me to take them away.'

She took his few shabby presents with her, said Allan to himself. Perhaps they had been nearer to each other because they were both poor.

'When I finished reading it,' continued Hector, 'the Spanish idiot said that the señora had told her that she wouldn't be back for dinner, so would the señor let her cook him a paella? She was from Valencia, and the best paella is the paella of Valencia.' He would tell Theresa, thought Allan, to try her hand at a paella. 'Believe me, I had no paella that night.' He got up, and went to stand with his back to the fireplace. 'I'm not vengeful, I'm not nasty, Allan, but I did want to find out why she left me, to round it off, I suppose. But how to set about it? I remembered that she had a woman friend.'

'Miss Jackie Tomkin.'

'That's the one, an aggressive female, don't you think?'

'I met her only twice, but they did ring each other from time to time.'

'I met her about four times; didn't take to her. Success has not eluded me because I know how to plan and work things out.' This one you didn't, Allan couldn't help saying to himself. 'The next day I went to see a private inquiry agency, the best in town. I had Miss Tomkin's flat watched, she lives in Swiss Cottage, and I was certain that sooner or later she would go to see Miss Tomkin. The private sleuth had her likeness, a snap taken at Saint-Tropez. Two days later she turned up with a long-haired bearded bum, the sleuth followed them to some dreary lodging in Camden Town, then phoned me the address. I told him to go back and take a snap of the bum without him noticing it. The last thing I wanted was to go there and meet him.'

'He might have offered you a flower.'

'A flower?' Hector frowned. 'I didn't want to see her either. With me, my dear fellow, the mind rules the heart. The sleuth brought me the snap taken in their sordid street. They were walking with their arms round each other's shoulder. The man was the bum from Saint-Tropez.'

'I guessed as much.'

'Not difficult. Well, that's how it ended. Thank God I'm back here, and I can assure you that I won't go philandering again, but if I do,' he dropped his voice, 'I won't take it seriously.'

That is, Allan thought, if you don't meet another Patsy.

'Now I want to talk about you,' Hector said. 'Peggy and I had a long chat about you last night. She told me what a good and staunch friend you were during her ordeal.' He sat down beside Allan on the sofa. 'I hate to see you buried here in this village. You told me once that you didn't enjoy playing the farmer.'

'Things have changed.'

'Fundamentally things don't change. Look at me. When I left I thought that I'd never see the Court again, yet here I am. What I want to say is this: I'm certain that I could get you a good job with my team. I'm sure you have the push and dash to make a go of it. The rest will follow.'

Allan was moved, for it wasn't necessary, and for a moment he liked Hector because he was ready to do something that wasn't necessary. 'It is kind of you,' he said, 'but I have to stay here. My brother Harold didn't leave very much, and I must make a success of the farm, otherwise my niece might find herself in want.'

'But surely . . .'

'That's the exact truth. My brother was climbing to the top, death caught him halfway up, so he rolled back, as simple as that. Another five years and he could have turned the farm into a skittle alley for old people, but he wasn't granted those five years. I must stay and make a job of it.'

'All that for that little girl.' Allan nodded twice. 'Well, you know best, yet I for one think you're wasting your time. Never do anything for a relation.'

'It isn't because she's a relation. She relies on me.'

'But she'll grow up, find some long-haired fellow, marry him and you'll see her perhaps once a year, provided she has the time.'

'That's quite natural.'

'What a waste of time for you,' Hector said, helping himself to more brandy.

'It isn't. She's already done a lot for me.' He smiled because he knew that Hector would feel embarrassed and consider him almost indecent. 'For instance, she's made me believe in God, and I'm seriously considering becoming a Catholic.'

'Really, Allan,' said Hector, blushing for him.

'There were people, I was told, who converted because they saw God in the bottom of a beer mug; I saw Him while I watched Theresa being told on the phone that her parents were killed in an air crash. More edifying, don't you think? Or is it the same?'

'I'm really not the one to answer such metaphysical questions,' said Hector, looking at the seascape above the chimney-piece.

'The beer mug or the telephone,' said Allan, more to himself than to Hector. He stood up. 'Speaking of my niece, I must go and fetch her. Thanks again for your offer. It moved me.'

'Don't mention it, my dear fellow,' said Hector, accompanying him to the door. 'Will you look in tonight? Bring the little girl.'

'I'll ring later in the day,' said Allan, and when he shook Hector's hand he no longer thought of the actor.

The fog still held sway. Like a sail that's fallen on top of you Allan said to himself as he groped his way to the Land

Rover. Then, in spite of the little visibility, he forgot the fog. Frankly, he was proud of Patsy who had left him so treacherously and whom he would never see again. She was true to herself. She had said she was an animal and she remained one. Animals don't argue, don't haggle, think only with their instincts; that is don't consider pecuniary interests. He saw it clearly, wishing he could see the road as clearly, too. She had gone against her grain when she chose successful Hector, but probably that wasn't true, probably Hector's vast income was only an excuse to go off with him, the truth being that at the time she enjoyed going to bed with him. A bitch follows a dog without thinking of the bones he might dig out for her. It was the consolation of the poor man, backed by his vanity, to interpret her departure as there being one law for the rich, and a different one for him. A rabbit just managed to get out of his way.

When Patsy lived in the lap of luxury the bearded fellow appeared, begging a few francs from Hector who sent him packing. He knew Patsy too well to see her as an avenger of the injustice the rich meted out to the poor. She had looked at him, liked his beard and long hair, and in all likelihood she was by then tired of the lap of luxury, but above it all the bum (to use Hector's expression) attracted her. Hadn't he, Allan, been a bum too when she came to live with him? She must have tried out the bum on the beach of Saint-Tropez and found him satisfactory. His conversation, or maybe his silence, was less pushful and forceful than Hector's. The fine dresses and jewels she left behind; she had taken with her all Allan's mean offerings. That was her strength, and by that alone could she be judged. And when the time was ripe to leave the bum she would take with her the garland he had given her. Yes, he was proud of Patsy for not having let down herself, proud yet with no desire to see her again. She must have forgotten him completely, and that was as it should be. While she was with Hector she might have remembered him; now, if she remembered anyone, it could only be Hector. If he found the strength to defeat his mental sloth and was received into the Church he would pray for Patsy because, taking it all in all, she did deserve it.

That took him back to Mother Mary Philomena, regretting for the hundredth time that he hadn't been more forthcoming when he saw her the day after he heard of Harold's and Elisabeth's death. Why couldn't he have told her that there was no fear of his mistress coming back or of him marrying her? Already then he was perfectly aware that there was no danger of that. Anyhow, it didn't matter any more. He shook his head. He was wrong, for it still mattered a lot. When he went up to London on a Saturday in November to take Theresa out, the fat mother superior talked to him for a long half hour, emphasising in almost every sentence Theresa's attachment to him. He hadn't the courage to tell her that he would do nothing to upset her. 'She's a very possessive girl,' Mother Mary Philomena had said. His answer was, 'I don't mind that,' instead of declaring that he wouldn't take Patsy back even if she wanted it. Shapes loomed up in the fog, villagers on their way to old Fred's funeral. In twenty-thirty years' time, Allan mused, they would be much older than Fred, yet would continue to refer to him as old Fred.

He reached the house, got out of the Land Rover, and as he approached the front door a voice spoke to him, nearly making him jump. 'Hullo, sir,' said Horace who was standing beside the door. 'Did I frighten you?'

'You almost did.'

'Sorry, sir, but I didn't want to miss you, and it's so easy in this fog.'

'Come in,' said Allan.

'Oh, thank you, sir.'

Why, Allan wondered, was Horace so suspiciously polite?

Mrs. Bramm had made a fire, the logs dry because they were kept in the old stable where the Friesian bull calves had lived before he had sold them. The fire blazed and orange-coloured gay flames lit up the gloom. 'Very cheerful in here,' observed Horace.

'When did you get back?' Allan asked. The boy had grown, but boys always seem to grow if one hasn't seen them for a few months.

'Last night,' said Horace. 'A kindly father, not mine of course, dropped me here. The fog was even thicker, and for some reason, for which I can't be blamed, the door of the vicarage was open, so I went straight in, and when I made my entrance into the study I frightened the life out of my pa.'

'I don't blame him.'

'It wasn't my fault, it wasn't me who left the door open. He spent the rest of the evening telling me about evil ghouls who try to frighten people by putting white sheets over their shoulders, lurking in churchyards, and appearing before bereaved widows and widowers or decent sons and daughters who mourn their parents, the ghouls' intention being to make 'em drop dead. There was more of it this morning at breakfast, and now it'll be sheer hell till the school report comes in. "I don't want to make a guess," he says all the time.' While he was speaking he turned round in small circles.

'What can I do for you?' Allan asked, smiling.

'I just looked in to say hullo to you, sir,' said Horace in an ingratiating voice. 'I nearly knocked into Mr. Lindsey in the fog. Now if anyone looked like a ghost . . .' He noticed that Allan appeared to be in a hurry. 'I quite forgot to tell you that my pa is a great admirer of yours, speaks of you all the time.'

'Your father?'

'My father,' said Horace with a cunning light in his eyes. 'He says it is a fine Christian thing to take a little orphaned niece under your wings. He loves birds, you know. He says few men who aren't yet very old would bother to do that. That's exactly what my pa says.' He swallowed hard before he asked in a voice he tried to make as casual as possible, 'Is Theresa coming here for her hols?'

'Most definitely, in fact she's coming today.'

'At what time, may I ask?'

'Her train arrives at eleven-thirty, and I'll have to set off in a moment because of the fog.'

'It's very thick, sir.'

'Would you care to come with me? I'm sure she'll be pleased to see you.'

'Yes, please,' said Horace, quicker than he intended.

His conscience was clear in every respect; he could look Theresa straight in the eye, that is if he bent down enough, for he had given her back the ten shillings he had paid as deposit for the bicycle. Giving it back wasn't the precise truth because when he held out the four half-crowns, usefully forgetting the other ten shillings he had spent on smokes, she said she didn't need them, but as he pocketed them quickly he saw her make a gesture of surprise. She must have forgotten that by now.

Theresa got into an empty second-class compartment at
Waterloo station. The last time her fond parents had insisted
on her travelling first. Now even the thought of it was far from
her. At the end of October there was a collection at the convent for the White Fathers, a White Father in person having
explained to the girls all his Order had achieved in Africa.
Theresa wrote to Weatherton, asking him to send them ten
pounds; Weatherton came in person to the convent, asked permission to see Theresa; Mother Mary Philomena summoned
Theresa, and when she came in she left them alone. Weatherton didn't believe in beating about the bush : he flattered himself on always coming to the point; and in simple words he
told her that he had sent only one pound because Theresa
couldn't afford more as she wasn't as well off as she had been
when her daddy was earning vast sums. Theresa took that in
her stride, observing that she was sorry on account of the
White Fathers. That moved Weatherton so much that he said
that he would raise it to two pounds. 'Please do that,' said
Theresa. 'I need a new coat for winter. I'll tell Mother Mary
Philomena to get me one that costs two pounds less.' That
moved Weatherton even more, and before departing he asked
Mother Mary Philomena to spare no expense. He went away
regretting that he hadn't sent the ten pounds, and Theresa
went to bed contented, thinking that she was as poor as her
Uncle Allan, and what more could she want?

A corpulent woman accompanied by two girls appeared in
the corridor, looked into the compartment, smiled, then said,
'There's another girl in here, so you'd better travel with her.
Where are you going, dear?'

'To Yeovil.'

'My nieces are going to Sherborne, so you'll keep each other
company.' She let the girls peck her cheeks, then got off the

train with a sigh of relief. She came to the window, made a sign, the two girls stared dumbly, but Theresa understood and let down the window. 'Thank you, dear,' the woman said. 'Come here.' That was for the two nieces. 'Tell your mummy that I'll ring her in the morning.' She hurried off as though afraid of being called back.

The nieces sat down facing Theresa, who examined them with smileless eyes. The bigger was her age with round cheeks and round eyes and no nose to speak of. The smaller was her replica except for the nose, which was long. They weren't the sort of girls she liked talking to. The train pulled out; the bigger looked hard at Theresa while the smaller smiled at her sister. 'Hols?' asked the bigger.

'Hols,' said Theresa.

'You're from Dorset?'

'I'm from Somerset,' said Theresa.

'Zomerzet,' said the smaller, giggling.

'That's how they speak there,' said the bigger.

'Some might,' said Theresa.

'Zome might,' laughed the smaller.

'Neither my uncle nor I speak like that,' said Theresa.

'You're going to your uncle?' Theresa nodded. 'We're going home to daddy and mummy. Where are your daddy and mummy?'

'They're away,' said Theresa.

'Far?'

'Very far.'

'So you're spending your hols with your uncle?' said the bigger. Her sister leaned forward, waiting for the answer.

'He's my guardian,' said Theresa.

'Jennifer has a guardian too,' said the smaller.

'But then you're an orphan,' said the bigger.

'Not necessarily,' said Theresa. Not necessarily was one of Mother Mary Philomena's favourite expressions.

'But Jennifer is an orphan,' insisted the smaller.

'I don't know her,' Theresa said coldly, and took a bar of chocolate from her coat pocket.

'You're allowed to eat chocs?' the bigger asked. 'We're not allowed to.'

'I won't tempt you,' said Theresa. 'Temptation is wicked.'

'If I had chocs I'd offer you some,' whined the smaller.

Theresa bit into the chocolate, the two girls watched her greedily, their eyes on the bar, and Theresa sighed because it was so difficult to keep to one's principles. 'Have some,' she said, and the sisters' eyes lit up. Theresa divided the bar in three parts. 'Like Gaul,' she smiled.

'What's that?' asked the smaller, taking her part.

'Gaul was divided in three parts,' said Theresa. 'Haven't you reached Caesar?'

'We've reached Shakespeare,' said the bigger. 'We've got a mistress at our school who recites Shakespeare beautifully.'

'We have a nun at my convent,' said Theresa, 'who recites Racine beautifully.'

As the sisters had no idea who Racine could be, the conversation languished till, having finished her share, the smaller asked, 'Has your uncle a beard?'

'Why should he have a beard? My uncle is too handsome to have a beard.'

'We've one who has a beard,' said the bigger. 'He's a solicitor. What does your uncle do?'

'He has a farm, a very big one.'

'We've a chicken farm,' said the smaller.

'Four thousand battery laying hens,' said the bigger.

'My uncle doesn't need chickens. We get our eggs from Mrs. Simson.'

'Who's Mrs. Simson?' asked the smaller.

'My uncle's farm manager's wife,' said Theresa grandly.

'It must be a very big farm,' said the bigger.

'I told you it was,' said Theresa.

'Your daddy and mummy,' said the smaller, 'must like your uncle very much to leave you with him.'

'They trust him completely. They know that he's the best uncle there is.'

'Have you an auntie too?' asked the smaller who, perhaps because of her long nose, was more inquisitive than her sister.

'My uncle has no wife, and he'll never marry.'

'Why's that?' asked the smaller.

'Because he doesn't need to. I'm his housekeeper, and I cook for him.'

The bigger was amazed, so said her silence and her eyes. However, her sister was undefeated. 'Then what does he do while you're at school?'

'He eats very little, but when I get back I give him lots to eat.'

'And then he gets fat?' asked the bigger.

'He doesn't get fat. I know how to balance a meal.'

'What's that?' asked the smaller.

'To balance a meal,' said Theresa, 'is not to serve two courses with starch or with similar things in them.'

'What does that mean?' asked the smaller.

'For instance you can't start with a potato salad and then give mash. Or you can't give a potage Saint-Germain and then peas with the entrecôte.' She eyed the two girls triumphantly, then immediately regretted her superior attitude. 'I think I've more chocolate in my suitcase.' The smaller jumped on the seat to help her get her suitcase down. Both watched her rummaging for the chocolate, and when she found it she divided it in three parts.

'You're lucky,' sighed the bigger.

'Our mummy is very fat,' said the smaller, 'and that's why she's against chocolate.'

'And puddings,' said the smaller. 'Does your uncle give you plenty of chocs?'

'A cook-housekeeper hasn't time to eat chocolates,' said Theresa.

Then followed the routine questions: where was she at school, how old was she, and when would her parents come back? 'I'll go to them,' said Theresa.

'Soon?' asked the smaller.

'That depends on God's will, but I think He wants me to stay awhile with my uncle.'

'Because you cook for him,' said the smaller.

Conversation turned back to their schools. The sisters were at school in St.-Leonards-on-Sea, Theresa spoke of her convent, then they talked of girls and mistresses, and the train hurried on under a low sky, and as it approached Sherborne it nosed its way through fog. The sisters got their suitcases down, reminded each other not to forget the school trunks, and before alighting they asked Theresa when she was going back, and which train she would take. They sighed, thinking of chocolate, as she told them that she was returning two days after them.

'Perhaps end of next term we'll travel together again,' said the smaller.

There wasn't much time to waste on holiday plans between Sherborne and Yeovil. Still Theresa decided to visit the jay's grave tomorrow, and the day after to ask her Uncle Allan to take her to Uncle Justin's. What had Horace said? If Uncle Justin hadn't died she would be cooking for him too. She wouldn't mind, but she definitely preferred to cook for Uncle Allan alone. She had in her pocket a recipe for a Christmas pudding, and she sent up a quick prayer asking St Teresa to intercede for her and not let her make a mess of it. The train slowed down with a jerk, stopped and there was Uncle Allan, and she laughed as she caught sight of Horace.

The fog began to lift as though tired of its efforts. 'Here I am,' she said as she ran up to Allan. One can see that, said Horace to himself. 'You haven't grown much,' he said aloud.

'I think you've grown a lot,' said Allan.

'I'll never be tall,' said Theresa. 'I'll be like mother.'

'You don't need to grow tall,' said Allan, and received her luminous smile.

'There's the same porter as last time,' she said. 'I'll ask him to get my trunk.'

'I'll get it for you,' Horace said.

While she and Allan waited for Horace they hardly exchanged a word. He nodded once or twice as if answering an unformulated question, and she continued to crane her neck and smile at him.

'Here he comes,' she said. 'I'll help you, Horace.'

'I don't need any help,' he said, panting.

The fog had taken itself away by the time they left the town behind. As they reached the open country they saw a lot of commotion on the road and in the fields nearby. Four police cars and an army bus were parked on the edge of the road, and in the fields advanced policemen with police dogs and soldiers in a wide half-circle.

'A man-hunt,' said Horace in an excited voice.

It wasn't a man-hunt. They were searching for a girl of Theresa's age whom (still unknown to them) Lindsey had raped then strangled under the cover of the silver fog the afternoon before.

'How are Mrs. Simson's budgies?' Theresa asked.